KING'S KNIGHT

This is a work of fiction. Names, characters, places and incidents either are the product of the author's imagination or are used fictitiously. Any resemblance to actual events, locales, business establishments or persons, living or dead, is coincidental.

KING'S KNIGHT
Copyright © 2016 Regan Walker

Paperback ISBN: 978-0-9968495-6-2
Print Edition

ACKNOWLEDGEMENTS

There were many who provided me their expertise for this book. Katie Sterns, a gifted horseback archer, graciously read my scene of Merewyn shooting from the back of her Welsh pony. My friend, Chari Wessel, my consultant for ship scenes, stayed with me for this book and contributed from her fine mind. Scott Moreland, my editor, is a constant encouragement, helping me in those doubtful moments, of which there are always many.

I must thank photographer Laura Olenska for the image of Merewyn on the back cover of the paperback. It captures well Merewyn's delicate features and her determination. Interestingly, I saw the image years ago when I was doing the cover for *The Red Wolf's Prize* and thought it perfect for Serena. Since she was "the prize" I thought to put her on the front cover. But Laura and I didn't get together until after that cover was done. Now Laura has generously given me her permission to use her photograph for Merewyn, who is very much like Serena, her "mother of the heart". (The link for Laura's website is on my Books page at the end of the story.)

Lastly, I thank my street team, Regan's Ravens, who believe in my stories and help other readers to find them. I am so blessed to have you all!

AUTHOR'S NOTE

Following the Norman Conquest of England, William I reigned over a kingdom consisting of Normandy and England. Because he gave lands confiscated from the English to his Norman followers, many of his nobles possessed lands on both sides of the Channel. But a quarter of a century later, all was not peaceful in the kingdom.

Rebellions flared in both England and Normandy and the Conqueror's eldest son was not in his favor. William was busy trying to hold his kingdom together, so perhaps that explains why he was an inconsistent, if not a poor, father. His sons' flawed characters were the result.

The Conqueror died in Normandy on September 9, 1087. Although his father considered Robert, the eldest son, a weak leader, he inherited the dukedom of Normandy, arguably a more prestigious position in those days than England's king.

As for William, his middle son, the Conqueror expressed the desire that he should succeed him as King of England. William was quick to seize the opportunity. Called "William Junior" by his contemporaries and dubbed "Rufus" by historians because of his ruddy complexion, William II was skilled with a lance and well liked by his men. However, he frequently broke his word and constantly warred with the church, eventually drawing open disdain from the Archbishop of Canterbury for his male lovers who frequented his court.

The Conqueror's youngest son, Henry, received only silver at his father's death and was bitter for it, often changing sides between his two warring brothers when, by doing so, he could gain lands. While Robert was conveniently away on crusade in 1100, William Rufus was slain in the New Forest, some believe by Henry's order. Upon William's death, Henry quickly seized the throne, even though Robert was William's designated heir.

It is against this background of a dysfunctional royal family my story is set.

In 1090, nobles loyal to Robert and William were at war with each other in Normandy, a war instigated by William himself. Henry, who had purchased lands from Robert, fought on the side of his eldest brother, but was soon abandoned by both his brothers.

Early in the next year, William decided to personally intervene in Normandy, taking a force of knights with him. At the king's side stood a noble and valued knight, Sir Alexander of Talisand, son of the legendary Red Wolf, whose men, out of respect, called him the Black Wolf.

For such a knight, only a woman of extraordinary character would do, one who had triumphed over hardship and shame, one who was not afraid to hunt with a wolf.

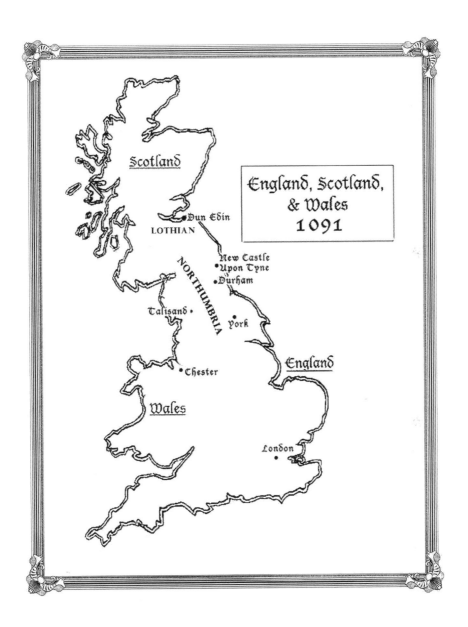

Scotland

England, Scotland,
& Wales
1091

•Dun Edin
LOTHIAN

New Castle
•Upon Tyne
•Durham

NORTHUMBRIA

Talisand •

•York

•Chester

England

Wales

London
•

CHARACTERS OF NOTE
(BOTH REAL AND FICTIONAL)

Sir Alexander of Talisand, son of the Red Wolf

Merewyn of York

Sir Rory, son of Sir Maurin de Caen and Cassandra

Sir Guy, son of Sir Geoffroi de Tournai and Lady Emma of York

Sir Renaud de Pierrepont, Earl of Talisand (the Red Wolf)

Lady Serena, Countess of Talisand

Maggie, Talisand's head cook, Cassie's mother and Rory's grandmother

Maugris the Wise, a seer

Sir Geoffroi de Tournai, husband to Lady Emma and father of Guy and Bea

Lora, daughter of Sir Alain and Aethel and sister to Ancel

Sir Jamie, captain of the house knights at Talisand

Father Bernard, Talisand's priest

Hugh, Vicomte d'Avranches, Earl of Chester

Lady Ermentrude, Countess of Chester

Nelda, maidservant to Lady Serena

William Rufus, King of England

Robert, Duke of Normandy, older brother of the king

Ranulf "Flambard", advisor, priest and treasurer to the king

Adèle de Vermandois, daughter to the comte de Vermandois

Herbert, comte de Vermandois

Sir Nigel d'Aubigny, one of the king's barons

Sir Duncan, eldest son of Malcolm, King of Scots

Malcolm Canmore, King of Scots

Edgar Ætheling, brother to Margaret, Queen of Scots

Steinar, Mormaer (earl) of the Vale of Leven in Scotland and Alex's uncle

Owain ap Cadwgan, a prince of Powys in Wales, Rhodri's nephew

Love wants a chivalrous lover
skilled at arms and generous in serving
who speaks well and gives greatly,
who knows what he should do and say,
in or out of his hall,
as befits his power.
He should be full of hospitality, courtesy, and good cheer.
A lady who lies with such a lover as that
is clean of all her sins.

From the 12th century poem *Be'm plai lo gais temps de pascor*
By the knight-troubadour Bertran de Born

PROLOGUE

Merewyn escaped into the woods, dashing between trees, her heart beating like a frightened fawn. Crushing bracken beneath her bare feet, she ran as fast as her twelve-year-old legs would take her, outrunning the boys who pursued her but not their horrible taunts.

Behind her, she could still hear their echoing shouts, like the cries of mobbing crows. *"Bastard! Whore's daughter!"*

She knew well enough she was bastard born, but her mother had been no whore. Lady Emma, her mother's closest friend, had told her Inga had been young and beautiful, the only child of the finest sword maker in York. Though common-born, she was noble of spirit and kind to all she knew. But the Norman knight who took her by force cared naught for her innocence. To him, she was merely one of the conquered, his rightful prey.

Pain stabbed Merewyn's side and she paused in her running to rest against a tree, panting out breaths while looking behind her, listening for running feet. The only sounds were the leaves rustling in the breeze and a bird, disturbed by her presence, taking to flight.

Relief washed over. She was alone.

Memories of her mother were few and shrouded in mists of child-hood, half-forgotten. Sweet had been her kisses but too soon they were gone. Merewyn vaguely remembered a stepfather, Sir Niel, but he was often away with the other knights and died in battle when she was only

1

four. Days later, her mother had died trying to give birth to his son. The midwives had shooed Merewyn from her mother's bedchamber, closing the heavy door to keep her from seeing the thrashing white body and the sheets stained scarlet, but nothing could block the sound of her mother's screams. They had haunted Merewyn all the years since.

"Here she is!"

Panic seized her as a half-dozen leering boys, older than her by several years, emerged from the trees to surround her like ravenous dogs.

One with shaggy brown hair stepped in front of the others. "Swive with us and we'll leave ye be." He was too young for a beard but his thick-chested body told her he worked in the fields. Fear clawed at her belly and dread settled over her. She knew the meaning of the word he had used. The kitchen wenches had whispered about the couplings between the earl's men and the village whores.

"Keep away from me or you will be sorry!" she cried, but her voice quavered. Their predatory looks told her they did not take her warning seriously.

The thick-chested leader stepped closer.

She pressed her back into the tree, the rough bark digging into her tunic.

He reached out to grip her chin, twisting her face back and forth, his rough fingers scraping her soft skin. "She'll nay be so bad to look at once the mud is gone."

She swatted his hand away.

He grabbed her wrist and yanked her into his chest. He had a foul smell of one who had not washed for a long while. She drew back her foot and kicked his shin hard.

Expelling an oath, he squeezed her wrist harder, his dark eyes narrowing. "Ye'll pay for that."

She sank her teeth into his hand, determined to fight with whatever she had.

"Bitch!" he spat out, thrusting her away.

The other boys closed in, like dogs after a cornered rabbit.

Merewyn screamed, a shrill cry echoing through the woods.

The leader reached for her again just as heavy footfalls crashed through the underbrush.

"Halt!" came a shout. A lad, taller than the rest, with black hair and brows drawn together in a frown, emerged from the dense growth of trees to scrutinize the half-circle of boys standing around her.

Alexander, the Red Wolf's son.

Her heart still pounding, she looked toward her savior. He was only a year older than she, but just then Alexander looked much older, much larger than she remembered. His black hair framed gray eyes shooting silver sparks beneath his dark brows. A fierce apparition, his broad shoulders and lean muscled limbs promised strength and his presence gave her hope.

"What goes here?" he demanded.

"Just a bit of fun," said the shaggy-haired leader. " 'Tis only Merewyn, the whore's daughter."

Alexander backhanded the other boy, a blow that sent him reeling. "Never call her that again."

The boy brought his hand to his injured cheek. "What is she to ye, cub of the Red Wolf?"

Merewyn knew Alexander hated the nickname, but the only sign of his anger was his clenching jaw and his intense glare aimed at the leader. "If you value your skin, you will leave *now*."

The leader sneered. "There are many of us and only one of ye," he boasted, puffing out his thick chest. His companions, however, were beginning to look doubtful.

"So be it," said Alexander. "You will be first."

Where he had learned to fight, she did not know, but Alexander reared back and planted his fist in the miscreant's face, sending the other boy sprawling in the mud.

Raising his hand to ward off the next blow, the boy said, "All right, ye can have her." Rubbing his jaw, the leader struggled to his feet and shot Merewyn an angry look before slipping into the woods. His companions slunk away after him.

Alexander turned to her. His gray eyes that had been stormy only moments before were now calm, but in their depths she glimpsed concern. "Are you all right?"

She let out a breath. "Yea, but I would not be had you not come. I am in your debt."

He tossed her a grin. " 'Tis one of the rare times I am glad my father casts a large shadow. 'Twas not *my* fists they feared but the wrath of the Red Wolf."

The hint of a smile crossed Merewyn's face. He might be loath to claim credit but she knew well who had saved her. From that moment on, he was the hero of her heart.

CHAPTER 1

Nine years later, Avranches, Normandy, March 1091

Alex left the meeting with William Rufus, pausing in front of the king's tent to gaze across the bay toward Mont Saint Michel. The rugged granite crag reaching hundreds of feet above the vast muddy plain always filled him with awe. He could well imagine that three hundred years before, as the Bishop of Avranches had claimed, the Archangel Michael had pressured him into building a church on top of the island. The Benedictine abbey sitting on top of the granite rock stood like an offering to Heaven.

It was the perfect place from which Henry could take his stand against his brothers, the King of England and the Duke of Normandy, who had combined forces to lay siege to the fortress sheltering their rebellious younger sibling.

That is, if Henry had no need for fresh water, for there was none to be had on the rock that was Mont Saint Michel.

Henry's mercenaries and loyal knights knew well the unstable ground around the island, so they could avoid the treacherous quicksand better than could William's knights. Alex hated their routine sallies from the fortress to harass William's men while seeking the water Henry so desperately needed. Some of their forays had been successful, only postponing the siege.

Out of the corner of his eye, Alex glimpsed Rory striding toward him, shoving his tangled red hair back from his face.

"Alex, do you see Henry's knights riding on our side of the bay as if indifferent to the king's tent flying his banner within their sight?"

"Aye, I have been watching them. What say you we remind Henry's men 'tis William Rufus who has come to call and not some baron of low rank?"

Rory greeted Alex's response with a grin. "I will get Guy and some of the men."

Guy and Rory were Alex's closest companions, knights from Talisand like himself, serving England's king.

Moments later, Rory had gathered the men. Alex mounted Azor, his black stallion, while keeping his eyes focused on the score of mounted knights in the distance making their way along the edge of the bay.

"They will not taunt us for long," Alex muttered to himself.

Just as he raised his hand to give the order to charge, the king plunged from his tent, wearing mail and a plain iron helm. "I will not sit in my tent drinking Robert's wine when a fight can be had!" shouted William. "I am coming!"

"My Lord," Alex said, bowing his head, " 'tis our pleasure to follow you into the fray."

They rode forth, the king in the lead, and soon they were engaged in close fighting with Henry's mounted knights, their swords clashing furiously in hand-to-hand combat. The men they fought were as well trained as they were, some likely having been squires in Rouen with William before he was named king.

Engaged in his own battle, Alex looked over his opponent's shoulder just as one of Henry's men thrust a lance into William's horse. The stallion screamed in panic and reared, causing the king to fall. The horse ran, dragging the king behind him, his foot caught in the stirrup.

Alex slashed his sword, dispatching the knight with whom he'd been fighting, and dug his spurs into Azor's side in pursuit of the king.

Just ahead of him, the king's horse came to a sudden halt and pitched to the ground, dead. Beside him lay his fallen master. The king's eyes were closed and his mud-smeared face pale beneath the dirt.

Behind him, Alex heard the sound of Henry's men galloping toward him. From their vile remarks, they thought he was running. They were wrong.

Alex whirled, his sword flashing in the sun.

Five of Henry's knights faced him, reining in their horses to sneer. The first one, a powerfully built knight, charged forward. Alex cut him down with one strike of his blade, standing in his stirrups to add force to the blow.

With his legs, Alex maneuvered Azor to one side as he turned to face another. Shifting his sword to his left hand that held his shield, he drew his lance and launched it at his opponent's neck. The man grunted and toppled sideways, blood gushing over his mail, as he pitched to the ground.

A third knight urged his horse in front of the other two who remained. Grimacing, he said, "You will not have me so easily!"

Behind Alex, the king moaned. *William lives!*

Alex studied the face of the helmed knight who confronted him, the way he held his sword, his horse's nervous dancing. Overconfident and arrogant with less control than he believed, Henry's knight spurred his horse forward. Using his legs, Alex turned Azor to the side, escaping the man's blade. As the knight passed, Alex's sword sliced through the back of his neck.

Before the two who were left could attack, William roused and shouted, "Stop, you fools! I am the King of England!"

The remaining two knights apparently believing it was William who had spoken, ceased their pursuit of Alex and stared at the king, their faces ashen beneath their helms.

Alex dismounted and helped William to rise.

One of Henry's knights quickly slid from his saddle and gave over his horse to the king.

William swung into the saddle, acknowledged Alex's help with a nod and eyed the soldiers before him. "Which of you killed my horse?" he demanded.

The one who had thrown the lance stepped forward. "It was me. But I did not know you were the king. I thought you were only a knight."

William must have been in a generous mood for he appeared amused, not angry, and his next words surprised Alex.

"By the face of Lucca, from now on, for your courage and spirit, you will be my man and in my service get a proper reward."

The man dropped to his knee. "As you wish, My Lord."

William turned his horse and galloped away. His new man, taking the horse of one of his fallen companions, mounted and followed.

Having finished their own battles, Rory and Guy and the rest of his men rode up staring at the king riding away.

"Do not ask," Alex said to them. "Only know this, William has been saved from death this day and gained himself a new liege man in the process."

Alex had witnessed the king's vile temper on more than one occasion but today he had witnessed his magnanimity. In so doing, William had won Alex's respect.

★　★　★

Talisand, England, July 1091

The summer sun found its way to the green undergrowth around her, its golden light dappling the ground as Merewyn lifted her bow and looked into the distance. A tree stood in challenge, her target a small spot of sunlight on its dark bark.

Taking her stance, she nocked the arrow, lifted her bow and pulled the string back to her cheek, an action so familiar she had no need to think about the separate motions, only the result. She let out a breath and loosed her fingers. The arrow flew, a blur too fast for the eye to follow.

"Thwack!" The satisfying sound echoed through the woods, confirming the shot, a difficult one, had hit its mark. In her hands, the bow had become her constant companion and a terrible force, a symbol of the strength she had acquired in Wales. Never again would she be vulnerable to men who, because of her beginnings, considered her an object of scorn, or worse, easy prey.

Pleased, she quickly nocked the second arrow, but the sound of thundering hooves and bleating sheep had her jerking her head around. Heart pounding in sudden alarm, she fixed her eyes on the meadow in front of the palisade. Who would ride toward Talisand at such a pace, tearing up the sod and scattering ewes and their lambs that only moments before were peacefully nibbling on grass?

When no clarion call sounded from the gate tower, she squinted into the morning sun and watched as a dozen riders hurtled down the green slope heading toward the open gate. Over the jingle of bits and harnesses, they exchanged jests and insults, egging each other on.

Despite the years that had passed since she had last seen him, Merewyn recognized the rider in the lead at once.

Alexander.

His sable hair, now long to his shoulders, whipped behind him. Clad in mail, he sat as straight as a lance atop a huge black stallion. Moving as one with the great horse, he raced like a threatening storm toward Talisand's gate.

Even beneath his mail, she could see his body was now that of a warrior. Powerful shoulders, a lean, muscled frame and spurs marked him as one of the king's knights.

He sped by without a glance in her direction. Inwardly, she chided herself for the joy she experienced at seeing him again. In the months after her return to Talisand, she had heard tales of him whispered about the hall. Vicious on the battlefield and domineering in bed was how the women described him. An arrogant, swaggering knight and, to her mind, just like the others. The kitchen wenches spoke of his many conquests with women with a gleam of envy in their eyes.

She wanted no part of it.

One day, he would take his place as the Earl of Talisand, lauded as the king's favored knight. Such a man would not even remember the girl he had once saved from a pack of village boys. Why should she give him another thought? After all, she was now her own defender.

In the year after the ruffians had surrounded her in the woods, Alexander's presence had shielded her from harm. But when he left for Rouen to train as a squire, those same boys, keenly aware her protector was gone, began to leer at her once again.

What began as rude comments, muttered in passing, soon became indecent invitations. Whenever she ventured into the village, a group of idle boys was always waiting, their eyes following her as they called out bawdy suggestions. It was only a matter of time before they found her alone and cornered her once again.

The increasing peril driving her, Merewyn had sought help from the

Lady of Talisand. A countess, Serena was also Talisand's best archer. Merewyn had begged Serena to train her in the way of the bow. She was only beginning her lessons when the Welshman, Rhodri, and his Scottish wife, Fia, came through the demesne on their way to Wales.

In his youth, Rhodri had been Serena's teacher of the bow and a bard of some renown. Now, he ruled Powys with his two brothers. He had married Fia, a noble Scotswoman, during his sojourn at the court of Malcolm, King of Scots.

When Rhodri observed Merewyn shooting, he complimented her on her rapid progress and suggested she might accompany him to Wales where he could see to her further training.

Merewyn had been only too glad to go.

It was in Wales under Rhodri's tutoring that she had perfected her skill, eventually drawing the respect of his most senior archers. No one in Powys inquired about her origin or her parentage. Impressed with her archery skills, no one cared.

But now she was back and the day she both anticipated and dreaded had arrived.

★   ★   ★

Alex pulled rein in front of the manor, the cloud of dust settling around Azor's hooves. The bailey's inner courtyard swarmed with men-at-arms, villeins and servants welcoming them home.

He swung from the saddle, his spurs jingling as his heels hit the ground. Tired from the road, he was happy to be home and waved to the men and women whose smiles greeted him.

Talisand's great hounds rushed to his side, scattering the geese shrieking their protests. The wolf dogs were so tall their shaggy heads reached Azor's elbow. Swift in the hunt yet docile around the hearth fire, the hounds were favorites of Alex. Patting the hound's grizzled gray head nuzzling his gauntlet, Alex breathed in the scent of the beast. The familiar odor comforted him even if it was the smell of unwashed dog that had lain too long in the mud and rolled in moldy straw. "'Tis a welcome sight you are, Cathal."

Casting his gaze about the large open space of the bailey, his eyes were drawn upward to the great mound of dirt, the motte, now covered with summer's grass. On top sat the huge timber castle, towering above all. It was the landmark he had followed as he tore down the slope. One day, when it was his turn to rule Talisand, he would see it reinforced with stone.

A short distance away from where he stood was the two-story whitewashed manor he called home. Adjoining it was the larger, wooden hall that could hold more than a hundred men.

On the far side of the bailey were the armory and stables set against the palisade fence. Smoke billowed from the smith's forge and the sound of metal being tortured on the anvil added to the discordant sounds around him. But it was home.

To the north, he could just see the daub and wattle cottages that marked the village. Whiffs of smoke from the hearth fires rose through the thatched roofs.

On three sides of the palisade wound the River Lune like a natural moat. In Talisand, far from Normandy's battles, there was peace.

Children pushed their way through the crowd to stare at the knights, the boldest waving their hands in hearty welcome.

Alex's youngest brother, Thibaut, separated himself from his friends and raced to Alex. "You're home!" The boy's eyes shone with excitement. "Did you have many adventures?"

Alex chuckled and tousled Tibby's brown curls. "I did, but the telling of them must wait."

His youngest brother returned him a momentary pout, but was soon grinning once again. Tibby, only ten summers, could never be dour for long. Of the Red Wolf's four sons, he was the merriest and the most indulged. Like Alex's other brothers, Tibby had the brown eyes of their paternal grandfather in Normandy. Only Alex had his father's gray eyes. And only Alex, as the eldest, had been fostered away from Talisand. With his fostering and his training to be a squire that followed, Alex had spent more years away than at home.

A stable boy eagerly rushed to meet him, reaching for Azor's reins. Alex thrust them into the boy's hand. "Give him a good rub down and oats. I've ridden him hard this day and he did a destrier's service in Normandy."

"Aye, Sir Alex," the lad said with a grin.

Alex's squire stepped to Azor's saddle and removed the shield and helm from where they were secured. "I will see these to the armory, sir."

Alex nodded as the squire walked off and the boy led Azor toward the stables, the stallion briefly tossing his head.

Still at his side, Tibby said, "I will help," and ran to catch up with the stable boy.

Nearby, Rory and Guy slipped from their saddles and handed the reins of their horses to their waiting squires. The rest of Alex's men waved goodbye before going in search of their families.

Doffing his gauntlets, Alex watched Rory wending his way to him.

"Who is that stable boy?" Alex asked when Rory reached him. "There are so many children at Talisand now, I can scarce remember to whom they belong." The boy looked familiar, one of the groom's sons most likely.

" 'Tis young Leppe," said Rory.

Alex watched Tibby and the stable boy nearing the stables. Leppe stroked the stallion's neck to calm its agitated snorting. Azor had scented the stables and was impatient for his stall, but the boy's deft touch worked its magic and the stallion settled. "I remember him now. He is the grandson of one of the old guards who served my grandfather."

"The child has grown up among us Normans," said Rory. "Like so many of his friends, Leppe even speaks a few words of Norman French."

When his father had first been given Talisand by the Conqueror, he'd had to win the trust of the English who were there, survivors of the Conquest and fearful of their Norman overlord. The Red Wolf's reputation for savagery on the battlefield only made them more anxious. But his father had won their respect, along with that of Talisand's lady, Serena. Alex would not mar that trust for it was the legacy that would one day be his.

"Is it possible Talisand's numbers have grown while we were away?" Rory asked, looking around. "I see many new faces."

Alex remembered the conversation he'd had with his father before he left for Normandy. "The last time we were home, Father told me the king's levy for his many wars made more men-at-arms necessary."

A pretty serving wench passed by with a slow smile aimed at Alex. Returning it, he said, "Some faces are familiar."

Rory's mouth formed a mocking smile. "Mayhap you bedded her when last we were here and have forgotten. Obviously she has not." With a shake of his head, Rory added, "You pile up conquests with women like you do bodies of the king's enemies."

"And you exaggerate. 'Tis the Red Wolf the men spoke of over the night fires in Normandy."

"Not since that day in Avranches when you took on five of Henry's men and managed to cut through three of them before help arrived. Now they speak of his cub, the Black Wolf. Did you know?"

Alex chuckled. "Nay, but I suppose it fits. My hair, my horse—"

"Your way with woman," teased Rory.

"More likely, my scowl," Alex returned.

His face suddenly serious, Rory said, "The men admire you more than you know, Alex."

Alex raised his brows but said nothing. He had wanted to be like his father, but in truth, he could not claim to be the equal of the man he so admired.

Wiping the sweat from his brow with the back of his hand, he watched Guy, the younger of his two friends, sauntering toward him. Guy brushed a lock of his light brown hair from his forehead and turned to wink at the same serving wench.

"The swagger in his step is new," Alex remarked. "Was he doing that in London?"

Amusement danced in Rory's blue-green eyes. "Aye, it came with his knighting in Normandy. 'Twill pass the first time he loses a fight to another of the king's new knights."

Casting the woman a parting glance, Guy joined them. " 'Tis good to be home."

Rory rolled his eyes. "As if there were not enough women for you in London."

Guy sighed wistfully, gazing at the swaying hips of the woman as she walked toward the door of the hall. "We were not in London long enough for me to sample many. And you well know there are never enough women, particularly when the supply is limited by the need to

13

compete for our share. Alex leaves few comely women unattended."

" 'Tis true," Rory muttered.

"Enough you two!" Alex cut off his friends. But he could not deny that some unseen force drove him, as if life would be brief and he must taste it all before he left this world. He thrilled to the excitement of battle and lost himself in the arms of willing women, ever restless and always looking for the next challenge.

"Alex can endure anything save being idle," quipped Guy.

Ignoring the jests of his friends, Alex searched the crowd for the face of the girl he had not seen for many years, a girl who he had been told was recently returned to Talisand. "Where is Merewyn, I wonder?"

"Just there," said Guy. "Your gaze is set in her direction."

Alex scanned the people moving about the bailey. "I see no golden-haired girl."

"You must remember her as she was when we left to squire in Rouen. I grant you, it has been years and 'tis obvious Merewyn has not been a girl for some while. But even dressed as a lad, I would know her anywhere. We were raised in the same household."

Guy gestured with a nod toward a young bowman wearing a cap of brown felt, a leather jerkin over a linen tunic and loose green hosen tucked into brown leather boots.

"*That* is Merewyn?" asked Alex. "Looks more like kin to the Welshman who is friend to my mother."

The young bowman's head jerked up. Alex's words had carried across the bailey. Leaving his friends, he strode toward the slender figure in brown and green. As he did, the bowman bent down to pick up a quiver of arrows and a pale golden plait fell over her shoulder to touch the ground, a single concession to her femininity. Rising, she flipped the plait to her back and turned her appraising gaze on him.

"You have changed much, Merewyn," he said, arriving in front of her. His eyes took in her alabaster skin and the blue-hazel eyes he had never forgotten with their golden flashes amidst the vivid azure blue. He supposed she was a woman now but any curves she possessed were hidden beneath the jerkin and loose hosen.

"So have you," she said, her voice lower and more sultry than he remembered. "You are taller."

He was tempted to laugh, but uncertain she had meant it as a jest, he refrained. There were many things she could have remarked upon, which would have pleased him more. He took her reference to his height as avoiding them. "You might have noticed I gained my spurs since last we were together," he said, feigning offense at her failure to remark on his knighthood.

" 'Twas not unexpected," she said, her manner formal and distant. He sensed more than her attire had changed. Gone was the girl who had followed him about like a whelp, the vulnerable waif he had once defended. Before him stood a proud young woman who defied a woman's place with her bowman's garb. In her beautiful face, he saw a cold determination that had been absent when he had last bid her goodbye. What had happened? He was intensely curious but reluctant to ask while they stood in the midst of the crowded bailey.

"Alex!" Rory's voice rent the air.

Alex turned to see his companion standing at the door of the manor next to the Lord of Talisand. His father's chestnut hair had long been laced with gray but his body was still lean and well muscled. In his fifth decade, the Norman knight favored by the Conqueror and known for his prowess on the battlefield and his fidelity to both king and wife owned Alex's respect. But with the Conqueror's death and Alex's knighthood, the Red Wolf rarely rode to battle. In recent years, it was more often Alex who led Talisand's men.

Acknowledging his father with a raised hand, he turned back to Merewyn. "I must speak to my father, but I will look for you at the evening meal."

"I am not difficult to find," she said and abruptly turned and walked away.

He watched the solitary figure blend in with the men and women mingling in the bailey. Why had she never wed? There was no ring upon her finger and she was past the age when matches were made for young women.

* * *

"I bring news," Alex said to his father and followed him into the hall, crushing fresh rushes beneath his feet, sending the pleasing smell of dried herbs into the air.

The great hall had been there when the Conqueror and his knights had arrived before Alex was born. His father once offered to replace it with another, but his mother would not hear of it. The cavernous chamber had been built by her father, the old thegn, and was still the place they most often took meals, reserving the castle for war and royal guests.

Bright with many windows open to the bailey, at night candles and the central hearth fire provided light. Most of Talisand's men ate at two long trestle tables flanking the central hearth, but the place of honor, where his parents and their guests dined, was the table at the front of the hall set upon a raised dais.

With Rory and Guy on his heels, Alex moved farther into the hall where the aroma of meat roasting with spices wafted from the kitchens. "Dinner cannot be far off," he said.

"But first I must have ale!" wailed Guy in dramatic fashion. "Else I will die of thirst!" Ever the jester, Guy gripped his throat and feigned a gag.

Rory cuffed him on the head.

Maggie, Rory's Scottish grandmother and Talisand's housekeeper, bustled into the hall from the kitchens, brushing loose strands of gray hair from her eyes. She reached up to straighten her headcloth that marked her a married woman. Once a blacksmith's wife, she was now a widow. At her side, a serving girl carried a tray laden with cups, a pitcher of ale and a platter of bread and cheese.

Hands on wide hips, Maggie paused to look Alex and his two companions up and down. "Humph!" she remarked. "The three of ye look like ye rolled in the dirt. Ye're in need of a bath, but, if yer father allows, have a drink and a bite to eat before ye get yerselves to the river to wash."

Alex's father nodded his assent, his lips twitching up in a smile.

"You missed us, Maggie, admit it," Rory said to his grandmother, planting a kiss on her forehead, being careful not to touch her with his dust-covered mail.

"Aye, I suppose I did," she grudgingly admitted, "though the wenches needed the rest."

Casting a glance at Alex, Rory chuckled.

"We shall not be much of a burden," Alex said. "The king would have us here but a short while." He took the heavy tray from the servant girl. "Allow me to assist," and carried it to one of the trestle tables.

Maggie followed the three of them to the table. They detached their scabbards and set them aside, swinging their legs over the benches to sit, eagerly watching the servant girl pour the ale.

The girl winked at Alex before returning to the kitchen.

He lifted the large cup and drank deeply. "Ah, that is good and just in time, Maggie. You must have heard us coming."

"We heard ye all right, loud enough to raise St. Cuthbert, stirring up clouds of dust in the bailey. But 'twasn't me who knew of yer coming. Maugris told us ye'd be arriving this day. I've had the kitchens preparing a feast all morning at yer lady mother's direction."

"Maugris. I might have known. So the wise one has been seeing visions again." Alex had to wonder, did he have a vision of the king's court at Westminster? Did he see the brothel it had become when the king did not entertain his earls and barons? The old Norman who had come with the Red Wolf from Normandy missed little. Wise in his pronouncements, Maugris' words, be they caution or prophecy, were respected by all.

"What was that prophecy he had of you before we left?" Rory asked. Beside him, Guy set down his cup and leaned in to listen.

Trying to recall the seer's words, Alex rested his elbow on the table, his chin in his hand. "Something about my wandering..."

"The wolf's cub will wander, ever restless, until the wolf rampant flies above the red hart," Maugris intoned in his gravelly voice as he stepped to the table.

"Maugris!" Alex stood. "I see you still speak in riddles. Come, sit with us and share some ale."

Maggie raised her brows in question to the old man.

He nodded. "But Maggie, you know I prefer wine." Then to Alex, he said, "I have admired many things about your mother's people, but I never acquired a taste for English ale."

Maggie waved her arm, summoning a servant, then muttered something about having to see to the feast and headed toward the kitchens.

Alex was very fond of the housekeeper who kept Talisand's hall in order and of her daughter, Cassie, Rory's mother. A redhead like her son, Cassie was another sensible, hard-working woman, who seemed destined to assume her mother's role reigning over Talisand's kitchens, laundries and gardens.

Clothed in a fine blue tunic of Talisand wool, Maugris slid his lean frame onto the bench beside Alex. It always amazed him that the old one's face could be both ancient and ageless, as if he had been born with silver hair and skin wrinkled from the sun. But as ancient as he looked, Maugris' pale blue eyes sparkled with the excitement of youth.

Before the wine arrived, Alex's father left the man he'd been speaking with and joined them, taking the small bench at the end of the table.

A servant delivered a pitcher of wine and two goblets and Alex's father turned to him. "You are here, so I must assume William Rufus has successfully taken his older brother in hand. Is that your news?"

"Aye," said Alex, sparing a glance for Rory and Guy sitting across from him. "Once Duke Robert got a good look at the size of William's army, he agreed to terms without a fight. The two signed a treaty in Caen while William's knights sat around dicing and exchanging blows in a hastily arranged practice yard. 'Twas not the battle we expected, at least not then."

"What about Henry?" his father asked.

"'Twas Henry we fought. William's agreement with Robert stripped their younger brother of his lands in Normandy. Henry was bitter when he stomped away. We learned later he was holed up at Mont Saint Michel with his men, intending to defend his claims to the Cotentin." Seeing his father's expectant expression, Alex added, "The king ordered us to lay siege and we were only too glad to finally draw our swords."

"I wonder if that was wise on William's part," muttered Maugris. "Henry has a temper as bad as the king's. Worse, he switches sides between his brothers whenever it works to his advantage."

"What happened at Mont Saint Michel?" asked the Lord of Talisand, his gray eyes alight with interest.

Alex shrugged. "We had a few skirmishes with Henry's knights, but the ranks of Henry's soldiers dwindled each day as the king gained ground with Normandy's nobles. The last of the major supporters for Henry's cause fell when William persuaded Hugh de Avranches, the Earl of Chester, to cross to his side." Always one to calculate the course that was to his advantage, Alex was not surprised when Earl Hugh had decided in favor of William's greater power and wealth. "With the earl's defection, others quickly followed, swearing allegiance to William."

" 'Tis unfortunate Hugh felt he must fight for Henry and all to the good he is back in William's fold," said Alex's father.

Rory leaned forward. "Alex will not tell you but he displayed great skill, so much so the men are now calling him the Black Wolf."

Alex stared into his ale. As proud as he was of having the favor of the king and the other knights and as much as he had wanted Merewyn to notice, his accomplishments dwindled to the ordinary when he compared them to those of his great father. But when he looked up, he was pleased to see the pride in his father's face.

Guy chimed in, "The siege ended when Henry's men cried thirst and Duke Robert had water delivered to them."

The Lord of Talisand laughed. " 'Tis no surprise. Pliable, weak Robert would hardly allow his younger brother to perish of thirst."

"Those were nearly the duke's words when the king erupted in anger," Alex said with a smile. "William accused his brother of keeping a good store of enemies by giving them meat and drink. His face turned crimson and he began to stutter. For a moment, I thought he might run Robert through."

His father seemed to consider the possibility. "The two have come to blows more than once."

"Days later," Alex said, "Henry sued for an honorable surrender and his brothers granted it, pleased to see the back of him, I think."

Maugris asked, "Is William satisfied with his foray into Normandy?"

Alex took another drink of his ale. "Yea, I suppose. And Robert is with him, but the king came back to England earlier than expected."

His father raised his brows and Alex answered the unspoken question. "Word reached the king in Normandy that Malcolm, the King of Scots, had marched into England to besiege New Castle upon Tyne. William now prepares for war, gathering his army to march north. He will call a meeting of his barons soon. Will you go?"

"One does not refuse the king," said his father. "But your mother will not be happy to hear William Rufus has set his eyes upon Scotland. Your Uncle Steinar rides with King Malcolm."

"An uncle I have never met," Alex reminded him.

"Well, he has the same violet eyes and fair hair as your mother. And the same temper when aroused. Were you to encounter him, you would know the two are siblings."

"I will keep that in mind should I meet him on the battlefield." The possibility sent a shudder through him. The last thing Alex needed was to slay his mother's much beloved brother.

His father stared into his wine, his forehead furrowed. "I wonder why the King of Scots picked this time to invade England..."

"Well, for one, William was away in Normandy," Alex offered, "but there is also the matter of Edgar Ætheling, the brother of Malcolm's queen. He has been living in Normandy where he gained lands from Duke Robert. He was at the treaty signing in Caen."

His father's dark brows drew together. "You believe *he* is the reason Malcolm attacked New Castle?"

"I do. As a part of the agreement between William and Robert, Edgar was expelled from the duke's court. He left Normandy an angry man. With his brother-in-law a king, one does not have to wonder where he went."

"Scotland, of course," said Alex's father, shaking his head.

Maugris turned his goblet in his hand. "So, the Conqueror's son fears the Ætheling as did his father."

"Likely so," said Alex. "The king still has many enemies and Edgar, now in his fourth decade and a seasoned knight, would make a powerful ally of Robert's, especially if Malcolm were to aid them with his army."

"And then there are the Welsh," interjected Rory. "The king was none too pleased to hear of trouble on the border with Wales."

"We know of William's problems there," said the Lord of Talisand. "It was Rhodri's anticipation of war that caused him to send Merewyn home."

Merewyn. The girl with the beautiful eyes, now a woman, who dressed as a bowman. The last time he was home, she was still in Wales.

He expected her to return, but he had not imagined she would do so looking like one of Rhodri's archers. "The king has not been successful against the Welsh," he told his father, "and I cannot see him risking more of his men in that wild place when he gathers an army to fight Malcolm. The quarrelsome Scots fight like brawlers in a tavern but the Welsh fight like foxes at night in a chicken pen. You will see their feathered shafts in your dead, but you will never see the foxes."

Alex looked up to see his mother, Lady Serena, gliding toward them, elegant and beautiful. Her gown was silk, the same color as her eyes, and her flaxen hair neatly plaited.

Her face lit with excitement as she approached. "You are home!"

Alex rose and bowed. "I would offer you an embrace, but I still bear the dust of my travels."

"A kiss of greeting will do," she said, presenting her cheek.

He gave her the requested kiss as his two friends stood and bowed.

The Lord of Talisand rose from his seat to stand by his lady, kissing her on the forehead. "How go the preparations for the celebration, my love?"

"Well enough, though Maggie is having a time of it in the kitchens." With a smile for Alex's companions, she said, "Cassie and Emma will be glad to see you both. Your mothers have been anxiously awaiting your return. Your sisters, Rory, and yours, Guy, will be joining all of Talisand to welcome you home tonight. And tomorrow, there will be contests of strength and games so do not drown in your ale."

Alex did not mind his mother's chiding, which had always been tempered with love for him and his brothers. After traipsing all over Normandy with the king who fought his own brothers, Alex was glad he and his three brothers were friends, which reminded him he had not seen Raoul or Roger anywhere. "Tibby greeted me when we arrived but where are Raoul and Roger?"

"Raoul is away on Talisand business with Sir Alain and some of the house knights," his father informed him. "Now that your brother has his spurs, there is no holding him here, so I have set him a task. Roger is serving his namesake, the Earl of Shrewsbury. Once Roger is knighted, I expect he will be as eager to serve the king as Raoul."

"What was Tibby doing when you left him?" his mother asked.

"Off to the stables."

"By now, he has probably found some trouble," his mother put in. Glancing at Rory, she added, "He follows your younger sister, Cecily, wherever she leads. The two were chasing chickens with Aethel's son, Ancel, the last time I saw them. But as long as the three mischievous imps are out of Maggie's way and her strawberry tarts are safe, 'tis best."

"Is my mother about?" asked Rory.

"Cassie is in the kitchens with your grandmother. Maggie has no doubt told her of your arrival but they are deep in flour, kneading dough for the bread ovens and watching closely the servants so they take care in turning the roasting spits. I will tell her you have gone with Alex and Guy to wash off the dirt."

Alex got to his feet. "Come, lads, let us test the waters of the Lune and scare a few trout."

CHAPTER 2

Merewyn waited in the shadows of the stable until Alex, Rory and Guy left the armory, their squires following after them with fresh clothing. Knowing the men would be at the river for some time, she left the shadows and headed for the manor. She did not wish to encounter Alex again so soon. Her stomach twisted in knots as she remembered her bedchamber was only a stone's throw from the one Maggie had told her Alex shared with Raoul.

She entered the manor just as Lady Serena came through the wide opening that led to the hall, the two buildings being joined. "Oh, Merewyn, I have been looking for you. There is something I want to show you."

"Yea, my lady?"

" 'Tis in your chamber."

They ascended the stairs to the chamber that was Merewyn's alone. Lady Serena opened the oaken door and gestured her inside. In front of her stood the table where she laid her bow and quiver of arrows. Beyond the table, sunlight from the window streamed in through the open wooden shutters. To her left was a small bed and, on the right side of the room, a larger one to which Lady Serena walked. Merewyn followed.

There, lying upon the fur-covered bed was a beautiful gown of amethyst silk. The bodice and matching hooded cloak were trimmed in an elaborate gold weaving.

" 'Tis lovely," said Merewyn reaching out to touch the silk, shimmering in the light from her window. She had never owned a gown the equal of this one.

The Lady of Talisand smiled. "It is for you, Merewyn, to wear this night."

"I am more than grateful, my lady, but why?"

Lady Serena gave her an indulgent smile. "I know you are content with your archer's clothing and your simple gowns of linen and wool, but tonight is special and you are now a woman grown. I would have you attired in clothing to match your beauty. Rory and Guy's sisters will be in silk, as will Lora. Emma would be angry with me if I allowed you to dress in less fine a manner than her daughter. She still thinks of you as hers."

"Lady Emma is very kind, but I have not lived with Sir Geoffroi and her for many years." They had taken Merewyn into their home after her mother's death, but after she took up the bow, Lady Serena had invited her to live in the manor. When she returned from Wales, it was to Serena's home Merewyn had gone. "You are more a mother of the heart to me than any other."

"It pleases me to hear you say it." Lady Serena sat on the edge of the bed, next to the gown. "You have become the daughter I once thought to have, Merewyn."

She beamed at hearing the words. "Truly?" She was still living with Lady Emma when Lady Serena had lost a girl child, born a few years before Tibby. It brought Merewyn great joy to think she might have filled the void left by the loss of Serena's child.

"Indeed, yea." She stood. "Now, say no more and accept the gown. The gold necklace Emma gave you will be beautiful with it."

Guy's sister, Bea, and Rory's oldest sister, Alice, were a few years younger than Merewyn's friend, Lora. In the time Merewyn had been back, she had noticed the three women were much admired. With powerful knights as their fathers, Merewyn was certain they had never feared being caught alone in the woods. Mayhap it would not hurt for her to dress like them in the hall.

She met the older woman's expectant gaze. "I will wear it and gladly."

Lady Serena gave Merewyn's clothing a long perusal. "I expect you should have a bath. I will see that the lads bring hot water and a tub to your chamber. My maidservant, Nelda, can assist you with the gown when you are ready."

★　★　★

Merewyn sank into the steaming water with a sigh, inhaling the flowery scent of the soap while reflecting upon her encounter with Alexander. She had noticed more than his towering height. No longer was his body that of a stripling lad. His broad shoulders that had once promised strength had gained muscle with his knight's training and his face had lost its boyhood look, gaining instead a man's strong jaw and high cheekbones. Together with his long black hair, they rendered him darkly handsome. She did not wonder the women spoke of him in hushed whispers.

She had expected her childhood adoration of him to fade with time and distance, that seeing him again would free her of the memories that had bound her to him during the years she had been away. But she had been wrong. The moment she had gazed into his piercing gray eyes and heard his voice, it had all come rushing back. Only the wave of longing that had washed over her was not a girl's adoration of a remembered hero. It had been a woman's desire.

She ran her fingers through the warm water and imagined running them through the waves of his long hair and touching the dark hair on his chest she had glimpsed from the neck of his tunic. He would pull her to him and her breasts would be crushed by his weight as he held her.

Her nipples formed tight buds and the caress of the water became his caress as her breathing became more labored. What would it be like to lie with him?

Her bow, leaning against the wall of her chamber, spoke a word of silent condemnation for her wild imaginings. "I know who he is and who I am," she said aloud to the bow. "You do not have to remind me." She shook her head, her wet hair splashing water over her face, waking her out of the fantasy and reminding her of Alex's reputation and what she could expect from such a knight.

He was arrogant; a knight who'd had many women. Beyond that, he was Talisand's heir and she a bastard of ignoble birth. He would wed a highborn lady, a marriage likely arranged by the king, and she would not marry at all. Having compared all men to Alex for so long, how could she wed another?

Her heart constricted at the possibility of Alex with a more worthy woman. Mayhap when that day came, she would be far away in Wales where Rhodri's archers would welcome her bow.

Did Alex suspect his absence had been the cause of her interest in archery? Nay, he would not have guessed that when he left to become a squire, she had been alone and afraid, in need of a weapon to defend herself. But now things were different. The change had come with her first archery contest after her return home. The men stared in admiration and kept their distance.

She looked again at her bow. "You have gained me respect in men's eyes. For that, I will always be grateful and, thus, I will heed your warning." Her archer's clothing had been carefully made to conceal her womanly curves. It was what she had wanted, this distance from men, mayhap even as to Alex, for were he to draw close and see her as a woman like the others, vulnerable to his masculine presence, she feared she would be helpless to resist him.

But tonight, for Lady Serena, she would don the gown of a lady.

$$\star \quad \star \quad \star$$

Alex took his seat on the dais between his father and Sir Geoffroi, Guy's father. He would have been happy to sit at the long trestle tables where his father's men ate, but tonight he and his companions were in the place of honor, as sons being welcomed home from war. It was a stark contrast to the cold nights in Normandy and those on the way home from London when they had crouched before an open fire with only a few hares to share between them.

In battle and traveling the length of England, he and his men had been gray, dust-covered figures passing in a blur. Often they were coated with mud from the rain-soaked moors. But tonight, the men-at-arms had doffed their mail to don fresh linen tunics, the knights wearing woolen and velvet. Only the king's court presented a more opulent display.

Because it was expected of the Red Wolf's son, Alex had worn a fine woolen tunic of midnight blue embroidered with silver thread on the shoulders, a gift from his mother. The Lady of Talisand had expectations for her sons' appearance, particularly Alex as the eldest. He was glad when she had taken no issue with his longer hair. His father had reacted to it with raised brows, but said nothing. All of William's younger knights had grown their hair long to mirror their sire. Alex was happy to go along with the new fashion because it freed him from cutting his hair. It was enough that he must shave his face for he could not abide a beard.

He had left his sword in his bedchamber, knowing none would be permitted in the hall this night. But the dagger at his belt, a gift from the king, was no less formidable a weapon. He could kill with it and had. In the four years he had served William Rufus, Alex had ended the life of more than one man at the king's command. It was a knight's service and he accepted it.

Servants hurried into the hall, placing trays of meat on the tables and the trenchers that served to hold their food.

A kitchen wench filled his goblet with wine. Alex nodded his thanks and, ever hungry, filled his trencher with slices of venison, spooning over it the juices into which he would dip his bread.

Maggie had outdone herself with a fine feast of venison, roasted in a vinegar and pepper sauce, hare spiced with what smelled like rosemary and thyme, and a peacock skinned, roasted and redressed in its own feathers. The delicacy was not often served at Talisand. He had first tasted the peafowl's rich, dark meat in Chester at the home of his foster father, Earl Hugh.

Biting into the chunk of peacock, Alex shot a glance at Guy, eating on the other side of Sir Geoffroi. The young knight was flirting with the young women at the tables, enjoying his new status.

Alex took a drink of his wine and looked up at the rafters. Where once, his mother told him, there had been bright ornamentation, now the images on the carved timbers were faded and darkened with soot from the central hearth fire. On his mother's side, his roots were deep in England's soil. But his father was a Norman, as were most of Talisand's men-at-arms.

Turning to his father, Alex asked, "How many new men-at-arms do we have?"

"A score in anticipation of trouble in the north, but there may soon be more if the king is assembling an army to fight Malcolm."

"He will be some time in doing that," said Alex, "for he waits not only for the men who owe him service but for the ships he would take to Scotland."

"Following in his father's steps," said Talisand's lord. "Mayhap a prudent step. 'Twas what the Conqueror did when he invaded Scotland."

Alex's mother, apparently catching their conversation, leaned across his father. "War was averted then with an agreement and your father returned unscathed. We can only pray that Malcolm and William Rufus will have sense enough to do the same."

His father took his wife's hand. "Do not worry, my love. All will be well."

She looked into his eyes. "It was my fervent prayer when I met with Father Bernard this morning."

Just beyond Alex's mother sat Maugris in his usual place, nodding in agreement. One never knew what vision the old man might have seen. Knowing the wise one advised his father gave Alex comfort. Whatever happened, he had to believe Talisand would stand.

Beyond Maugris, Alex glimpsed Sir Maurin with his dark head bent to his son, Rory. Like Alex's father, Sir Maurin had outlived the Conqueror and helped to bring peace to England. Once, Sir Maurin, Sir Geoffroi and Sir Alain were young knights, who, along with Alex's father, left Normandy to seek lands of their own. Now it was up to their sons to secure England's future. Alex was glad he would have at his side men like Rory and Guy, as well as his brothers. Jamie, too, for the house knight who had once been page to the Red Wolf, was devoted to Talisand.

Alex let his gaze drift about the hall, watching the men and women enjoying Maggie's feast. A long table had been added to the two they typically had in order to accommodate the crowd gathered for the homecoming feast. Because of the bachelor knights and new men-at-arms, the men outnumbered the women. But it was the women with their gowns and long hair that drew Alex's attention, a feast for his eyes, as Maggie's meal was a feast for his stomach.

Content, he reached for his wine just as a woman gowned in silk the color of dark violets slipped into the hall like a faint cool breeze. He set down his goblet, his senses coming alive as his gaze tracked her every move. Pale flaxen locks pulled back from her delicate face cascaded down her back, as her gown rippled around her. He imagined it rustling as she walked, the sound like leaves falling to the forest floor. Around her neck sparkled an intricate gold necklace. The queen of fairies walking among them.

Merewyn.

This afternoon she had appeared a diminutive Welsh archer. Now, attired like a lady of royal birth, she held his attention as no other woman in the hall.

He leaned into his father. "Have there been no suitors for her?"

His father followed his line of sight. "Merewyn?"

"Aye. She is one and twenty and not yet wed."

"Well, to begin, Sir Alain has yet to give his daughter, Lora, to anyone and she is of an age with Merewyn. But the truth is the girl would have suitors aplenty were she to smile at any one of my men, but she holds herself apart. Above reproach, your mother believes, afraid to encourage any because of her mother's fate. The men do not know what to make of her. Possibly they fear her arrows should their overtures not be welcomed."

"For good reason, I understand. The men say she can shoot well."

"Yea, she can. Tomorrow you will have to attend the archery contest."

"I just might." Normally, he would have headed straight for the sword matches but tomorrow he would begin with those testing their skills in archery.

Alex's gaze continued to rest upon Merewyn as she took a seat next to Lora and Jamie. It was not difficult to see why she had sought out those two. Jamie had been an orphan, just like Merewyn, when Alex's father made him his page. And Lora's mother had once been leman to Alex's English grandfather. In the eyes of some, Lora would be tainted by her mother's former life just as Merewyn was marked as a child of rape. Such blots against a woman were rarely forgiven by the merciless.

Merewyn's eyes scanned the hall before alighting on him. Her face bore a look of discomfort, as if she was reluctant to be here. Hoping to put her at ease, he smiled and dipped his head in greeting. Her eyes met his for only a moment before looking away.

*   *   *

Sipping her wine, Merewyn tried unsuccessfully to avoid looking at Alexander as she listened to Jamie recounting stories of his knightly pursuits while she'd been in Wales. He was generous in his compliments of Talisand's lord and modest in telling of his own feats, as he always was.

Jamie had been a knight for several years when she had gone with Rhodri to Wales. Now, just into his third decade, he was a well-favored man with a head of sun-bleached curls and a winsome smile. He often aimed that smile at Lora whose exotic beauty drew admiring glances from many men. But Lora's eyes seemed focused on the dais where Alex sat between his father and Sir Geoffroi.

Did Lora long for Alex? Merewyn hoped not, for her friend could have no claim on the heir of Talisand any more than she could.

"Tomorrow there will be tests of strength and contests," said Jamie, the sparkle in his eyes conveying his eagerness for the coming day. "Will you be attending the matches?" He had posed the question to the two of them but Merewyn was certain 'twas Lora's answer he awaited.

Lora returned him a small smile. "Yea, all of Talisand will be there."

"I will look for you then," he said. "And you, Merewyn, will you compete against Talisand's archers?"

She let out a breath, acknowledging to herself the mixed feelings she had about competing against the other archers. Though she disliked being on display, she could not resist the thrill of the competition. "I will. I was hoping Lady Serena might shoot. 'Tis been long since I have witnessed a demonstration of her skill."

"She does not often compete against the archers anymore," Jamie said. "Young Tibby and her work in the village keeps her occupied most days."

Lora chuckled and directed her next words to Merewyn. "My brother, Ancel, and Tibby follow that little vixen, Cecily, around like puppies."

"Aye, I have seen the three of them tormenting the chickens," Merewyn said.

"You should have seen them this afternoon," said Lora. "Their faces were smeared with the remnants of Maggie's tarts. Cassie had gone home to change and Maggie was in the hall directing the servants. The three imps found the cooling tarts sitting in the kitchen and apparently could not resist. I could hear Maggie's shouts to the front door of the hall when she found them."

"That must have been a sight," said Jamie, shaking his head.

"It would have been amusing," Lora said, smiling, "had not Maggie informed them they had just had their sweet for the day and would get no more. Their loud protests for what they considered a great injustice echoed through the hall as Maggie chased them from the kitchens."

Jamie laughed, as did Merewyn, trying to picture the scene. There had been children in Wales, dark-haired little ones she had adored, including those belonging to Rhodri and Fia. They had returned her affection, calling her "Merry". For as long as she remained among them, the name had described her well. In Wales, she had forgotten the shame of her youth. But always in the back of her mind was the memory of the raven-haired lad who had saved her in the woods.

✴   ✴   ✴

Alex stabbed a slice of venison with his knife and brought it to his trencher, listening to Sir Geoffroi with only half an ear, as he watched Merewyn. Lady Emma stopped by Merewyn's table to speak a word to her and he was reminded that she had once lived with Sir Geoffroi and his wife. When Merewyn laughed, men turned their heads to glimpse her. Did she know how attractive they found her? How attractive he found her?

"Has the king mentioned an intention to betroth you to a woman from one of Normandy's noble families?"

His attention roused, Alex faced the knight whose dark blond hair was now gray at his temples. "What?"

Sir Geoffroi's stark blue eyes took on a serious mien. "Surely the possibility comes as no surprise. Now that he has gained new lands in Normandy from his brother, I expect William will want to bind his young nobles to those lands."

"The king has said naught of it to me," Alex replied contemplatively. Crossing his arms over his chest, he added, "I would prefer to choose my own bride when the time comes."

" 'Tis not likely you will have the freedom. You know how your father came to wed your lady mother."

"Aye, I know the story. Neither was given a choice. But that was the Conqueror."

" 'Tis possible his son might feel differently. I do not know William Rufus well enough to say. But if you think to take a bride from Talisand, consider my daughter, Beatrice."

Alex looked to where Bea sat with Rory's sister, Alice. "She is very comely," he said half-heartedly. At eighteen summers, Guy's sister was living up to the name "Beautiful Bea". With her silken light brown hair and gray-green eyes, she was every bit the child of her mother, Lady Emma, who sat close by her daughter. But that was just the point. To Alex, Bea was a child and a compliant one at that. He looked beyond her to the woman who fascinated him.

"If you are gazing at Sir Alain's daughter, Lora, you may have competition from Sir Jamie. 'Tis why he is still unwed."

"Aye, I can see he is attentive to her," said Alex. He had not missed the attention Jamie paid to Lora and was not unhappy she was the one who garnered smiles from the captain of his father's house knights and not Merewyn. Why had Sir Geoffroi not suggested Merewyn? Was it the circumstance of her birth, her orphan status, or her unwomanly choice of pursuits?

"Well, there is also Alice, Rory's sister," Sir Geoffroi went on, "but I'm told the redhead is difficult."

Alex's brows drew together in a frown. "Marriage is not on my mind." He reached for his wine.

Sir Geoffroi lifted his goblet, giving Alex a sidelong glance. "Taking after your father? Until he met your mother, the Red Wolf was not his only name. The Conqueror's men called him 'the warrior priest'."

Alex laughed, covering his mouth to keep from spurting his wine on the table. Breaking off a piece of bread, he sopped it in the juices in his trencher. "There are many things they might call me, Sir Geoffroi, but 'priest' is not among them." He took a bite of the tasty juice-soaked bread. "Still, I thank you for the warning about the king's intentions. I have seen enough of Normandy to last me a long while. I have no desire to bind myself to it. There is no peace to be had in that nest of vipers."

Sir Geoffroi laughed heartily. "Now you know why your father and I were happy to accompany Duke William to England. The rewards came later."

After that, Alex turned to his other side and spoke in low tones to his father about the king's court and all he could expect to find there. " 'Tis not like that on campaign," Alex assured his father, "but in the king's palace at Westminster, his favorites wear their hair longer than mine and mince about gowned and perfumed like women."

"I do not look forward to that," said his father, "and your lady mother, who has no love for Norman kings, will have yet another excuse not to like this one."

Alex knew well his mother's opinion of the Conqueror for he had heard her expound upon it numerous times. With William Rufus' strange proclivities and his disdain for the church, she would like this Norman king even less.

Once the honeyed fruit tarts were served, conversation in the hall died as two minstrels in colorful robes of green, gold and scarlet approached the dais, carrying lyre and pipes. Candles flickered and the fire in the hearth slowly faded to embers as the minstrels' music lifted enchanting sounds into the air.

When the gentle music ended, the tables were moved against the walls and more lively music replaced the soft sounds in anticipation of the dancing that would ensue.

Men began to choose partners for the dances. Rory jumped from his seat and headed straight for Guy's sister, Bea. Guy, likely in an effort to get even, headed for Rory's sister, the redheaded Alice. When Alex saw Jamie take Lora's hand, leaving Merewyn alone, he quickly got to his feet and strode in her direction. He was of a mind to see if she danced as well as she was rumored to shoot her arrows.

* * *

Merewyn watched Alex crossing the hall to where she stood, oblivious to the eager looks from the women he passed. Her heart soared to think he would brave the disdain of others to seek her out for his partner. Mayhap he was not so arrogant as she had imagined.

When he bowed before her, offering his hand, she took it.

The shiver that snaked up her arm shocked her. It was the first time he had touched her so, the way a man touched a woman for whom he had affection. He was so much a man now, his strength revealed in his muscled shoulders and arms. She had promised herself she would stay away from him as she did the other knights and here she was partnering with him in a dance.

He led her to the large area where couples were forming squares. The group they joined set a fast pace keeping time with the music. Soon, she and Alex were matching the quick steps, laughing and smiling.

She was powerless against the joy she experienced being with him. If she allowed herself, she might imagine they were a couple, for they moved easily together as if it were not the first time they had partnered. She had learned to dance in Wales and savored the exhilaration of abandoning herself to the music.

And now it was Alex who held her hand.

After another dance, the room grew over-warm leaving her cheeks heated and her heart pounding. When the music came to a dramatic end, Alex lifted her high into the air, her hands on his shoulders. Caught up in the moment, she laughed as he set her down. But around them, she glimpsed frowns on the faces of some older women.

Alex must have noticed, for he pulled her toward the door that led to the bailey. "Walk with me, Merewyn."

Flushed with wine and heated from the dance, escaping the disapproving looks into the cooler air lured her almost as much as the temptation to be alone with him. "Aye, very well."

He guided her out the door but did not let go of her hand. She should not allow him to touch her in so familiar a manner, but she could not bring herself to take back her hand.

Above her, the moonless sky was filled with a radiant circle of stars, their brightness dazzling. "It matters not how many times I see the stars on a clear night," she remarked, "I am always in awe."

He joined her to stare up at the brilliant display of stars. " 'Twas the same for me when I looked into the night sky over Normandy."

She had often tried to imagine him in that land, worried her champion might be wounded or worse. As a squire, he had followed the knights to battle and later, as a knight, he confronted the swords of other men. He could have died; many did.

She peered at him out of the corner of her eye, admiring his strong profile set against the light from the windows of the hall. "Did you sleep outdoors in Normandy?"

"Some. The last months were often warm. We had tents, of course. But other times, some of us slept in the hall of one of the nobles in Normandy. William Rufus likes his comforts, even on campaign."

They walked through the bailey. All was quiet save the guards at the gate tower who spoke a greeting to Alex before returning to gaze outward from the palisade.

Alex rubbed his thumb over her knuckles, sending little ripples of pleasure through her. She forced herself to keep her mind on their conversation. "What is he like, the king?"

"He is still unwed, unusual for a king in his third decade. And he is not much like his father, who, I am told, respected the church. But like his father, he is a worthy knight and can be fierce in battle. He can also be dangerous when confronted." He laughed. "Like an angry bull."

She tried to imagine the Conqueror's son who had become king upon his father's death, but she could not recall one good thing said about him in Wales.

"When he is not wearing mail," Alex went on, "he favors luxurious clothing adorned with gold and jewels."

She glanced at Alex's dark blue wool tunic, now black in the moonlight, fitted to his lean muscled form. How much more elaborate was the king's attire? "Is he a difficult king to serve?"

"Not on the battlefield. And he is generous when pleased."

It seemed he might say more but he hesitated and then was silent. Was he brooding? Often, his dark looks could seem threatening. There was so much she did not know about Alexander the man.

They drew next to the stables and it occurred to her she would like to see his great stallion. "Would you show me your horse, the huge black one you ride?"

"Aye, but you will have to approach him with care since you are new to him."

Inside the long stable building, a lone candle burned in a copper lantern. At the entrance, a stable boy stirred in his sleep. Alex brought his finger to his lips and beckoned her farther into the stable's depths.

Horses moved about in their stalls, a few looking over the ropes across the open doors as they passed, greeting them with soft nickers. Near the back of the stable on the right was a large stall. The black stallion raised his head over the rope and, seeing his master, nickered loudly, his ears coming forward.

Alex reached out and stroked the stallion's neck. "Missed me, did you?" Then, looking at her, he said, "I acquired Azor in Normandy."

"Will he let me touch his muzzle?" she asked, tentatively reaching out her hand.

"If you speak to him with soft words, aye."

Merewyn loved horses but she was certain this one tolerated only one master. Gently, she ran her palm over the stallion's soft muzzle and reaching up, slid her hand down his forehead. "You are a handsome fellow." *Like your master.*

The light was dim but there were sparks in the stallion's eyes as he raised his head. "He is magnificent," she said. Larger than her Welsh pony, the black horse appeared to her a confident beast. "And I think he knows it," she said with a small laugh.

Alex turned her to face him and placed his hands on her shoulders. "He does. He's a proud beast like his master."

She knew she should move away but his strong hands somehow anchored her feet to the ground. Before she fully understood his intent, he pulled her to him and set his lips upon hers, claiming a kiss she could not deny him. It was her first, long imagined and now realized.

His warm mouth moved over hers, the effect like strong wine, lulling her to ignore the objections her mind was shouting. She brought her hands to his arms feeling the muscles flexing beneath his tunic and hung on as he swept her into a swirling mist of sensations.

Her lips still sought his as he raised his head. "I have been wanting to do that since you first entered the hall tonight."

"You would claim a woman's kiss merely because you desire it?" Mayhap it worked with others, but she refused to be one of his conquests. Bringing her hands to his chest, she pushed him away. "You have grown presumptuous." She knew of his reputation. Few, if any, women ever told him nay. 'Twas said the wenches who had gone to his bed did not leave disappointed. It made her angry to think they had some part of him she never would.

He drew close and whispered, "We were once friends, Merewyn. We could be more."

She jerked her head back. "Nay, I will not be one of your women." Angry with herself for so willingly falling into his arms, she stepped away. Even now, his nearness caused her heart to flutter in her chest and her body to want more of his kisses. "Are they all willing?"

"Most are, but I did not invite every woman to walk with me, Merewyn. Only you. 'Tis not all women I want." He stepped closer. "But I do want you, Merewyn."

His bold assumption that he might have her if he but wanted her was the final stroke. She turned on her heels and ran out of the stable.

CHAPTER 3

Alex slept well his first night home, glad to be in a bed and not on the ground. He woke with the memory of the kiss he had stolen from Merewyn. A very pleasant memory until he recalled her reaction. He might have acted too soon. Too, he must remember that she was the woman who, as a child, he had protected from the lust of others.

Her words of condemnation still rang in his ears. Was he so arrogant as to think he could have any woman? Possibly so. And Merewyn might fear becoming one of those nameless, faceless wenches and village girls he'd slept with on the way to becoming a knight, or the ladies who now willingly offered him their favors.

But she could never be one of those.

In the years she had been gone, she had grown into an alluring woman, but nothing like the women who typically came to his bed, experienced and willing.

She is an innocent.

He had an overwhelming desire to protect her, even from himself. But, as he determined to do so, the memory of the way she had responded to his kiss, a warm kitten in his arms, still lingered and his body stirred in response. Would she again open to his kiss? And if she did, would he take her as he wanted to or would he refrain with her innocence in mind?

His stomach growled, reminding him of other needs. Rising, he dressed in the shorter tunic he would wear to the sword fighting match.

After a hasty meal of bread and cheese and a few words with his father, he left the manor and strode through the palisade gate, drawn by the noise of people at play. Above him, the sun beamed down from a clear blue sky. The day would be warm.

Stretched out before him, covering the large expanse of green in front of the palisade, was a festival to rival those he had seen in Normandy. It appeared all of Talisand had arrived for the festivities.

To his right, the sword matches were just beginning. The clang of metal meeting metal resounded through the air as knights and men-at-arms tested their skill against each other in a circle set off by brightly colored pennons flapping in the breeze.

Alex looked briefly in that direction, noting Rory's red head moving about as he squared off against the more senior Jamie. Alex would join them soon, but first he wanted to observe the archery contest. He had heard much about Merewyn's skills. Now he would see them for himself.

Passing the huge blue and white pavilion raised against the summer sun where ale and honey wine would be served, he strode to where his mother stood at the edge of the crowd gathered to watch the archers, who were just stepping to the line.

"You are not competing?" he inquired.

She shot him a glance before turning back to watch the archers taking their stances. "Rising late, are you?"

"I was talking to Father about the summons I expect he will receive from the king," he muttered. "You did not answer my question. Will you shoot?"

"Not today. I am more interested in seeing how Merewyn fares. She was my student before she was Rhodri's. Did you know?"

"Nay, I did not."

" 'Twas after you left to squire in Rouen."

He scanned the line of archers preparing to shoot. Merewyn's fair hair, golden in the morning sun, was easy to spot where she stood at the line with three male archers. She had never appeared more beautiful even though she was, once again, garbed as the slender Welsh bowman, her hair confined to a single plait.

As one, the archers nocked their arrows, lifted their bows and pulled back the strings. The tension in the crowd was palpable as the archers narrowed their eyes on the target.

"Loose!" shouted an official.

The arrows flew with a great rushing sound. He had heard it often enough on the battlefield to find it familiar.

By the bright fletching of Merewyn's arrow, Alex saw her arrow had hit the target dead center, as did the arrows of two others, both men.

He waited, knowing they would move the target back another twenty feet.

Father Bernard joined him and his mother. "Good day, my lady," he said. " 'Tis good to have you home, Sir Alex." In his sixth decade, the priest who had taught them all to read, now had a tonsure of white hair. He was one of those priests who had married, but was now a widower, as much loved by the people of Talisand as Maugris.

" 'Tis good to be back, Father."

"Have you come to watch the archers?" his mother asked the old priest.

"I have," he said with a grin. "The skill of the young woman returned from Wales is much spoken of."

"You will enjoy seeing Merewyn shoot," said the Lady of Talisand.

"As much as I used to delight in your skill with the bow, my lady?"

Alex was aware of the friendship between the priest who had blessed his parents' marriage and his mother and had heard them teasing each other before.

"Mayhap more," his mother said.

As the archers prepared to shoot, Alex, his mother and Father Bernard turned to watch. The arrows were loosed and once the target was examined, only Merewyn and one man's arrows remained. The target was again moved farther away so that it was now standing amidst the trees.

" 'Tis a long shot," he said.

"Merewyn has hit targets farther away than that," his mother noted in a calm voice.

With a "thwack", Merewyn's arrow hit the center of the target. The man's arrow fell short. The archer offered his hand to her in congratulations as the crowd roared shouts of praise.

"The young woman is, indeed, skilled," remarked Father Bernard.

Alex nodded in agreement. "I vow she is as good as you, Mother."

"She is better, Alex. You will see."

Alex returned his gaze to Merewyn as she handed her bow and arrows to a waiting attendant and swung onto the back of a white pony. She claimed only three arrows from the quiver he held out to her, grasping them in the same hand as her bow. With her free hand, she turned her pony toward the edge of the wide-open area while the servants set up two targets side by side, strips of wood standing like trees.

Knotting the pony's reins, Merewyn laid them at the base of the horse's neck. Using only her legs, as he did when commanding his destrier in battle, she trotted the mare forward and then urged the horse into a canter, circling once around the large meadow. With a "Hah!" she and the pony were racing at a full gallop.

A knot formed in Alex's throat and the crowd held its breath as Merewyn raised her bow, nocked an arrow and, crossing before the targets, let the arrow fly. With a resounding "thump" the arrow hit the first target dead center.

Shouts of loud acclamation rose from the crowd as Merewyn slowed, patted the pony's neck and began to circle again.

"I have never seen the like," said Alex.

"Nor I," said Father Bernard.

"She is not done yet," said his lady mother, her voice filled with pride.

The crowd quieted as Merewyn again raced the pony in front of the targets, twisting lithely in the saddle to loose one arrow, then another. Two arrows smacked into the two targets in rapid succession.

The crowd erupted in shouts of praise.

Alex shook his head, amazed at the skill of this sprite of a woman who moved like the wind and contorted her body to wield her bow with deadly accuracy from the back of a galloping horse. Observing the way her slim thighs had gripped the pony's flanks, in his mind he saw those same thighs wrapped around his body. Silently, he cursed himself for having such thoughts, especially in the presence of Talisand's priest.

"William's archers do not shoot from horses," he said to his mother.

She returned him one of her knowing smiles that told him she was about to teach him a lesson. "Your father told me the Conqueror could draw a bow that no one else could wield while spurring his steed onward. The bow Rhodri designed for Merewyn may be smaller, but your father's archers are still in awe of her."

Remembering his king's fondness for young men, Alex said, " 'Tis best William Rufus not see her in the bowman's garb."

Father Bernard stifled a cough.

His mother shot him a puzzling look.

Unwilling to explain in a place where people could overhear, he turned his eyes back to Merewyn. She handed her bow to the waiting attendant and swung down from her saddle to stroke her pony's neck.

"The mare was a gift from Rhodri," his mother said. "Merewyn trained her in Wales and gave her the Welsh name Ceinder. The two have a strong attachment to each other, as you can see." With a wistful sigh, she added, "I am so proud of Merewyn."

"You have reason to be," said Father Bernard. "The girl has overcome much to become the young woman she is today." With those words, he wished them well and strolled away.

Alex considered the words of his mother and those of the good father. No other woman he knew, save his mother, had both ethereal beauty and a warrior's spirit. Watching his mother walk to join Merewyn where she was accepting the congratulations of the other archers, he considered the two women were much alike. Both were intelligent, strong and well able to defend themselves.

★   ★   ★

Merewyn walked beside Lady Serena as they made their way to the tent where ale was being served. Cecily ran up to her. "You were wonderful! I want to be just like you when I grow up!" the small redhead proclaimed breathlessly.

Her curly-haired companions, Tibby and Ancel, caught up with her, nodding their agreement. Ancel was the youngest of the three at only eight summers, but no less enthusiastic.

Cecily gazed up at Lady Serena, the child's red hair falling about her small shoulders. "Will you teach me, too?" she pleaded.

Lady Serena paused. "Heaven help me if you ever take up the bow, Cecily. Your mother would never forgive me."

"I did not begin so young," Merewyn said to the girl. "You have many years to learn."

The boys shrugged, but Cecily's lips formed a pout. Merewyn knew the girl would not let Lady Serena's words get in her way should she want to learn. In Cecily, Merewyn recognized a spirit like her own.

As they neared the tent, the smell of fresh-baked tarts wafted through the air. "Tarts!" shouted Tibby. With that, the three children scampered off in search of their favorite treat. Merewyn watched them for a moment, wistful at the idea of children of her own. 'Twas a dream she did not expect to see realized.

"Little Cecily is correct," said Lady Serena. "You did well today."

Merewyn was not unhappy with her performance but she wanted to do better next time. "Thank you, my lady. Mayhap next time I can add another arrow. What do you think?"

"You could do it, I've no doubt. Did Rhodri teach you the feat?"

"Nay, Rhodri's archers fight from the trees, not from a galloping horse. 'Twas another." Lady Serena looked at her expectantly. "Owain, a prince of Powys and a good friend."

They entered the tent and accepted cups of ale, then took them outside to stand under the trees where there was shade and privacy.

"I expect Rhodri had you following his archers all over the Welsh mountains," said Lady Serena.

"Not at first." Merewyn laughed, remembering Rhodri's worries. "He was afraid if anything happened to me you would take up your bow against him."

"And so I would have, the scoundrel. It is well you are home, for I think 'tis time you became a lady."

Merewyn was about to object that it seemed unlikely she would ever be considered a lady. She was not even the daughter of one of Talisand's knights. Serena must have seen Merewyn's doubt but misunderstood its cause.

"I, too, had to give up a man's tunic and hosen when I became Ren's wife. The day draws near when we must find you a husband. It will help if you dress in a manner to attract one. Do any of my husband's men appeal?"

Only one man appealed to Merewyn and she was certain he was not among those Lady Serena would list as potential suitors. "Nay."

"Well, you have been home only a short while. Time will show you the one. Meanwhile, I have been thinking that when the king summons my lord to the meeting of his barons, you and I should go along. I had little respect for the first William and mayhap I will have less for this one, but you have seen so little of England outside of Talisand, I would have you go."

Merewyn had never been to London and she admired Lady Serena. To be with her on such an adventure would be a great pleasure. "I would gladly go with you, my lady." But Lady Serena's hopes for her might be too high. Could she ever leave behind her past? Would the king's court be filled with those who would think less of her for it?

Lady Serena must have read her thoughts. "Do not think of the past, Merewyn. Your beginning does not have to define you. 'Tis the woman you have become that is important. You have grown into an intelligent, spirited young woman. It will be important for you to be accepted at the king's court as one who has the favor of Talisand's lord. 'Tis even possible you will find a suitor there among the king's knights."

Merewyn returned Serena a tentative smile. She would find no suitor at the king's court and she still had reservations about appearing at the king's palace. "I do not know how to behave before the king."

"But surely you do," Lady Serena insisted. "Emma raised you in your early years and she is a highborn lady. Her father was one of King Harold's nobles before the Normans came. I know she taught you French."

"Aye, I can speak the Norman tongue."

"And you were with Rhodri for six years," Lady Serena continued. "Did not his wife, Fia, tutor you in the ways of a lady? And were you not accepted in Rhodri's court?"

"Yea, but that was Wales."

Lady Serena gave an uncharacteristic snort. "From what I have heard, there is more dignity in Rhodri's court than in William's, but we shall see. I have not joined my husband in his visits to London since William Rufus was crowned four years ago. It is past time I do so. Now that I think of it, Alex's foster father, the Earl of Chester, will be there. Mayhap I can convince my husband to call upon the earl and his countess on our way south. You would enjoy Ermentrude."

When they had finished their ale and Lady Serena bid her good day, Merewyn bent to retrieve her quiver of arrows and saw a man's shoes in front of her eyes. Raising her gaze, she took in the long hosen-clad male legs with cross straps of leather, a dark blue tunic and, finally, as she stood, a smiling Alexander with his arms crossed over his chest.

"Are you avoiding me, mistress?" His manner was teasing but she detected a hint of annoyance in his voice. In truth, she had been avoiding him, embarrassed by his kiss in the stables and her reaction to it. But she would never admit it. "I was shooting in the archery contest."

"I know. I was watching. Your talent with a bow rivals that of my lady mother."

"It was Lady Serena who first taught me, but I do not consider myself her equal."

"You are modest. 'Tis a fine virtue for a woman, but in this case, mayhap misplaced. My mother claims your skill with a bow exceeds her own. After seeing you shoot from your pony, I would not say her nay. Nor, I suspect, would anyone at Talisand."

Merewyn smiled at his words, for against her better judgment, it pleased her to think he had watched her and admired her skill. "You do not think it unseemly?" She cared desperately that he should approve. But no matter his reaction, she would never give up the weapon that made her safe.

"How could I when they still tell the stories of my own mother donning a lad's clothing and killing a Norman knight with her arrow to save my father? Still, I prefer you in the gown you wore last eve. 'Twas very becoming."

His gray eyes bore into hers and she knew he was remembering not her gown but their kiss. So intense was his gaze, she had to look away, her cheeks flaming. "Thank you."

When she returned her attention to him, he was looking toward the clearing where the sword fighting was taking place. "My match is about to begin. I hope you will attend." Without waiting for an answer, he bowed and left her, striding toward the area set off by pennons.

Merewyn followed slowly, watching until he reached the roped off area. She wanted to observe his skill, for she had heard he was accomplished with a blade. Even at thirteen summers, he had wielded both fist and sword well. What was he like now?

By the time she arrived, Alex was facing off with Jamie. The two knights circled each other, their swords drawn and faces set in determination.

Even in the shade of the tall oaks, the air was overwarm. Neither man wore mail or helm, only a short tunic over hosen. Alex had confined his long black hair to his nape with a leather cord. Already his forehead beaded with sweat.

Seeing Lora watching from the other side of the clearing, Merewyn went to join her.

"First blood and not much of it," the Lord of Talisand, overseeing the match, reminded the knights, "and no hits above the shoulders."

A crowd of men gathered around, shouting encouragement to their favorite, eager to see the Red Wolf's son fighting the captain of the house knights.

Jamie moved first with a downward strike, but Alex quickly blocked the blade with an upward thrust. The older knight had powerful arms and a decade more experience than Alex. Jamie's skill had been honed in sparring with the Red Wolf nearly every day. But Alex, with his agile strength, moved gracefully, more like an animal than a man, allowing him to avoid the older knight's blade with his quick twists and turns.

After that, the blows came in rapid succession, steel meeting steel, as the two opponents forced each other back and forth over the uneven ground.

Alex's blade slid along the edge of Jamie's sword, the shrieking metal setting Merewyn's nerves on end. It was not a real battle but close enough for her to hear in her mind the sounds of many swords clashing. She could easily imagine Alex as he might be in battle: his powerful muscles flexing with every slash of his sword, his black hair flying about his shoulders and the look on his face one of dangerous intent.

Alex suddenly twisted around so fast he was a blur, his blade striking Jamie's twice before it stilled. Given the startled look on Jamie's face, Merewyn was certain he had not expected the move. The men watching shouted their approval. Neither had they. She glanced up at Alex's father whose face bore a grin. Had he taught Alex the move?

Children cheered from the sidelines. Cecily jumped up and down, flanked by her two companions. Alex's younger brother, Tibby, watched Alex closely, his admiration for his older brother shining in his eyes.

Jamie paused and Alex shot a glance to where Merewyn stood next to Lora. Taking advantage of the lapse, Jamie swung hard, forcing Alex to block the blade close to his body. It appeared Alex would prevail, but suddenly he stumbled and went down.

★ ★ ★

The tip of Jamie's sword pressed into Alex's chest. A bit more pressure and it would pierce his tunic and draw blood.

"Yield, Alex."

He smiled up at the blond knight. "Aye, 'tis your win, Jamie." The older knight offered Alex his hand and he took it.

"You are being very gracious about this loss, Alex."

"Mayhap, but I expect a rematch and soon," said Alex. They laughed about their various moves as they strode from the clearing. Once Jamie left him, his two friends rushed to his side, incredulous looks on their faces.

"What was *that*?" Rory questioned. "You never lose your footing, no matter the ground."

"Yea," said Guy, his forehead furrowed. "I have never seen you clumsy afore this." The younger knight furrowed his brow at Alex's amused grin. "Are you ill?"

Alex laughed. "Nay." Speaking under his breath, he confided, "Jamie might have won without my help, but 'twas my intention to assure he did."

His friends stared back at him, open-mouthed. "Why?" they asked as one.

He raised his brows. "Have you not observed Jamie is smitten with Lora but she pays him little attention? When I saw Lora closely watching, I thought to give Jamie a boost in her eyes."

"Ah," said Rory. "I begin to understand. 'Twas great-hearted of you.

But your lord father will think you are slipping."

"Nay, he will not," said Alex. "After I've defeated the two of you," he said with a grin, "I will meet him."

"Ho! The arrogance of our leader!" cried Rory.

"Then let the next match be mine!" said Guy.

"You shall have it," said Alex, a slow smile crossing his face. Guy was the youngest of Talisand's knights. His most difficult tests lay ahead of him and Alex was glad to show him the way.

In the next two rounds, Alex defeated his friends. Guy had learned much in Normandy but his lesser experience showed in the end. Rory made a single error that Alex quickly seized upon.

When he finally challenged his father, Alex was winded, but determined. He approached the Lord of Talisand who stood observing the remaining matches. " 'Tis you I would next lock swords with, Father."

The Red Wolf turned to face him, proud, erect and secure in his ability. His reputation on the battlefield was legendary even before Alex was born. His chestnut hair was now streaked with gray and framed a lined face that bore witness to the decades he had served the Conqueror.

"Are you certain you do not need a brief rest to recover?" his father asked, amusement twinkling in his eyes.

"Hardly. And do not go easy on me, Father. I would have a real test of my skill. We've not sparred since I left for Normandy."

The Red Wolf returned him a predatory gaze. "Very well."

The crowd's conversation faded to a hushed silence as father and son faced off in the center of the clearing, circling each other slowly. Alex reminded himself of his father's reputation. He might limp at times from the old riding accident, but as he circled Alex, 'twas not apparent.

Gray eyes met gray eyes as each took the other's measure. Alex had been schooled by his father not to be hasty but to consider the other man's moves before attacking. Hence, they continued to circle, eyes narrowed, each waiting for the other to strike. Alex was determined to be patient.

"I suppose I must begin this," his father said in a low voice, "else we will be here all day. And your mother watches with a worried face from the sidelines as it is."

The Red Wolf stepped back and with a powerful arc of his sword sending flashes of light into the air, brought his blade down hard upon Alex's sword raised in defense.

As one, the crowd inhaled, the air hissing through their teeth.

The blow sent a wave of shock through Alex's arm, but he held firm. "You will not end it so easily, Father. I have grown stronger."

His father grinned back. "I have noticed."

The Red Wolf tapped the end of Alex's blade, testing his reaction. Alex did not leap into the void, but waited until the opening he had wanted appeared. With quick reflexes, he slashed his sword first right and then left, the sound of clashing blades loud in the clearing. He had not confused his father, as he had hoped, but he'd gained movement forward nonetheless.

Striking again and again, he drove the Red Wolf back, but the older knight recovered and came at him with another powerful blow.

Their swords crossed, bringing their faces close together over the blades, two pairs of gray eyes shooting sparks at each other, their chests heaving short breaths.

Another long round of their clashing blades followed, at the end of which, his father loudly proclaimed, "I declare a tie!" Stepping back, he raised his sword in front of his face, pointing the tip to the sky, a signal the match was concluded.

"A tie it is," said Alex, sheathing his sword and bowing before the knight he respected above all others. If he had to stand in anyone's shadow he wanted it to be this man's.

The crowd seemed to approve. Loud shouts of praise were followed by "Ale for Talisand's wolves!"

His father laughed. Wrapping his arm around Alex's shoulder, he led him to the blue and white tent. " 'Tis time you had your own banner, Son. What do you say to a black wolf?"

"Aye," said Alex, accepting the large cup overflowing with amber liquid. "Mayhap on a crimson field."

His father smiled his approval. "So be it!"

Joined by their fellow knights and men-at-arms, expounding on the fine points of the morning's contests, Alex and his friends happily imbibed the ale that was set before them. It was another hour before they left for the hall, Alex's steps unsteady and his speech slurred. But it had been a good day and he regretted naught of it.

At the door of the hall, he waved off his two friends and headed for the manor, his only thought a comfortable bed where he might sleep for a few hours before the evening meal.

★ ★ ★

After the matches were finished, Merewyn and Lora walked along the bank of the River Lune speaking as two friends long separated. It was one of several conversations they had enjoyed in the months since Merewyn had been back, most of them concerning changes at Talisand.

In her hand, Merewyn still carried her bow, hardly aware of it or the quiver of arrows slung over her shoulder.

"Tell me more about Wales," Lora asked. "You seem so different since your return."

Images of warriors clad in brown and green flickered in Merewyn's mind. "They are fierce in a fight, each one skilled with a bow. Few of the women seek to have such skill, but they did not discourage my interest. Rhodri's encouragement and his approval gained me a place among them."

"Why did it mean so much to you to go? I missed your company."

"I had to go, Lora. I wanted to be able to protect myself. You know what I faced here. And you know the stories about Lady Serena as well as I. Imagining her dressed in an archer's clothing, killing a Norman knight to save the Red Wolf, I wanted to be like her."

"You very nearly are. The men now speak of you with admiration."

Merewyn smiled to herself. "Mayhap they will respect the bow where they did not respect the girl and stay away."

"You *want* the men to stay away?" Lora asked, a look of disbelief on her face.

"Aye." *Most of them.* She would not speak of her feelings for Alex she kept locked in her heart or the change that had occurred in her thinking about him. Turning her friend's attention to the match, she said, "The sword fighting was exciting, do you not agree?"

"I liked the fight between Earl Renaud and his son. Except for the years that separate them, the two fight in similar fashion. Alex was so… powerful."

Merewyn had hoped Lora would speak of Jamie, but having seen her watching Alex, she was not surprised this contest had drawn her friend's attention. The Red Wolf had seen many battles and his experience showed in his practiced moves and his powerful strikes, but Alex's skill did nearly equal that of his father. " 'Twas exciting to see them spar, even frightening, but there were other matches. Did you not think Jamie did well?"

The dark-haired daughter of Sir Alain smoothed the skirt of her leaf green gown, while appearing to ponder the question. She stood taller than Merewyn, her height gained from her father, the huge knight who carried the Red Wolf's banner.

"He won," Lora finally said, "but only because Alex stumbled, else it might have ended differently."

Merewyn wanted her friend to see the good in the golden-haired English knight who, like Merewyn, had been taken under Lady Serena's wing. "Earl Renaud has much confidence in Jamie," she said. " 'Tis an honor to be named captain of the house knights."

Lora tossed her thick hair behind her. The sun glistening in the long strands made them appear like burnt umber. It was not difficult to imagine why Jamie was so enamored of her. And Lora had a good heart, using her knowledge of herbs, gained from her mother, for others.

"Jamie is an honorable knight," Lora admitted. "But I have known him all my life. He was already the Red Wolf's squire when I was born."

Merewyn laughed. "Yea, but he is not old. Have you never asked yourself why such a well-favored knight is unwed?"

"I just assumed 'twas because of his service to Talisand's lord."

Merewyn shook her head. "Nay, I think not." She fingered her bow, wondering if she should say the words that were on her tongue. Mayhap they would help Lora see the prize that was hers to claim. "The man is too shy to speak his heart, but you can see his words in his eyes." Meeting her friend's dark gaze, she said, " 'Tis you, Lora. Whenever you are near him, he looks nowhere else."

Lora stared at her with a perplexed expression.

"Aye," said Merewyn, "I was right in thinking you were unaware. I only tell you so that you do not discourage Jamie overmuch."

"Jamie? Interested in—" Her words trailed off as she looked toward the grass growing at the edge of the river.

Merewyn put her arm around her friend. "To win the affection of one like Jamie is not a small thing. There are many women at Talisand who would gladly have him, but he waits for you."

Lora's eyes filled with tears and she turned and hugged Merewyn. "Thank you."

It pleased Merewyn to realize she had done the right thing in speaking to her friend. "Go tell him how well he did today and see his eyes light like the sun."

Lora nodded and hurried back toward the palisade gate.

Merewyn walked on by herself for a while, enjoying the sun-filled afternoon and the peaceful flow of the river, remembering the match between Alex and his father. Deep in her thoughts, she nearly bumped into Maugris, who suddenly appeared in front of her.

"Oh!" she exclaimed. "I did not see you."

The old seer greeted her with a smile. "Good day to you, Mistress Merewyn. I see you still carry your bow and wear the apparel of one of Rhodri's archers. Your shooting today amazed all."

"You are kind to say so, Maugris."

She meant to pass by, but he held up a hand. "A word if I might."

"Of course," she said turning to face him.

"Remember, the archer controls the bow and not the bow the archer."

She blinked twice. *Whatever does that mean?* The wise one was known to speak in riddles and this bit of advice was beyond her understanding. Did he know of her conversations with her bow? After all, he knew things no one else did.

At her puzzling look, Maugris smiled, his face a sea of wrinkles and his blue eyes twinkling. "Do not discount the words of an old man. I have faith in you," he said as he turned to go.

"I will try and remember that," she said to his back. What vision had he seen that caused him to speak so?

Still pondering his words, Merewyn strolled back to the manor and climbed the stairs to her chamber, thinking to please Lady Serena by changing into a gown for what would likely be another feast, this one to celebrate the tournament's champions.

She entered the dimly lit room, closing the door behind her, and set her bow and arrows on the table. "You did well today," she muttered to her bow, "but you need not look so smug." She walked to the window and threw open the shutters. The afternoon sun flooded the chamber and a pleasant breeze caressed her face as she looked beyond the river curling around the palisade to the green hills beyond.

Turning into the chamber, she froze. On the far side of the chamber, asleep on her bed was Alex, curled up on top of the furs with his back to her, his long black hair free of its leather tie a dark cloud on her pillow. The sunlight falling on his long lean body made her think of a sleeping Hercules.

She looked toward her bow. Silently, it warned, "Do not trust him! Remember his reputation." The bow spoke the truth. She could not allow anyone to find him here for they would think the worst. And if he remained in her bed she might be tempted to succumb to his seductive charm.

Walking to the bed, she gently prodded his still form. "Alex, what are you doing here?" she whispered, afraid someone might hear. "You must leave!"

Alex rolled over to face her, one gray eye barely opening under a dark arched brow. "Have you come to join me?"

He smelled of ale and his words were slurred. *Drunk.* She might have known he and his friends would be celebrating the matches they'd won. Did he even know where he was? "Alex, you are in *my* bed, not your own."

He closed his eye and sighed contentedly. "I am merely resting and I like it here." He rubbed his cheek against her pillow. "It smells very pleasant."

His measured breathing told her he had gone back to sleep.

She took in his masculine form. Even at rest he appeared formidable and so sensual that a part of her wanted to crawl in beside him. Shaking off the scandalous thought, she shook his shoulder. "You must wake up!"

This time both his eyes opened and he reached for her, his powerful arms pulling her onto the bed and drawing her tightly against him. "I do like you in your bowman's attire," he said, nuzzling her neck. He inhaled deeply. "You smell like a field of flowers."

She tried to wiggle free of his embrace but his strength held her to him. "Alex! Stop this at once."

"Do not scold, Merewyn," he said, tightening his grip and brushing his lips over her neck. "I like having you here. So soft. Can you not stay?"

It would have been laughable had she not been concerned about what others might think and where this could lead if she did not stop him. "This is *my* bed, not yours, you fool!"

Ignoring her protest, he rolled on top of her and brought his mouth down upon hers. The moment his warm lips kissed her, she forgot her scolding. She could not bring herself to refuse what she had longed for. He tasted of ale, his warm lips easing hers apart. Slipping in his tongue, he gently explored her mouth. 'Twas alarming and wonderful at the same time. Small ripples of pleasure coursed through her and an ache formed deep in her woman's center. With any other man she would have reached for her bow, but this was Alex. She did not fear him, as she would have another man.

She threaded her fingers through his thick raven hair, finally able to touch what she had so long admired. In a moment, she would pull away, she told herself.

He wiggled his hips until they parted her thighs. His hard arousal pressed between her legs, moving against her woman's flesh. Only his hosen and hers separated them. "I want you, Merewyn."

He knows who I am! Reason came back to her. She would have to be the one to stop this. Reining in the passion rising within her, she placed her hands on his shoulders and hissed, "Off! You must get off! This is unseemly."

He took her hands from his shoulders and raised them above her head, threading his fingers through hers. Pinned by his body and secured by his hands, she could not move.

His mouth sought the tender flesh of her neck where he trailed kisses down her throat, the stubble on his chin tickling her sensitive skin.

"You do not want me to get off, I can tell," he muttered. His speech was still slurred and she was not certain he was fully awake. But when his hips pressed into her causing her to sink deeper into the soft bed cushion, desire threatened to intoxicate her as surely as the ale had robbed him of his wits. "You are so warm and soft and smell so good," he murmured against her throat.

His words roused her from the fog into which she was slipping. "And you smell like the bottom of an ale barrel," she said shortly. Afraid she would soon succumb to his seduction if she did not move this instant, she brought her mouth to his ear. "Alex, 'tis *my* bed you are in and you were *not* invited."

She must have reached him in his stupor, for he raised his head, looked into her eyes and blinked. "Not invited?"

"Nay," she insisted as firmly as she could, meeting his startled gaze.

"Oh." Shaking his head, he let go of her hands and pushed his weight from her to sit on the bed, leaving her aching and wanting for his touch, but resolved to see him gone.

As soon as she was free of his body, she pulled her legs beneath her and scrambled back away from him on the bed.

He flung his legs over the side and turned to look back at her, blinking again as if trying to focus. Casting a glance around the chamber, he spoke in a clear voice. " 'Tis not mine."

"I have been trying to tell you that, you drunken sot." She was not really angry with him. Drunk, he had stumbled into the wrong chamber, but his nearness had stirred her senses, his kisses made her want more and her heart hammered in her chest with the excitement of touching him as a lover might.

With a deep sigh, he got to his feet and walked to the door. Turning to look at her, he said, "You are beautiful when disheveled, Merewyn, but 'tis quite apparent I am not wanted."

He opened the door to leave and she bit her lip to keep from speaking.

He could not have been more wrong.

CHAPTER 4

Alex speared a piece of smoked salmon with his knife and popped it into his mouth, savoring the salty, somewhat oily taste before washing it down with ale. A few days had passed since the contests and he had finally recovered from his celebration, his appetite returning full force.

His mother, dressed in a ruby-colored gown, glided toward his table and he welcomed her to the seat beside him.

"Do you go to the practice yard this morning?" she asked.

"I cannot avoid it. Rory and Guy want a rematch from yesterday's practice and some of the men-at-arms are itching to have a chance to trounce the three of us."

"I shall have a busy day myself. Aethel and I are taking herbs to the village women," she said as she accepted the bowl of gruel a servant set before her.

"Sir Alain's wife knows much about herbs and such."

"She does and they count upon her knowledge. Lora will be joining us a bit later."

All the while he ate, his eyes kept straying to where Merewyn sat at the next table with Lora, planning their day, no doubt. Since that afternoon in her chamber, now a vague but pleasant memory, Merewyn had been avoiding him. Had he really lain beside her? Held her? Kissed her again? He who, since coming to manhood, had never missed a woman's presence was missing this one's. Truth be told, it bothered him greatly. He'd not had a woman since returning home and he was beginning to suspect the cause was Merewyn.

The day after he'd wandered into her bed, Lora had moved into Merewyn's chamber, saying the two wanted to spend time together before Merewyn left for London. He had to wonder if Merewyn had sought Lora's company to protect herself from him. Surely she knew he would never harm her. He had not meant to stumble into her chamber, had he? He'd been drunk as a villager after harvest, but even floating in ale, some part of his mind must have known whose chamber it was.

Had he hoped she might welcome him? It was hardly noble to entertain such thoughts about a woman who had once sought his protection, but then she had been a girl, now she was a woman grown. As much as he tried, he could not deny the attraction between them. He was certain she had returned his kiss, at least for a few moments. Even with the ale, he remembered the enticing taste of her and her scent.

Letting out a sigh, he reached for the dish of wild strawberries, popping one into his mouth. The taste of it was sweet. *Just like Merewyn.*

As far as he could determine, she spent her mornings with Lora and her afternoons with Talisand's archers. When she donned her bowman's garb and headed toward the archery field, little Cecily trailed behind her like her shadow.

At one time Alex and Merewyn had been friends. The year before he'd gone to Rouen, she was always close by, her eyes large and adoring. 'Twas why he had looked for her the moment he'd heard she was back, curious to know what had become of her. In all the years he'd been away, he had never forgotten the beguilingly beautiful girl with her blue-hazel eyes, fragile features and golden hair. No longer adoring in her gaze, her manner was wary. But he sensed an inner strength in her that matched the beast in him. Her skill with the bow only made her more fascinating. She was making him think differently about other young women, too. No longer did he see them as merely potential bed partners. With Merewyn re-entering his life, he had to consider other women could be as intelligent and skilled.

He rose from his bench, belted on his sword and bid his mother good day. He was just about to reach the door of the hall when Merewyn and Lora passed by. Holding the door for them, he asked Merewyn, "Will you take part in the hunt this afternoon?"

She paused, allowing him time to peruse her simple gown of blue linen that brought his attention to her unusual eyes. "I might. It would be my first with the men of Talisand."

"Good. I shall look for you as we depart."

"I should never like to hunt," Lora said. "I am content to tend the herb garden and wait for the hunters to return."

"There is place for that, too, my lady." He bowed and watched the two women walk arm in arm from the hall, so very different. He had new respect for each of them, but only one had the courage to hunt with a wolf.

★ ★ ★

By the time the hunting party formed in the bailey, Merewyn had donned her archer's clothing and Ceinder was saddled and waiting. She grabbed the pommel and slid her foot into the stirrup. Lifting herself into the saddle, she made sure her bow was secure and her quiver was at her right shoulder where she had only to bend her elbow to fetch an arrow.

The hounds, excited for the hunt, barked and howled as the men made ready to depart. Lady Emma's husband, Sir Geoffroi, kept large sight hounds, offspring of Emma's beloved Magnus she had brought from York. One Christmas, Sir Geoffroi had given some of the pups to Talisand's lord and now their offspring hunted with him.

In Wales, Rhodri had hunted with rough-coated hounds that bayed to alert the hunters when game was sighted. She and Ceinder had hunted together in Wales but this would be the first time she would hunt with Talisand's men, the first time she would hunt with Alex.

A dozen riders, including Jamie, Alex, Rory and Guy, waited for the signal from Talisand's lord. Merewyn could not take her eyes from Alex, sitting atop his great black horse. He wore only a tunic and hosen, but he was still every bit the knight, armed with sword, spear and knife.

Chasing after the deer with him presented a test, for she must concentrate not on Alex but on the hunt, avoiding the men's horses and spears while she loosed her arrows. Some of Talisand's archers had gone ahead on foot to await them in the woods. She would have to avoid them, too.

Since that day in her chamber, her mind strayed many times to the handsome heir of Talisand. Alex might not remember that afternoon as drunk as he'd been, but her memories of his body pressed into hers and his kisses trailing down her neck were all too real. Alex had awakened a desire in her that had once been only imagined. Now it was all too easily brought to mind. She pressed her lips together, fighting to keep her mind on the hunt. She no longer thought of him as an arrogant beast, but he was still a man.

When the signal was given, the score of riders spurred their horses to a canter, the knights in the lead, following the dogs. She chased after the men, keeping to their pace. Trees rushed by as the hounds howled and the horses crushed the dense undergrowth beneath their hooves. She was thankful that Ceinder had an eye for obstacles and a steady gait that made riding to hunt with bow and arrow easier than it would be on a larger, bolder horse.

Merewyn slowed, guiding Ceinder around branches that jutted from trees blocking her path.

Shouts echoed through the woods, followed by the hounds' baying. Deer had been sighted. Ceinder's reins were already knotted. Now she laid them at the base of the pony's neck, reached for her bow and rode on.

In the distance, three deer leapt from the cover of the woods and raced across the meadow. The men galloped after them.

In front of her but behind the men, a hart sprang out of the woods, crossing her path. Seeing no other archer, she nocked an arrow, raised her bow and loosed the arrow.

The deer leapt high, as if trying to take wing, and then went down in a flailing tangle of legs.

Slowing Ceinder, Merewyn dropped from her pony and carried her bow to where the deer lay, wanting to assure the animal a quick death.

The deer lay quiet and unmoving, its tongue lolled out, its red sides still. *A clean shot.* She smiled to herself. Tonight they would dine on venison. Hunting was not merely sport, but necessary to add to their store of meat and she was proud that she could contribute to the meal this eve. July was a hungry month when grain stores were low and the people foraged, waiting for August's harvest.

She straightened, her eyes searching the woods for a servant who might be following the hunt. Before she could summon help to lift the deer, she heard a snorting sound from the bushes. Turning, she glimpsed a brown snout rising above the green underbrush less than twenty feet away. On either side of its hoary snout were wicked curved tusks as long as her hand. A whiff of musky taint hit her nostrils.

Oh God, a wild boar in rut!

Heart pounding, Merewyn reached for Ceinder's reins, but the normally calm pony rolled her eyes, showing the whites, and backed away, blowing and snorting.

With a guttural sound, the beast stepped from the brush, sniffing the air. Ceinder let out a high-pitched scream. The boar's tiny eyes glittered as it snorted and pawed at the ground, agitated by the pony's panicked dance.

The beast let out a fearful squeal sending chills up Merewyn's spine. What should she do? Her arrows would not stop a charging boar. Afraid she might only madden the animal if she wounded it, she began to back away. The boar squealed again and charged.

Ceinder fled and Merewyn ran, terrified. She could never outrun the wild beast gaining on her.

Pounding hooves shook the ground. A quick glance over her shoulder revealed Alex galloping into the clearing. He swung out of the saddle, landed running and flung his spear all in one powerful motion. The boar crashed to the ground and slid, plowing up the loam, before smashing into Merewyn, knocking her to the ground. One of its tusks pressed against her leg. The spear quivered, jutting up from the beast's armpit where it pinned the boar's heart.

Merewyn stared, open-mouthed, still shivering in fear. Part of her bow was beneath her, her quiver of arrows pressing into her back.

Without a word, Alex reached for her, pulling her free of the boar. Lifting her from the ground, he swept her into his arms, holding her tightly against his chest. "By the grace of God, you are safe."

She clung to him and the hard strength of his body, her heart hammering in her chest. "You... you saved me."

He pulled back to look at her. "Did you not see the boar?"

"Nay!" she spit out. "I went to check on the deer and the boar was in the bush. He caught me unawares. How did you know to come back?"

"I was heading back to find you when your pony screamed. In these woods it could mean only wolves or boar."

The sound of pounding hooves made her push away from Alex to stand apart, her arms wrapped around her leather jerkin. Her bow still lay on the ground but the quiver of arrows remained over her shoulder.

Into the clearing rode Alex's father, Sir Geoffroi and Jamie followed by Rory and Guy.

Talisand's lord gave the scene a studying perusal: the dead boar with the spear protruding from its wiry hide lying next to the deer with an arrow sticking from its body, Alex and Merewyn on either side, more intent on each other than on the beasts between them. With a concerned look, he asked, "You are both unharmed?"

"Aye," said Alex. "A fortunate shot stopped the beast."

"Fortunate?" scoffed Sir Geoffroi. " 'Twas not mere luck, that. 'Twas more like miraculous."

"You have rescued the fair damsel," said Guy with a grin.

"It was a close thing," said Alex, glancing at Merewyn and then looking away.

"If it had not been for Sir Alex," she said to his father, "I would not be alive."

*   *   *

Alex's hand shook as he grabbed the pommel of his saddle and swung onto Azor's back. The pounding in his chest was only beginning to subside, but a quick look at Merewyn assured him she was well.

What horror had gripped him when he'd ridden into the clearing to see the boar's tusks mere feet from Merewyn's slender body. He remembered little of what followed, certain he'd gone mad. Enraged, he had flung his spear at the beast. Surely God had been with him to enable him to pierce the beast's heart as he had dropped from his horse in a blur.

He'd had close calls in battle and faced death more than once. But never had the life at risk been Merewyn's. The pain he felt at the thought of losing her was like no other he had experienced. The moment he'd realized the boar was intent on taking her life, killing the beast was his only purpose.

During the ride back to Talisand, he pondered what the girl meant to him. Kissing her had told him he wanted her in his bed, but his feelings had gone well beyond lust for a beautiful woman. He could not abide the thought of any harm coming to her—or of another man having her. And he had no desire to take another woman to his bed though several made clear they were willing.

Rory and Guy had sought their pleasure and were quick to tell him of their conquests. When his companions noted his unusual abstinence, Alex had said nothing.

"Are you certain you are not ill?" asked Rory one morning when Alex ignored a village girl's flirting at the practice yard.

"Do I appear ill?" he snapped back. Alex had just defeated Rory in their sparring, thus he expected the reply that followed.

Rory took in Alex's appearance, which, except for the sweat on his forehead from their lively swordplay, conveyed his readiness to spar again. He was not even winded. "Nay, you do not seem ill."

When Guy, who had been listening to their conversation, suggested the cause was Merewyn, Alex returned him a dark scowl. He would not allow her name to be bandied about.

In response, his friends grinned widely. "You'll hear no complaints from this quarter," Rory said with a smirk. "Leaves more women for me."

"And me," put in Guy.

Alex no longer wanted to be a part of his friends' search for comely wenches to bed. Their pleasure excursions now seemed shallow and his former behavior dishonorable. Being in Merewyn's company was somehow more satisfying even if he could not touch her.

After they returned from the hunt with the animals they had taken, Alex and his companions left for the river to wash and then change for the feast that would follow. When the time for supper drew near, the enticing smell of boar, spiced with sage and roasting in its own juices, filled the hall, making his mouth water.

As the men and women gathered for the meal, the roast boar was carried into the hall on a huge wooden plank and set on a special table where it was carved. Wine flowed freely as he and his companions ate with Merewyn, Lora, Bea and Alice at the end of one of the trestle tables nearest the dais.

Jamie joined them, commending Alex on his kill. He was glad to see Merewyn appeared to have recovered from her encounter and was exchanging pleasantries with Guy.

They were still eating when Alex looked up to see a man dressed in the king's livery step into the hall and stride toward the dais.

"From the king," the messenger said, bowing before the Earl of Talisand and thrusting the scroll toward him. His father accepted the parchment, broke the seal and quickly read the missive. Then he asked the man to hand it to Alex.

The message contained only one line:

You are summoned to Westminster for a meeting of the barons in a fort-night.

A scribe had no doubt written the message, for the king was unlettered, but it was signed with William's mark. A date was scrawled below which, according to Alex's figuring, left them ten days to reach London.

The messenger handed his father another scroll. "This, too, my lord."

His father took it and read the second message but did not pass it to Alex. Instead, he proclaimed, "The king's summons has come." Turning to Alex's mother, he asked, "Do you still wish to go, my love?"

"I do. 'Tis time I called upon your king." Then glancing toward Merewyn, she said, "My student of the bow has never been to court. She will attend as well, as we have discussed."

His father nodded, seemingly content with his wife's plans. Mayhap he was pleased she would go. Alex knew his mother would never claim a Norman as her king but his father told him she had once entertained the Conqueror at Talisand for the sake of her husband's honor and her brother's life. Her willingness to go to court now and bow before William Rufus suggested age had softened her.

Alex looked across the table at Merewyn, studying her expression. What would it be like to be with her on the road for many days? There would be two other women on the journey, his mother and her maidservant, Nelda, and for that, he was glad. 'Twas best he and Merewyn would not be alone.

"Can you be ready to depart at dawn tomorrow?" Alex's father asked his lady.

"Since I expected the summons, Maggie and Nelda have been readying the chests that will go with us. We need only one cart and it can be loaded this evening."

Before Alex left the hall, Maugris came to speak to him. "Might I have a word?"

Alex drew the old one aside, wondering what vision he had seen now, hoping it was not a harbinger of doom. "Aye."

"Honor is revealed in the face of temptation, my son, and courage in the face of fear. You have passed one trial but still face another. It is near, even at your door."

With that, Maugris wished him a safe journey and abruptly turned and walked through the door to the bailey.

Alex stared after him, mystified.

$$\star \quad \star \quad \star$$

Merewyn stifled a yawn and accepted the groom's help mounting Ceinder. Unused to rising before dawn, she was still tired from the restless night before. Then, too, as she dressed, she and her bow had exchanged words about her decision to accompany Lady Serena to London. But in light of Maugris' counsel, she ignored her bow's scolding. London would be an adventure, one she eagerly anticipated.

Since they would be stopping in a village and then going on to Earl Hugh's castle in Chester, Lady Serena had wanted her to wear a gown for the travel. Merewyn was so pleased to be included she did not complain of having to struggle with skirts and Nelda had been there to help with the laces.

The linen gown she chose, the color of rust, would bear up well under the dust of the road. On her head she wore a straw hat like many of the villeins did when working in the fields. Her dark green cloak was tied behind her, secured to her saddle with her bow and quiver full of arrows.

Alex dipped his head to her and his mother as he rode to the head of the column where he joined his father. The knights wore no mail and, because they did not ride to war, their destriers, even their squires, remained behind. Still, every man had his sword and a long knife at his belt.

The sun was rising on her left as Merewyn and Lady Serena fell in behind Alex and his father. Following the two women were Sir Geoffroi, Guy and Rory with several men-at-arms behind them. A male servant brought up the rear, driving the cart in which Nelda, Lady Serena's maidservant, rode with the chests, tents and food stores.

Lady Emma, Sir Geoffroi's wife, had not come with them. All knew the reason. After the Norman Conqueror's devastation of her home in York, she would have nothing to do with the Conqueror's son. Merewyn, too, had reservations. At Talisand, she had known Norman knights of noble character like Earl Renaud and Sir Geoffroi, but her own mother's terrible fate had taught her many were not like them. She hoped never to meet a knight like the one who had sired her.

A few hours later, the sun beamed from the sky full of puffy white clouds that reminded Merewyn of the white roses growing wild near Talisand. They would miss the harvesting of crops that had just begun, but mayhap the harvest of spring grains would still be going on when they returned.

With no rain on the horizon, she settled into her saddle, looking forward to the day's journey. The countryside opened before her, broad and green, with tree-covered hills in the distance. Her spirits lifted as they made their way south, following the old Roman road toward Chester. The huge gray stones placed there by the ancients a thousand years before still provided a wide path and marked the way. It was the same road she had traveled less than a year before when she had returned from Wales and the one Rhodri and Fia had led her along six years earlier when she had first gone with them.

But this time it would take her to places she had never seen.

She tried to imagine the wonders that lay in London. Even Chester would be new to her. When Rhodri had taken her to Wales, they had passed close to the city but he had not stopped there. No Welshman would be welcome in Chester. Ten years before, Gruffydd ap Cynan, who had only just been named the King of Gwynedd, had been captured by treachery and imprisoned by Earl Hugh, the Norman lord Rhodri called Hugh the Fat.

When her eyes were not on the countryside, they were on Alex, riding in front of her atop his great black horse. The two of them seemed a matched pair: long black manes, muscular bodies and power restrained by force of their will.

One day, Alex would take his father's place as the Earl of Talisand and she would return to Wales to fight and mayhap die with the Welsh who had been so good to her. She did not shy from her fate but the longing for what could not be tore at her heart.

At midday, Alex turned in his saddle to look back at her just before his father called a halt to water the horses. Alex dismounted and came to help her down from her horse. She might have managed without him but it was a kind gesture since her skirts made dismounting awkward. "Thank you," she said as she placed her hands on his shoulders trying to avoid his eyes. But when his powerful hands circled her waist, his heat invaded her body and she turned to meet his penetrating gray gaze. Then her feet were on the ground and he dropped his hands.

They walked their horses to the stream not far from the road. Merewyn removed her hat and wiped her brow. The shade and cooler air beneath the canopy of trees was welcome. They stayed long enough to eat some cheese and dried venison while sharing their thoughts on the countryside they had passed.

Just as she was finishing, she felt Alex's dark eyes upon her. "Do you consider me peculiar, sir knight?" she asked, trying to make light of his unrelenting gaze.

"I find you fascinating. A beauty, aye, but a fierce one with your bow and that look in your eyes, more like a warrior's than a woman's."

"I assure you I am a woman." She had never considered herself a beauty, not like Bea, Guy's sister, and she was not a warrior as the strongest of the Welsh were. "It has taken me much practice to become proficient as an archer."

"I know of only one other woman who has done so."

"Your lady mother?"

"Aye. Maggie told me that when my mother was your age, she hunted rabbits for Talisand's kitchens."

"An unusual pursuit for the daughter of a thegn. In my conversations with Lady Serena, I learned she first took up the bow for sport.

Later, it came to mean much more to her, as it has for me."

He looked at her expectantly, as if he thought she would say more, but she could not. She did not want him to know she had been a frightened girl when she'd asked Lady Serena to teach her archery. It was enough that he admired her skill and compared her to Talisand's lady.

He tossed her one of his amused smiles. "And, like my mother, you have added to our stores of food."

"The deer—"

"And the boar."

"You make light of what was a harrowing experience," she said, frowning.

"Just teasing you." His slight smile confirmed his words. She supposed it was best to find some cause for laughter in the incident, although she would always shudder to recall how close she came to being speared on a boar's tusks.

"I will never forget that you saved my life."

He chuckled. "Given your inclination to danger, I expect there will be other opportunities."

A call from Sir Geoffroi returned them to the road where they resumed their travel. That night, they stayed in the village of Wigan on the River Douglas where the local priest arranged lodging for them. Merewyn had no complaint, for the company was good and the rabbit stew they were served satisfied her hunger from the long day's travel. And being with Alex made any place grand for she noticed little else but him.

The next day, they pressed on toward Chester.

'Twas a long, tiresome journey that finally brought them to the city that lay a stone's throw from Wales. Merewyn knew of it from the many evenings she had spent around the hearth fire with Rhodri and Fia. It was the place the Normans had decimated. Then they built a great castle set against the ancient Roman walls, the place where the Earl of Chester lived, a Norman dreaded by the Welsh.

Merewyn looked from one side of the road to the other, trying to absorb all she was seeing. Her life had been spent in small towns and villages and here was a walled city. They passed cottages nestled closely together inside the city's red stone walls. In the distance, next to the River Dee, she glimpsed a tower.

"That was once an old Saxon church," said Lady Serena, "but a few years after Chester was securely in Norman hands, Peter, the Bishop of Lichfield, moved his see here. The old church was not good enough for him, so he tore it down and began a grand new one. The sandstone walls of the new tower were his creation."

Merewyn eyed the jagged appearance of the building next to the tower. "It looks unfinished."

"The bishop was still building the cathedral when he died six years ago. I am told work continues to this day. But the bells in the tower work well enough. You will hear them ringing out the hours from Matins to Compline."

Talisand's church lacked a bell tower but Father Bernard had asked one be installed so that he could call the faithful to prayer.

They rode on, the castle's wooden tower looming high above where it sat upon a great motte. Around the motte on two sides flowed the River Dee. As they drew closer, the castle seemed to grow in size.

A brief conversation between Earl Renaud and the guard at the gate and they were allowed to enter the bailey.

The head groom and his stable boys took their horses.

Merewyn accepted Alex's help and slipped from her saddle, his hands on her waist lingering long enough for her to find his masculine presence disturbing.

"You are all right?" he asked.

After so many hours in the saddle, her legs were sluggish and it took a moment for her to walk comfortably. "Aye, just a bit unsteady."

Once she was walking with ease, she followed Alex to where her fellow travelers stood as a group in the bailey.

"I was here with the Conqueror nearly a score of years ago when he took this city," remarked Sir Geoffroi " 'Twas a terrible winter and a worse memory."

"I have heard tales, awful things," she said. "Was it as bad as they say?"

Sir Geoffroi regarded first Alex, then Rory and lastly, her. "The three of you were mere babes at the time and Guy had yet to be born."

Shaking his head, he continued, "As bad as they say? 'Twas worse. The Conqueror showed no mercy to the English. As he did in York, he killed many and ordered us to destroy the food stores and salt the land to assure there would be no support for a future rebellion. The people were starving."

Talisand's lord placed his arm across Sir Geoffroi's shoulders and said to the others, "Geoff and Alain risked William's wrath to help as many as they could reach a nearby abbey where there was food."

"You did what was right," said Lady Serena. Her words were met with nods from the men. Alex's father squeezed his friend's shoulder and then moved to stand next to his wife.

"I like to think so," said Sir Geoffroi. Then raising his eyes to the timber castle, he added, "Chester was the last of England to be subjected to the Conqueror's will and when it was done, William ordered the castle you see to be built."

All of England knew the timber castles stood as symbols of the Normans' power and authority and, in many instances, the Normans' cruelty. Merewyn admired Sir Geoffroi for his courage to defy his king in order to help the people.

"Would that I had been with you and Sir Alain," said Talisand's lord.

" 'Twas best you were not," remarked Sir Geoffroi. "We could hide among so many knights, but the king's wolf never could."

" 'Tis a time best forgotten," offered Lady Serena.

Guy eyed his father, admiration in his expression. "Is it not strange to return here, Father?"

"Yea, it is," admitted Sir Geoffroi. "I only hope this summer finds the land at peace with the Conqueror's son." Then, turning to Alex, "You fostered here and must know Earl Hugh well."

"Aye," said Alex. "Five years of my youth were spent here. But I have seen the earl many times since. He was with us in Normandy, though he joined William late in the fight."

Merewyn had wondered about his time away. He must have seen much fighting and many deaths.

"Earl Hugh is a good knight and was respected by the Conqueror," said the Lord of Talisand. " 'Twas why I chose him to foster Alex."

"I expect William will soon have Earl Hugh fighting the Welsh again," ventured Alex.

Merewyn spoke the one truth she knew of the Lord of Chester. "The earl still holds the King of Gwynedd as his prisoner."

Lady Serena nodded, her expression somber. "Rhodri told me of it many years ago."

They ascended the stairs to the castle. At the door, Earl Hugh and his wife greeted them and introductions were made. Merewyn judged him to be in his fourth decade and his countess in her third.

Though he was attired in garments befitting a high-ranking lord, the earl still had the look of a warrior, his craggy face brown from the sun, his demeanor intense. He was clean-shaven and his dark hair cut in the shorter Norman style, like that of Earl Renaud and Sir Geoffroi. But unlike Talisand's men, Earl Hugh had a large belly his cinnamon-colored tunic strained to cover.

The Lady of Chester must have been sharing her husband's trencher, for her elegant pale gold gown did not conceal her plump figure. But, unlike the earl, Countess Ermentrude had a pleasant face and a warm smile, one that was very welcoming. Merewyn assumed her hair was brown from her brows for the woman's headcloth entirely covered her hair. "Welcome to Chester," she said and took Lady Serena's arm, leading her into the castle. "It has been too long!"

Merewyn followed the two women as they spoke of their children. Behind her, the Earl of Chester inquired of Talisand's lord, "I trust your journey was without mishap, Ren?"

"Yea, 'twas pleasant with fair skies, but long enough your hearth fire and some of Normandy's wine will be most welcome."

Earl Hugh laughed. "And a soft bed, no doubt. 'Tis been many years since we found sleeping on the ground an adventure."

The earl welcomed Sir Geoffroi and the other men into the castle, beckoning them toward the hearth fire in the large hall.

Two rough-coated hounds came to greet the visitors. They were slightly smaller than the ones at Talisand but no less friendly. One hound trotted up to Alex and nuzzled his hand. "Remember me, do you?" Alex said, scratching the dog's ears and patting his head. To Merewyn, the two seemed great friends.

Earl Hugh glanced at Alex, Rory and Guy, who had joined the other men around the fire, and said to Earl Renaud, " 'Tis been but a short while since I was with these three in Normandy. I expect we will soon ride together with the king to deal with the Scots."

Merewyn did not hear the response as her attention was drawn to the grandeur of the hall, larger than the one at Talisand that sat next to the manor. Light from torches and candles illuminated the intricate tapestries decorating the walls. The weavings were very large, making her wonder if they hid alcoves.

"This is your first visit to Chester," stated the countess. "Do you like the tapestries?"

"Oh yea, they are wondrous." Merewyn could not suppress the awe in her voice for the tapestries looked almost like paintings so intricate was the weaving. Light from the blazing fire and many candles made the figures depicted seem to come alive: the animals of the hunt raced through the woodlands and the ladies smiled at their gallant knights.

"The ones we have in Talisand's old hall are small," put in Lady Serena, "but the castle at Talisand has larger ones."

In addition to the dais and trestle tables, there were small tables and benches scattered around the edges of the room in between the tapestries.

Since they were the earl's only guests, Countess Ermentrude told Merewyn there was plenty of room and she would have her own chamber. Nelda would have a room in the servants' quarters.

Serving women bustled into the hall, setting pitchers of wine and silver goblets on one of the long tables. Once the wine was poured, Earl Hugh lifted his wine in a toast, "To the health of the king!"

"To the king!" echoed the travelers and downed their wine. Even Lady Serena, who had no love for Norman kings, joined in.

It took Merewyn a few more gulps than the men to drink her portion, but she was glad she did as the potent red liquid lifted the weariness from her bones and warmed her blood. She watched Alex down his wine with great enthusiasm, exchanging barbs with Rory and Guy, but more than once he glanced to where she stood with Lady Serena and Lady Ermentrude. Each time, her heart hammered in her chest as their eyes met.

The two earls and Sir Geoffroi stood to one side, but close enough for Merewyn to hear them speak of the battles with the Welsh that had gained Earl Hugh and his cousin a good part of North East Wales. It horrified Merewyn to think Rhodri might be affected but, as she listened to the men speaking, she was comforted in the knowledge there had been no dire news out of Powys where Rhodri made his home.

A servant came to show the women to their chambers. Merewyn, together with Lady Serena and Nelda followed her to the floor above. Once inside her own chamber, Merewyn was pleased to see a fire in the brazier, candles on the table under the window and her chest of clothing at the foot of the bed. Opening the carved wooden box, she found the gowns Nelda had neatly folded. The dark-haired maidservant with fair skin, a round face and pleasant manner was a treasure. And she had been kind to help Merewyn when she was not her mistress. No wonder Lady Serena so valued Nelda.

While Merewyn waited for the hot water to arrive for her bath, she took out the gown she would wear this evening, an azure velvet that fitted her well. She would save the amethyst silk Lady Serena had given her to wear in London when she would meet the king.

She walked to the window and flung open the shutters, breathing in the cooler air of the evening. Just then she heard the bells of the church ring the hour of None. Looking past the motte and the River Dee, she glimpsed the peaceful village lying on the other side of the river. The cottages glowed with many hearth fires where she imagined the people were preparing their supper. She sighed, more content than she had been for a long while, for when Lady Serena had told Countess Ermentrude that Merewyn was her ward and the daughter of a close friend who had died, the countess had accepted the description without question.

Merewyn could only hope the shame of her birth did not follow her into the future.

CHAPTER 5

Alex washed the dust from his body, scraped the stubble from his face and clothed himself in a dark brown tunic he was certain would meet the expectations of Earl Hugh. He did not worry so much about Ermentrude, for the countess had always been a jolly soul with a pleasing disposition. But the earl demanded that his sons, including his foster son, dress as worthy young nobles.

Alex's gut roiled at the memories that assaulted him coming back to the place where he'd spent so much of his youth. At Talisand, he had been the favored, eldest son of the Red Wolf, more indulged than even Tibby was today. But at Chester, he was folded into the large family of the earl and his wife much like another lance was added to the armory.

Earl Hugh was a tyrant who tolerated no disobedience of his rigid edicts. Alex had rebelled early on until he tired of the whippings. The earl was always careful not to leave permanent scars that would draw the questions of Alex's father. By the time Alex had returned to Talisand in his twelfth year, he was a different lad. 'Twas one reason he had come to Merewyn's rescue so quickly that day in the woods. He could not abide anyone taking advantage of another's lesser position with the intent to inflict harm.

But now Alex was a knight in his own right and a friend of William Rufus whom he had served even before he became England's king. And the girl he had rescued had grown into a beautiful and fierce young woman. Was she drawn to archery as a means of defense? It had occurred to him when he had asked her why she had taken up the bow.

Closing the door of his chamber, he descended to the hall. Gathered around the earl and his wife were Alex's father, Sir Geoffroi and Guy and Rory. Alex's mother and Merewyn had yet to appear. The men-at-arms who had accompanied them would sleep in the barracks the earl kept for his own men, so Alex did not look for them. No doubt, they would be enjoying the village taverns and the village women.

"Alex!" Earl Hugh's voice sounded like a command. "You have timed your appearance well," he said with a smirk. "The wine has just been poured."

Ignoring the barb, Alex accepted wine from the tray carried to him by one of the servants. Greeting the others and seeing the elegant attire they had donned for the evening, he was glad he had dressed in similar fashion.

He had just taken a sip of the red wine when his lady mother and Merewyn descended the stairs. His eyes devoured Merewyn. Her blue velvet gown flowed around her as she walked. The candlelight had turned her hair a rich gold. Around her neck was the same golden necklace she had worn on the night of his homecoming. He took in her slender form, her long fingers held shyly at her waist and the delicate features of her face.

Setting down his goblet, he excused himself and slowly walked toward the two women who had just reached the bottom of the stairs. Acknowledging his mother, he bowed, "My lady mother."

The Lady of Talisand dipped her head and tossed him a knowing smile before walking past him without saying a word.

Alex bowed before Merewyn. "You are a vision."

Her blue-hazel eyes sparkled with mirth. "You mean because you recognize me now that I am free of all the dust?"

He chuckled. "Well, the same could be said of me. Nay, I only meant to admire your beauty."

" 'Tis the second time today you have complimented me in such manner. You must want something," she teased.

"Aye," he said. Gazing intently into her eyes, he decided to speak the truth he was just coming to realize. "I want... everything."

She inhaled sharply, her cheeks blushing scarlet. Holding out his arm, he whispered, "Do not worry, I will tell no one of my ambition toward you." Indeed, how could he speak to others of something he was only beginning to understand himself?

" 'Twould be best if you said nothing to me of it, either," she said shortly, placing her hand on his offered arm. "It would not be proper for Talisand's heir to dally with a commoner." The bolt of lightning that surged through him at her touch was mirrored in her eyes. He was pleased to see the attraction was shared.

He led her toward the others. "It matters not to me you are not of noble birth."

She let out a heavy sigh. "Surely it would matter to the king and your noble father."

He could not argue with her, not after Sir Geoffroi's warning of the king's likely intent. Their conversation ceased when he delivered her to the ladies.

During the evening meal that followed, he suffered through Earl Hugh's recounting stories from Alex's days at Chester as a foster son, minus the whippings, of course. Rory and Guy took full advantage, teasing him unmercifully for the tales of his once stumbling with his sword.

"For that," Alex informed them, "I shall have to trounce you at chess, a game Earl Hugh taught me and his sons well."

"He is a fierce player of the game," the rotund Earl Hugh said in warning to Alex's companions. "Look not for mercy."

Alex thought it an interesting comment from one who showed little mercy himself.

"Aye, we know," said Rory. "Our time in Normandy afforded us many nights where dice and chess were our only amusements."

"To us," put in Guy, "it was merely a way of passing time. To Alex, it was a battle to the death with carved horses, knights and kings."

"So be it," said Earl Hugh. "Tonight we shall have games of chess." Then looking at Alex's father, standing next to Sir Geoffroi, he added, "I welcome the opportunity to defeat my old friends."

"You will not find us so easily vanquished," said Alex's father. "Geoff, in particular, has recently shown great skill in the game."

* * *

Merewyn had been listening with great interest to the men's discussion of chess and now she watched carefully as the servants cleared away the trenchers. The men set up the boards for the two games on the small tables that they carried from the edges of the room.

None of the men had asked her to play. How were they to know in the six years she had been in Wales, archery was not the only skill she had acquired? In Rhodri and Fia's great manor in Powys, many evenings they played chess.

The game fascinated her because it reflected the world in which she lived: the king who could move in all directions because his will was law; a queen who could move only on the slant and one space at a time because women were rarely allowed to act directly; pawns, like the villeins, tied to their liege lord for the land they rented in exchange for his protection; rooks that had full access to the board but could only move in straight lines like the siege towers they represented; bishops, representing the church, whose movements were restricted but who could jump over others like the knights who protected the king, whose surrender meant the loss of all.

As she watched, Alex took a seat across from Rory at one table and Earl Hugh faced Sir Geoffroi over another. Merewyn sat with the ladies who kept their hands busy with needlework as they spoke of their children. She had no interest in needlework and she had no children. Instead, she kept her eyes on the play of the games and thought of the King of Gwynedd rotting in a cell somewhere in the castle. Rhodri had told her the Welsh king was descended from the great Brian Boru, High King of Ireland. A sad end for so great a man.

Except for her dismal reflections on the King of Gwynedd's current state, it had been an entirely pleasant evening. The meal had been a tasty array of many dishes and meats and now a lute player provided music that soothed her spirit. Even the earl's hounds were calm, sleeping before the hearth fire.

She sighed as the games of chess wore on. Patience had never been one of her virtues. But for the game she envisioned, she could wait.

A servant added logs to the hearth fire sending sparks into the air and then refilled the men's goblets. Merewyn refused more wine. She needed her wits if she was to play a decent game of chess.

78

Having defeated Rory, Alex now played against Guy, but Alex was restless, stirring on his bench with every move he made of the chess pieces. To her, he appeared like a stallion about to break into a run. Often, he ran his fingers through his long black hair and crossed and re-crossed his legs beneath the table.

From the exasperated sounds coming from Guy, Alex had to be an aggressive player. Only a well-thought-out strategy would defeat him. Could she do it? For some reason, it was important to try.

At the other table, Sir Geoffroi had defeated Earl Hugh, who took the loss with good grace, but demanded a chance to play against Talisand's lord. Earl Renaud was only too happy to comply and slid onto the bench Sir Geoffroi had vacated.

Merewyn waited for the right moment, eager to try her skill against Alex and hoping, when the time came, she would be allowed to play.

As the last games unfolded, her attention was drawn to Earl Hugh, who stared at the chessboard frowning at his remaining pieces. The faint smile on the face of Talisand's lord told her he was winning.

Alex quickly bested Guy and Merewyn knew her chance had come. Finished with his game, Alex looked up at Sir Geoffroi with a raised brow and head tilted in invitation, but the older knight shook his head.

"I can play," she offered, certain no one took her seriously.

Lady Serena glanced up from her needlework. "When did you learn the game?"

"Rhodri taught me more than the way of the bow, my lady." She grinned at Alex. "He taught me to play chess."

"Many ladies can play chess," interjected Countess Ermentrude in Merewyn's defense while pulling a needle through the cloth she held. Then winking at Merewyn, she added, "Do manage to win, young lady."

Merewyn smiled at the plump countess. "I will certainly try."

Earl Hugh glanced up only for a moment before returning his attention to the board in front of him, puzzling over his next move.

Rory and Guy nodded to her encouragingly. "You are our last hope to see Alex's streak of victories ended this night," said Guy.

With his open palm, Alex beckoned her to the empty bench across from the chessboard he was setting up with the pieces from his last game. "Let us witness this new skill you have acquired. Mayhap I can teach you a move or two."

Merewyn was certain he could teach her many things but whether chess was one of them remained to be seen.

* * *

Alex took a swallow of his wine and tried to relax, doubting Merewyn knew more than the rudiments of the game but happy to teach her more. Any reason to spend time with her pleased him.

The hearth fire blazed as a servant added another log, but the lute player had stopped playing for the moment. There were no other sounds in the hall, save for the occasional whisperings of his mother and Lady Ermentrude. Rory, Guy and Sir Geoffroi had gathered around the other game, leaving Alex and Merewyn alone for the moment.

His enticing opponent inhaled deeply and let out a breath as she took her bottom lip between her teeth and considered the board. The swells of her breasts pressed against the edge of her velvet gown. He tried to keep his mind on the game ahead but, in truth, her presence was distracting. Merewyn was far more interesting than any game of chess.

Glancing at the black pieces on his side of the board, he moved one of his pawns forward. As he had been taught, it mattered not which color began the game. "I will move first. That way, you will have time to think."

She looked down at the board and brought her elbow to the table, her fingers playing about her delicate alabaster throat. Turning her unusual blue eyes on him, she said, "I expected you to make the first move, but I do not need time to think, not yet anyway."

Her slender fingers wrapped around a pawn and caressed it before moving the piece forward.

His mouth watered. When he looked up, beneath her long lashes she watched him. His mind strayed to the afternoon he had wandered into her chamber drunk and encountered those same seductive eyes, then filled with anger. He blinked and forced himself to focus on the game. Mayhap he needed a knight. He moved the piece, carved and painted to look like a black knight, forward two squares and to the left.

He was feeling quite confident until Merewyn licked her lush bottom lip while studying the board. His groin swelled in response and he shifted on the bench, thankful his tunic covered his reaction. He was certain her seductive movements were innocent, but she could not have made him want her more had she set out to do so.

Merewyn glanced up once before moving her white knight forward.

His mind wandered, seeing again her thighs clenching the sides of her pony as she galloped by the targets, rapidly loosing arrows with deadly accuracy. Dragging his mind back to the game, he straightened in his seat and moved his bishop across from her knight. Satisfied with the move, he folded his arms and waited for her next move.

The game continued with both of them making careful moves, Merewyn surprising Alex with her skill. He had known she was intelligent, but the way she played chess told him she could be clever, as well.

Shifting on her bench, Merewyn appeared to carefully consider her next move. One of her long fingers played with a strand of flaxen hair lying across her shoulder. The strands caught the light from the candles turning them into liquid gold. His fingers itched to touch the silken strands.

Two more pawn moves and he captured her knight, thinking he had her. But then his eyes fastened on her hand moving to the delicate skin of her throat.

After what seemed but a moment's passing, Merewyn looked up and smiled. "Checkmate."

★   ★   ★

Thrilled she had won but reluctant to act too much the victor, Merewyn offered Alex another smile. "Fortune was with me." When she had spoken the word that proclaimed her the winner, Alex had looked startled, as if waking from a dream. With him watching her, it had taken all the concentration she could muster to maintain any strategy at all. Unsure she could do it, her hope had risen when he continued to appear distracted. Mayhap he had been tired of the game having played several rounds.

"You may have had fortune on your side," he said, "but you also displayed a fair amount of talent. Rhodri might have been a good teacher, but you must have been a keen disciple." He dipped his head to her. "Well done, my lady."

She thanked him. Because Alex's praise meant much, she resisted the urge to correct him for calling her a lady when she clearly was not.

Countess Ermentrude stood and gave a small cheer; Lady Serena nodded her head, smiling.

Rory and Guy left the other game and came to congratulate her and tease Alex. "Felled by the fair damsel!" proclaimed Guy with glee.

"We dare not tell the king of your loss to a lass," chimed in Rory with feigned terror.

Alex grinned at Merewyn. "We will see who wins the next game."

Pleased she had won, Merewyn did not think Alex minded the jests he endured from his fellow knights. Mayhap he would win the next game as the gleam in his eye portended.

Talisand's lord, having defeated Earl Hugh, rose from his bench. Joined by Lady Serena, he proposed a toast. "To the talented ladies!"

Everyone raised their goblets. Countess Ermentrude downed her wine and proudly said, "I love to see a bold knight vanquished at chess by a lady. 'Tis one of the few battlefields where we can be the victor."

Earl Hugh hastened to give his opinion. " 'Tis best it is so."

Lady Serena rolled her eyes and clinked her goblet against Ermentrude's, the two exchanging a grin.

"We had best retire," said Alex's father. "The bells toll Compline and our next stop is Shrewsbury. Beyond that, a long road awaits us to London."

Merewyn did not disagree and, with the others, ascended the stairs to her chamber, thinking of a rematch with Alex. She was not being very true to her plan to keep distance between them. In truth, she relished any chance to be with him, even if it meant losing a game of chess.

As it turned out, their stop in Shrewsbury was brief, but she got to see Alex's brother, Roger, whom she had not seen since she left Talisand for Wales. His chestnut hair, the same color as his father's, made him look much like the Red Wolf, save for his brown eyes.

Their host, the old earl, Roger de Montgomerie, had begged his friend, Earl Renaud, for time to show them the Benedictine Abbey he had founded. Merewyn was glad Earl Roger prevailed.

Talisand had a beautiful stone chapel built by Lady Serena's father, but it paled in comparison to the church at Shrewsbury. At least four times larger, the abbey church dedicated to Saint Peter had massive rounded stone arches the chapel in Talisand lacked. A long walk on a gray stone floor led to the magnificent nave with tall windows that allowed light to flood the church.

" 'Tis another Norman cathedral that replaced a Saxon church," remarked Lady Serena, "but this one is beautiful."

When Merewyn told Alex it was not like any she had ever seen, he was quick to reply. "Westminster Abbey in London is even more magnificent. 'Tis much larger and grander than this one. The Conqueror himself was crowned there as was his son."

CHAPTER 6

A foreboding like a black cloud hovered over Alex as they entered London, riding down the Strand toward the palace. It had naught to do with the dark sky above threatening rain, the foul-smelling mud splashing onto Azor's withers, or the dirty, narrow streets with their buildings pressed closely together.

The cause of it, he knew, was the king.

With his notorious temper and his strange proclivities, many knights disdained the royal court. In private he could be easy, tossing off jests as one given to frivolity, however, in public and when angry, he was given to fits of temper accompanied by stuttering. At times, William was barely able to converse. Then he would turn savagely cruel, seeking to intimidate those around him. Only on the battlefield could William Rufus be counted upon to act the leader of men like his father, appreciating boldness in others.

With Alex, the king had been generous. But what would he be with Merewyn?

If he could, Alex would spare her and his mother the evenings at court. But since they had come to London, their presence at court would be expected. While his father, who had attended the king before, would find little surprising, the women would be shocked at what they might see. For Merewyn, there was also danger. And not just from the king. Ranulf, the king's priest and advisor, ruthlessly pursued any beautiful woman he desired. Against both Alex vowed to guard her well.

Their party numbered more than a dozen since Earl Hugh and a few of his men had joined them in Chester. Alex was always amazed the earl could still sit a horse since he had grown corpulent, not unlike the Conqueror in the years before his death.

Alex remembered those years and the hectic days that followed the king's deathbed confession in Normandy. Once William Rufus learned he was to have England, he had made haste to cross the Channel and claim the crown, taking Alex with him. Upon their arrival, the new king had knighted Alex, then only eighteen.

The hooves of their horses splashed dirty water from the muddy puddles as they headed toward the River Thames.

"Our house should be ready to receive us," he said to his father, riding next to him. "I asked the king's messenger who came to Talisand to assure it was so when he reached London."

Talisand's lord raised a brow. "The king's messenger does your bidding?"

Alex smiled to himself as he remembered why the man had so quickly agreed, for Alex had once defended him before the king. "He owed me a favor."

His father's expression was assessing. Alex knew him well enough he did not fear him like he had once feared Earl Hugh, but it was still true that the knight called the Red Wolf could terrify weaker men with just a look. " 'Tis well and good our lodgings are ready. I would not want to try and find rooms at the king's palace."

"Aye, 'twill be crowded," said Alex.

Nearly twenty thousand people lived in London now and, with William summoning his army, Alex expected the numbers to swell as knights, men-at-arms and seamen poured into the city. Taverns would be overflowing with men and fights among them would be a common occurrence. Already the streets were filled with more people than when he had left.

From the other side of his father, Earl Hugh spoke. "As I am oft here, I have long maintained a house not far from the palace."

Alex turned in his saddle to look at Merewyn, riding alongside his mother. Both women appeared tired, their shoulders drooping like plucked flowers left in the sun. The air was thick with moisture, draining strength, making him glad he wore no mail. "We will soon be there," he encouraged.

At his words, Merewyn lifted her head and straightened her back.

He smiled to himself and turned back to face the streets of London. Merewyn had fortitude. She would not allow him to see any weakness.

A short while later, Earl Hugh and his men left them to head down a side street. The Talisand group continued on, arriving in front of the two-story manor that was their destination.

Their London house was larger than the one at Talisand because, while it lacked a hall, it possessed a large dining chamber with a hearth. It had windows, now shuttered, on both sides looking out on the street and, from the second story at the rear of the house, one could see the River Thames.

The manor's door was nearly on the edge of the street. A narrow strip of stones ran along the front of the house, a feature shared by many of the homes on the Strand. The trees and flowers so abundant in Talisand were missing altogether making the house seem dour in its mood.

Alex dismounted and handed Azor's reins to the young groom who waited before the door. "Did you receive my message, Ric?"

"Aye, sir, all is ready for his lordship. The stable boys will take the horses and see them fed."

"You have my thanks," he told the groom. Glad things had gone well, Alex helped Merewyn down from her mare. He was enjoying having his hands on her waist. For more than a sennight, he'd been at the task. Ignoring the jests of his companions at the attention he paid her and the occasional puzzled looks from his mother, he was always there to assist Merewyn. She had never complained about the long days yet he knew she was often weary. Each time he had helped her from her horse, she thanked him even as her sweet smell filled his nostrils, driving him half-mad for want of her.

Giles, the gray-haired steward who had served his father as long as Alex could remember, rushed out the door to greet them. "My lady, my lord, all is ready. The bath water is heating and a dinner of roast duck will soon be served."

"You have our thanks," said his father. "We are tired from the road and all you suggest will be most welcome." Draping his arm around Alex's mother, the two followed the steward into the manor. Sir Geoffroi walked behind them with his son, Guy. Alex, Merewyn and Rory followed. The men-at-arms tramped around to the stable where they would lay their pallets for the night.

Inside the house, drinks of spiced wine awaited them. Shedding their cloaks, they accepted the warm cups smelling of cloves and cinnamon, gratefully imbibing the sweet wine tasting of spices and honey. He was happy to see that the drink revived Merewyn. Like a flower given water and sun, she smiled, her cheeks reddening with the heady wine.

Their eyes met over their cups and the room grew more heated. "So, what do you think of London?" he asked her.

"I am overwhelmed. 'Tis even larger than Chester. And your home," she said looking around, "is beautiful."

Their London house was more richly appointed than the manor at Talisand but Alex loved his home in the north and preferred it above this one.

Nelda came down the stairs. "Your chamber is ready, my lady," the maidservant said to her mistress.

"Come, Merewyn," said Alex's mother, "let us have that bath Giles spoke of and shed these mud-stained garments for some clean gowns."

Alex's gaze followed the two women as they ascended the stairs, then he joined the other men as they strolled into the main chamber.

"It appears London has not changed," said his father looking out the window to the street. He turned into the room and faced Sir Geoffroi. "I doubt you have missed it any more than I."

Guy's father laughed. "Nay, I do not miss London. Nor do I miss York, or any other town. I prefer to remain on my lands near Talisand where Emma and I can live in peace. 'Tis enough to attend the barons' meeting and give what advice the king will take. Our sons can ride to battle with their young king."

Alex shared a glance with his two companions. "If the king has his way, we will soon be on our way to Scotland."

"First we must endure the king's court," said Rory.

"Aye," said Alex. Raising a brow toward Guy, he said, "Best not to appear too prettily dressed, else your youth and that handsome face of yours might be confused with the king's favored courtiers."

Guy looked affronted.

Sir Geoffroi scowled.

"That has not changed?" asked Alex's father.

"Nay," said Alex. "If anything, 'twas worse after we returned from Normandy."

⋆　⋆　⋆

Merewyn sighed with relief when she arrived at the chamber assigned to her. Her body ached from the long day's ride. The room was dim; the only light was the narrow band spilling in around the edges of the closed shutters. She opened them wide, eager to view the surrounding area.

The window faced east toward the river. On the far bank of the Thames stood a few buildings, but on either side of them the land appeared to be untamed marsh. Dark clouds hung low overhead, their brooding color turning the waters of the Thames a dull gray. A stench rose in her nostrils making her grimace. She could not tell if it was the river or something else. As they had ridden into London, the whole city seemed to smell of raw offal. She could not imagine a king living in such a place, but then Alex had told her William Rufus was not often here.

Behind her, a knock sounded.

"Enter."

Nelda peeked her head around the oak-paneled door, her blue-gray eyes scanning the chamber as her dark plait fell over her shoulder. "Can they bring the bathing water in now, mistress?"

"Aye, of course. And 'tis your chamber, too, Nelda. Lady Serena told me we were to share."

"Do not be concerned with me," the maidservant said, opening the door wide to admit two boys lugging pails of steaming water. "The chests will be here shortly so you will have fresh clothing after your bath. I will bathe while you and Lady Serena are at supper."

The girl was efficient as she moved the copper tub to the center of the room and gestured the lads to fill it. When they had done so, Nelda ushered the lads from the room and waited by the door as two male servants carried their chests into the room, along with Merewyn's bow and quiver of arrows.

Once the men had gone, Nelda made a quick survey of the chamber, a satisfied look on her face. "I will return after I've seen to Lady Serena."

"Thank you, Nelda."

Alone, Merewyn peeled off her gloves, her gown stained with mud, her undertunic, shoes and hosen. Taking the pot of soft soap from her chest and picking up a drying cloth from the stack left on her bed, she breathed in the scent of Talisand's flowers and stepped into the tub.

The light from the window fell across her body. Most of her skin was a pale ivory, but even with her straw hat, her face felt tight, as if it had gained color from the sun, for they'd had good weather.

She eased her body into the steaming water and laid her head on the edge of the tub letting the hot water soothe her. Her mind filled with images of their travel to London. She had loved seeing the countryside and places she had never been. The days spent conversing with Lady Serena had been pleasant. But most of all, she had enjoyed being with Alex, mayhap too much. She was fond of seeing him each day. He could be charming as well as commanding and often he had made her smile in their brief stops or at supper. Whatever there was between them, it had grown, at least on her part. It was there whenever he touched her, placed his hands about her waist or allowed his gray eyes to linger on her.

It was dangerous, but she could not bring herself to show him indifference.

In Shrewsbury, they had played chess again and he had won. She had been relieved. It was better that way. Friends traded wins.

The memory of the first night he had kissed her flickered in her mind. He had said they could be more than friends. What had he meant? She would not be his mistress and could never be his wife. What more was there for them? In truth, she feared she was playing with fire. But she could no longer deny her heart.

The bath water began to grow cold and, feeling a chill, she quickly rinsed her hair and reached for the drying cloth. Stepping from the tub, she dried herself and changed into a linen gown the color of green summer leaves. Nelda would return to help her with the laces. Would Alex think it feminine? Her archer's clothing had been sewn to conceal her curves. Though she was slender, she did have them and, for Alex, she wanted to appear more than a bowman.

Pulling her still damp hair back from her face, plaiting the sides and tying them together at her crown, she let the rest of her hair hang free.

She shot a glance at her bow, leaning against the wall next to her quiver of arrows. The silent rebuke she heard in her mind was not so strong as it had once been. As Maugris had advised, she would control the bow and keep her own counsel.

After Nelda had come and gone, Merewyn went downstairs. Everyone was there save Alex. Her searching gaze did not go unnoticed. Rory strolled to her. "Alex has gone to the palace to let the king know Earl Renaud has arrived. He will bring back news of the barons' meeting."

Embarrassed that Rory should have been so quick to see her interest in Alex's whereabouts, Merewyn thanked him and went to join Lady Serena where she stood with Earl Renaud and Sir Geoffroi on the other side of the room. She had just taken a sip from the goblet handed her when Alex appeared at the doorway, a frown on his face.

He darted a glance at her, then strode to his father. "The king has decided the barons will meet two days hence. Ranulf says nearly all have arrived. But William has called a hunt for tomorrow in Windsor Forest."

A hunt. With a night's sleep in a comfortable bed, Merewyn would enjoy racing through the woods after deer. Her brows lifted in question to Lady Serena. "Where is Windsor?"

" 'Tis the closest of the royal forests, a morning's ride away," replied Lady Serena. Then she turned to Alex, "Will we be expected to join the king for dinner at Windsor Castle tomorrow eve?"

"Nay, he plans to return to Westminster where we will dine with him and the barons. 'Tis likely to be a large gathering with so many in London."

The steward was good to his word and soon they were dining on roast duck cooked in wine sauce with cherries. The dish was a particular favorite of Merewyn's and she ate heartily from the trencher she shared with Alex.

It was a happy gathering that evening as the men discussed the king's hunt planned for the next day. Merewyn had never seen Windsor

Forest, one of the king's woodlands set aside for his pleasure. The men did not invite her to participate but she wanted to. A royal hunt!

That night, Merewyn lay in bed, listening to the rain pounding on the roof, the sound soothing and the breeze blowing in through the open shutters clean and fresh.

The next morning, awakened by the bells sounding the hour of Terce, she threw back the cover and walked to the window. In the distance, the Thames was a deep blue, the morning sun already turning the sky a paler version of the river. She inhaled deeply. The air, washed clean by the rain, smelled fresh. The rain had swept away the horrible stench, at least for a time.

Nelda stirred in her small bed on the far side of the chamber. "Oh, I am late rising." She sat up, already replaiting her hair. "Do you require my service before I attend Lady Serena? I am certain she is awake and Earl Renaud may already be breaking his fast."

"Nay, I am well able to dress myself, Nelda." Merewyn's voice was full of the excitement welling up inside. "I plan to join the hunt so 'tis an archer's clothing I will be wearing today." Then with a smile, she added, "No laces."

Nelda returned her a surprised look and then, bobbing her head, splashed water on her face, slipped her simple tunic over her undertunic and left the chamber.

It took Merewyn only moments to dress and plait her hair she was so anxious to take part. Grabbing her bow and arrows and her brown felt hat, she quickly descended the stairs and crossed the entry into the main chamber. The men were seated at the table and, as Nelda predicted, eating their morning gruel, bread and berries. Cups of ale dotted the table.

Alex looked up and scowled, his hand poised with a piece of bread in front of his open mouth. "Where do you think you are going dressed like that?"

Rory coughed and sputtered, his gruel flying out of his mouth.

Guy beamed at her. At least he was pleased.

Merewyn's gaze quickly took in the two older knights. Both Earl Renaud and Sir Geoffroi bore amused expressions.

In a fit of temper, Alex threw his bread on the table.

"I want to join the hunt," she calmly stated. "I have my bow and arrows and Ceinder can soon be saddled and ready."

Pounding his fist on the table, making the cups jump, Alex bellowed, "Absolutely not!"

His father raised a brow and cocked his head toward his son.

"I think 'tis a grand idea," said Guy.

"We know she can shoot well," chimed in Rory, wiping his face with a cloth.

"And I have you to protect me," she said to Alex, batting her eyelashes, "should I face a wild boar."

Sir Geoffroi laughed. "Emma would be proud."

From behind Merewyn, the voice of Lady Serena brought the discussion to an abrupt close. "Let her go with you," she said to her son. "Ren and Geoff will look after her. And Rory has the right of it. Merewyn can shoot well. You have witnessed her skill yourself. It might prove entertaining to see her outshoot the Norman king's men."

Alex turned to his father as if seeking support, but Talisand's lord remained silent in the face of his wife's approval.

"I like it not," said Alex, "but I can see I am outnumbered."

In a typical hunt, the men raced their horses after the hounds and, when they had cornered a deer, dropped to the ground to render the killing blow. But she could shoot from her pony, which gave her an advantage. Merewyn could hardly wait to see how she fared against the king and his barons.

Lady Serena draped her arm around Merewyn's shoulders. Having the support of the Lady of Talisand meant much. Alex might not like it, but Merewyn would go with them.

"I will wear my cap," she said to Alex holding up the brown felt, "so everyone will think me your page."

Alex let out a huff. "Indeed, that is just what I feared."

*　　*　　*

Alex held his breath as they approached Windsor Forest, hoping no one would remark on Merewyn's presence. Perchance he could keep her hidden among the others as they hunted in the thousands of acres set aside for the king.

Already, a group of more than a dozen men had gathered for the hunt, waiting beneath the tall beech trees that stood guard at the entrance to the dense woods.

Like his father before him, William Rufus was an avid hunter. Alex had hunted many times with him in the New Forest that the Conqueror had created southwest of London at the expense of nearly two score villages. It was close enough to Westminster for the king to spend a day away from court pursuing the beasts of the chase, the hart—the red deer stag he loved—and the wild boar. But most often, the king hunted in Windsor Forest because it was closer to London.

Only the king and his friends were permitted to hunt in the royal forests. Harsher than his father, William Rufus showed no mercy to anyone caught hunting without his permission. A man found taking one of the deer would be sentenced to death. To shoot at a deer would lose a man his hands and disturbing a deer would cost a man his eyes.

Alex considered the penalties cruel. The nobles complained about them and the poor cried foul, but the king remained unmoved, caring little about the ill will his harsh punishments brought him. The church also loathed the harsh forest laws and frowned on hunting for sport, but William Rufus gave little thought to the clerics' protests.

Alex and his father had discussed the forest laws, glad no royal forest had been declared a part of Talisand's lands.

His mother was quick to tell him the Anglo-Saxon kings had allowed the people to hunt freely. She argued it was beneath a king to care so little for his people and so much for his own pleasure that he would maim and kill those who hunted merely to feed their families.

Alex had agreed with his mother, but could do nothing, despite her urging him to raise the matter with William.

His father had sympathized, but in the end, shrugged. "Alex is the king's knight, Serena, compelled to serve his sovereign no matter his views on the matter."

The knights from Talisand, joined by Earl Hugh and the "page" accompanying them, approached the waiting men. Talisand's lord, Earl Hugh and Sir Geoffroi rode in front. Merewyn rode next to Alex where he could keep an eye on her. Rory and Guy moved up to flank them.

Glancing at Merewyn in her green and brown archer's clothing with her brown felt cap, he was struck by how young she looked. The description of a page was not far off. He suddenly wished her pony was a dark bay and not white, for its color, a stark contrast to the muted colors of the forest, drew the eye. 'Twas the only white horse in the hunt and given the apparent youth and sex of the rider, the king was certain to notice. The possibility disturbed Alex greatly.

"You are scowling," whispered Merewyn.

"I have good reason!" he hissed back.

"Welcome, Earl Renaud," said one of the barons from the midst of the hunters. Alex recognized the man. 'Twas Robert fitzHaimo, baron of Gloucester, one of the king's loyal subjects. Like the Red Wolf, fitzHaimo had served the first William and now served the second. The baron was slight of frame and his chestnut hair nearly the color of Alex's father's, only longer. The Red Wolf might be a decade older, but to Alex his father was somehow more virile, his presence more dominating than the other men.

"Do you wait for the king?" asked Alex's father.

"Aye," replied fitzHaimo. "His huntsman has been here with his scent hound so that we now know the path the deer will take. He is stationing the hounds ahead along the expected route."

"A messenger arrived some time ago," said a man Alex did not recognize, "advising us the king would be late. We expect him any moment."

Altogether a score of men waited for the king. The sun was now strong in the sky and the rain of the night before was causing steam to rise off the damp vegetation where the sun's rays reached to the forest floor.

"Go on," Alex told Rory and Guy. "Greet the others." Then frowning at Merewyn, he said, "I will stay with my *page*."

Merewyn raised her eyes to the trees.

Rory and Guy chuckled as they walked their horses around Alex's father and Sir Geoffroi to greet the knights with whom they were acquainted. Earl Hugh had already wandered off to converse with one of the barons.

Azor was restless beneath Alex. Neither of them liked to wait. Then, too, the stallion might be sensing his master's anxiety. He walked the horse in a circle, then brought it alongside Merewyn. She had not moved at all, her mare standing serene and seemingly content.

"Say nothing unless you are asked a question," he cautioned in a low voice. "If a question comes to you, short answers are best. In truth, I would have no one hear your voice."

She nodded. But he was not fooled. Now that she had what she wanted, she appeared compliant. But the glimmer of defiance in her blue-hazel eyes told him once the hunt began, he could not be assured she would remain at his side.

A horn sounded from behind them. In the distance, hounds bayed. *The king.*

*   *   *

Merewyn's stomach clenched as the king and his guards arrived. She had never met this William but she knew the Norman knight who had raped her mother had served the first one. She straightened her back, tugged her cap down on her head and stiffened her resolve. *I will not cower.*

Alex tossed her a look of caution, his gray eyes stormy. "You have nothing to worry about if you remain silent."

Of what does he worry? But she nodded all the same.

She knew instantly which of the approaching riders was the king. His resplendent attire captured her eye: a bejeweled, scarlet tunic over blue silk undertunic, the sleeves extending to his wrists. On his thick fingers were many rings, each displaying a different jewel. He had long yellow hair, a small red beard and florid cheeks. The horse he rode was a magnificent Spanish chestnut stallion. She was surprised to see how short the king's legs were, but his upper body was powerfully built. Yet the king had a protruding belly, like the richly attired man with dark hair who rode beside him.

She trembled as William Rufus fixed his eyes upon her. The color of his eyes was somewhere between green and brown, and they contained glittering specks like small fires. His intense scrutiny was unsettling.

Shifting his gaze to Alex and his father, the king said, "My wolves ride together. *Excellent!*"

"Sire," said Talisand's lord, bowing his head to the younger man as

Sir Geoffroi and Alex did the same. Merewyn bowed her head and said nothing.

"*Bonne chasse!*" The king proclaimed, bidding them a good hunt, and left them, walking his magnificent stallion toward the front of the party.

"Who is the one who rides beside him?" she asked Alex, noting a certain resemblance except for the dark hair of the king's companion.

"Duke Robert, the king's older brother. They are currently at peace since their treaty at Caen. The duke intends to accompany William's army to Scotland because he knows Malcolm."

She accepted that it was a knight's duty to serve his king, but she did not like to think of Alex riding to war. Dismissing her fears about Scotland, she watched the king and his brother riding off.

When the king was a dozen feet away, he turned in his saddle to look back at her before resuming his path to the front of the party.

"Was it my pony that drew the king's attention?" she whispered to Alex.

Alex gave out a frustrated sigh. "William has seen white horses before. Likely even Welsh ponies. Nay, 'twas not your pony. He may be wondering why I would bring a page to a hunt. Too, he will have noticed your bow and arrows. But more likely 'twas your womanly features that made him turn to study you further. I've no doubt he considers you a most winsome lad."

Her cheeks heated at the compliment Alex had paid her no matter she was disguised as a boy. "But I did naught to draw his attention."

"In truth, I fear you could not have avoided it. William likes lads, especially feminine ones."

What did Alex mean? Before she could ask, the horn sounded and the hounds bayed loudly from deeper into the forest.

The score of riders were suddenly off, cantering after the king. The earth trembled at the pounding hooves. Merewyn forgot all and charged forward, thrilling at their swift pace as they dashed through the forest, following the sound of the baying hounds.

At first, the path was straight and wide and Ceinder held a steady gait. But soon, the riders spread out and the path she was on narrowed and took a tortuous turn through the woods. Merewyn tried to hold to Alex's left side.

"Stay close," he cautioned, keeping pace with the others.

How could she stay close and still take a deer? She could not!

They raced on for a while, a daring chase, winding through trees while trying to stay clear of the other riders.

Ahead, the men's shouts told her some of the deer had changed course, doubling back. With the dogs barking loudly and scrambling to keep up, a deer darted into the meadow she had just entered, heading straight toward her. Seeing the horses, the deer leaped to the left, hurtling toward the cover of the woods.

Her eyes never leaving the deer, Merewyn laid her knotted reins on Ceinder's neck and galloped in pursuit, guiding the pony with only her legs. Keeping the deer in sight as it headed into the woods, she nocked an arrow, pulled back the bowstring and let the arrow fly.

Ahead, the deer dropped to the ground, the sound a heavy crash echoing through the trees.

Merewyn slowed as she neared the kill. "I got him!"

Alex rode up behind her, a frown on his face. "I suppose I should congratulate you on a great shot but I cannot be happy for the attention it will bring you."

As if his words were prophetic, the ground shook with the pounding of many horses coming toward them.

"Look! The page has taken a deer," a man's voice shouted. "A stag!"

Merewyn dropped from her horse to check on her kill, to be certain the hart was dead. The men gathered around her.

"*Parfait.* 'Tis a clean kill, master page," said the man she recognized as the king's brother. "A worthy display of skill, shooting from your horse. 'Tis few who would attempt such a feat."

"A page skilled with a bow?" queried the king riding up beside his brother to study her. "Most unusual. My brother has great skill at archery, young page. 'Tis high praise he gives you."

Merewyn bent her head and went down on one knee before the king and the duke, but remembering Alex's caution, said nothing.

"Rise, page," ordered the king.

Merewyn managed to stand, but her knees were shaking.

"I would have a name," the king said to Alex.

Alex hesitated, then spit out, "Mer... Merry."

"Meriwether," the king said, apparently reaching for the name he associated with the nickname. "A fitting English name for one who hunts on a day when the sun shines. Bring your page to the feast tonight, Sir Alex. I would see more of this Merry." And with that, the king ordered one of his servants to take the deer back to the palace and add it to the others the hunters had taken. "Tonight," the king pronounced as he rode away, "we dine on venison!"

When they were gone, she stood, looking up at Alex, who was frowning down at her from his horse. "Now you have done it."

"Whatever do you mean? I but shot a deer. Surely you deemed it possible? And tonight, I can go disguised as your page, can I not?"

Before Alex could answer, Rory and Guy rode up. "What happened?" asked Guy.

"I felled a deer," she informed him.

"And drew the interest of the king who wishes the page he now knows as 'Merry' to join the feast tonight."

Rory let out a whistle.

Guy's frown joined Alex's. "Oh, that does pose a problem."

Merewyn surveyed the faces of the three men, her gaze finally resting upon Alex. He ran his fingers through his long black hair. "Just so," he said.

Dropping from his stallion, he helped her remount and fixed her bow and arrows behind her. He was displeased, but why?

Alex lifted himself into his saddle. "Now I must decide if 'tis better for her to remain as my page and hope the king's interest wanes with his other diversions or have her dress as a lady and ward off the lust of the king's men. Either way, 'twill be an onerous evening."

Merewyn disliked being discussed as if she were not there. "I fail to understand how that is your decision, Alex. Besides, while I first thought to go as your page, if I am to join your lady mother and Earl Renaud in the king's hall, I will be expected to wear a gown."

"She has the right of it," said Rory, nodding his head. "My mother would expect the same of my sisters."

"So be it," said Alex with a look of resignation. "I will wear my sword should it be required. You may have brought us much trouble, my lady."

She could hardly see how women were responsible for the lust of the king's men. After all, there was nothing remarkable in her or her attire. All ladies wore similar gowns.

" 'Twill at least be an interesting evening," said Rory.

"Best we not consume much wine," cautioned Alex. "Come, let us find my father and yours, Guy, and see if the hunt continues. If not, we should make our way back to London."

On their return, Alex rode beside her, his eyes straight ahead, his face expressionless. She knew he worried over the king's notice of her. "How did you choose the name you gave the king?"

"I just took the first name that came to me."

" 'Tis odd you picked that one. It is the name I was called in Wales."

CHAPTER 7

Icy fingers of dread crept over Alex as he slowly descended the stairs of their London manor that evening and beheld Merewyn, standing beside his mother. The two of them were richly gowned for the evening.

The violet silk Merewyn had worn on his first night home again made her appear the ethereal creature. Gone was the page that had felled a red hart with his bow. Before him stood a beautiful young woman, her flaxen hair plaited on the sides and pulled back from her face. The rest of it spilled down her back, a waterfall of liquid gold. He had the urge to run his fingers through the long strands, but then he reminded himself he was still angry with her for insisting on joining the hunt.

Her skillful shot had brought about an awkward state of affairs. Dressed as a lady, she might be safe from the king, but she would not be safe from his brother, Robert—known to have sired several bastards—or every other rogue in the hall. At one time, Alex would have been one of those knights who sought her favors if she was a woman who freely gave them. Now he must protect her against his fellow knights, or worse, some nobleman of his father's rank.

Maugris had warned him of temptation that called for honor and courage needed in the face of fear. Tonight he would certainly need courage and his wits as he battled other men tempted by Merewyn's beauty. Was that what Maugris had seen?

His father stepped away from the others to join Alex at the foot of the stairs. "You seem to have taken an interest in my ward."

Still watching Merewyn, Alex said, "I worry for her in that den of debauchery we enter tonight."

"You have never worried for a lady's virtue before. Why Merewyn's?"

"I feel very protective of her."

His father's gray eyes narrowed on him. "The last time I looked at a woman the way you are looking at Merewyn, it was your mother."

Alex's brows drew together as he pondered his father's words. He compared the two women standing on the other side of the room, one a younger version of the other. "Do you think they are much alike?"

His father shifted his gaze to his wife and his ward. "Aye, I suppose they are. Both are unusual for their sex. Your mother used to hunt for Maggie, though not from the back of a horse. It was through her archery skills I found her hiding among the servants."

Alex recalled the story. "She smiles about it now."

"Yea, but I can assure you she did not smile then. She hated all Normans, especially the king who had given Talisand to me along with her."

"Would you have taken her if she were not the daughter of an English thegn?"

The look in his father's eyes told Alex his mind was lost in memory. "I nearly did."

He was glad to hear that his father had wanted his mother before he knew her to be the daughter of Talisand's old English thegn. His parents' beginning had been rough but love had come despite their differences.

Alex wanted Merewyn no matter the circumstances of her birth and if he decided to make Merewyn his, no man would take her from him, not even the king.

With a troubled look, his father cautioned, "Keep it at friendship with Merewyn, Alex. The king, no doubt, has plans for you."

"Sir Geoffroi warned me of such, but I would guard her even if she were only a friend."

"Then keep her close in the king's hall tonight. Geoff and I will intercede if necessary."

"Your offer is appreciated, Father, but I think I can handle this."

A smile crossed the face of the Red Wolf as he placed his hand on Alex's shoulder. "Aye, mayhap you can. I expect one day—and that day may not be far off—when the accomplishments of the Black Wolf will surpass those of the Red."

Alex gave his father an incredulous look, but inwardly he smiled at the approval he glimpsed in his father's eyes.

Soon after, they departed the manor. The distance to Westminster Palace was not far and they kept to a leisurely pace, avoiding the pools of standing water. Finally, ahead of them in the distance loomed the palace.

Passing Westminster Abbey on their right, beside him, Merewyn inhaled sharply. "That is the church?"

"Aye, the abbey is just there and, in front of you, the palace."

" 'Twas King Edward who rebuilt Saint Peter's Abbey," said Lady Serena riding ahead of them beside Alex's father.

"The Conqueror added to the palace," put in Alex's father. "He found it inferior to the ones in France."

"No doubt," his mother muttered.

"The king tells me he has plans to make Westminster a grand hall," Alex put in, wondering if William's plans were not spurred on by the desire to outshine his father. What must it be like for William Rufus to live in the shadow of the Conqueror?

"I expect he will," came his father's response.

"I have never seen the like," said Merewyn, staring at the abbey as they passed. Then looking ahead to the palace, she added, "I cannot imagine the palace being even larger."

By the time they arrived, many of William's subjects were waiting to greet him.

Grooms in the king's livery took their horses.

A few earls and many barons and knights congregated around the door of the palace. Alex recognized those who had hunted with them that morning as well as others from his time in Normandy. Earl Hugh waved to them from where he spoke to the king's chancellor, Robert Bloet.

Alex's father was well known and much respected. Thus, Earl Renaud and his beautiful English wife garnered considerable attention as they walked up the stairs.

Alex took Merewyn's hand and tucked it into the crook of his elbow. "Stay close," he whispered. She looked at him with trusting eyes but also a hint of fear. "I will not leave you," he vowed. She had to be feeling awkward and mayhap fearful to be in the presence of the Norman king and so many of his knights.

Finally, the group from Talisand neared the king, who was standing inside the door greeting his guests. As was usual, the king was attired in great finery, a crimson tunic, with jewels set into the fabric. On his fingers were many rings of gold.

Next to the king was his older brother, Duke Robert, dressed in similar garb, though mayhap a bit less extravagant. His hair, too, was shorter than William's.

On the other side of the king's brother stood Ranulf, dubbed "Flambard", or "torch-bearer", for his overwhelming personality.

Alex knew Ranulf to be clever, talkative and always full of ideas. He was the king's closest advisor and priest, but his chief occupation appeared to be raising money for the king's wars. In that effort, Ranulf was not above robbing the church. Alex deemed it likely it had been Ranulf's counsel that had left the powerful position of Archbishop of Canterbury vacant for so long, enabling the king to claim the rents as his own. But more concerning to Alex at the moment was Ranulf's reputation as a conspicuous pursuer of women. He collected them like trophies.

In truth, the handsome Ranulf might be the greatest threat to Merewyn which, to Alex, seemed an odd turn of events. At one time, he and Ranulf had competed for the affections of the women at court. Always more aggressive than Alex in seeking out willing females, Alex had tolerated the man for he had the king's respect. But no longer. Now Alex recognized the king's advisor for what he was, a predatory despoiler of women. Ranulf, he was certain, would not fail to notice Merewyn's loveliness. That she was not a nobleman's daughter only made her fair game.

Arriving in front of the king, William smiled at Alex and his father. "Ah, my wolves grace my hall! And with lovely ladies." He first greeted

Alex's parents and then turned to Alex. "But where is the young page whose arrow felled the hart?"

Alex cleared his throat. "My Lord, may I introduce to you Merewyn of York, my father's ward. I believe you know her as 'Merry'."

The king's unusual eyes captured the light as they narrowed upon Merewyn, his expression one of disbelief. "By the face of Lucca, what have we here?"

Still holding on to Alex's arm, Merewyn made a brief curtsey before the king. "My Lord."

"Do my eyes deceive me?" asked William. "This jewel is the page you called Merry?"

"By the marvels of God," exclaimed Duke Robert, " 'tis the page skilled with a bow turned into a beautiful young woman... *Ravissante, tout à fait ravissante!*"

The short dark-haired duke, barely taller than Merewyn, grinned broadly at her, grimly reminding Alex that whereas the king might prefer to take his pleasure with young men, Robert loved women. That he found her enchanting was hardly surprising.

Alex was about to move past the king when William Rufus held up his hand. "Sir Alex, there is someone I would have you meet."

Alex turned.

" 'Tis the young Adèle, here with her father, Herbert, comte de Vermandois. Her father's lands in Normandy are among those I now control."

Alex shot a glance at Sir Geoffroi who had turned back at the king's words. The knight's earlier speculation echoed in Alex's mind. *Now that he has gained new lands in Normandy from his brother, Robert, I expect William will want to bind his young nobles to those lands.* The last thing Alex needed was an arranged marriage but he would not openly defy his sovereign. He inclined his head. "Of course, My Lord."

They passed the king and his brother, arriving in front of Ranulf Flambard. The king's advisor took Merewyn's free hand and placed a kiss upon her slender fingers, his dark eyes searing into hers. "I shall look forward to a dance with you this night, my lady. I would see more of your beautiful face."

Alex scowled and tightened his grip on Merewyn. "The lady's dances have all been claimed, I am afraid."

Ranulf laughed. "We shall see, sir knight. We shall see."

"He makes me uneasy," said Merewyn casting a glance back at Ranulf as they entered the hall. The large space was filled with people engaged in conversation. Already, many seats were taken at the long trestle tables. "Who is he?"

"The king's chaplain, advisor and keeper of the treasury. And a scoundrel. Do not concern yourself with him. I will make sure the men of Talisand guard you well."

Before they took their seats, Alex left Merewyn with Rory and Guy and drew Sir Geoffroi aside. "Did you hear the king? It appears you were correct in your assumption. William wants me to meet some woman from Normandy."

"Aye and not just any woman. The daughter of Earl Herbert of Vermandois is rumored to be beautiful, but also treacherous. She has been thought to use poison, though I suppose 'tis normal for the women of Normandy." At Alex's raised brow, Guy's father explained, " 'Tis how they rid themselves of unwanted husbands."

"You have my thanks for the warning, but I hope never to put myself in such a position."

Alex returned to collect Merewyn. It was not enough he had to fend off the men who would be after the woman he vowed to protect. Now he must deal with a young noblewoman from Normandy known for her treachery.

Was his father aware of the king's plans? Even if he were, Talisand was a long way from Wessex and per chance the king might be persuaded to accept another in his place. The Earl of Chester had many sons, but at least two were sons of his wife. After what happened at Avranches, Earl Hugh owed the king a debt for his mercy in taking the earl back into the fold. One of those sons might be proposed as a candidate for the hand of Lady Adèle. Alex could only hope.

Soon they were seated between Sir Geoffroi and Rory, Guy on Rory's other side. Alex looked up to see his parents sitting with the king on the dais. The invitation to dine with the king was a high honor; one Alex was certain his mother would have declined were she able.

He took off his sword belt and laid it under his bench, then leaned in to Rory. "Do not leave Merewyn alone should I be drawn away. You and Guy must claim her dances if I cannot."

"With pleasure," Rory replied with a grin.

"Your eagerness is wholly unnecessary," Alex commented dryly. He would not be pleased should his fellow knight take a fancy to Merewyn.

*   *   *

Overwhelmed by the dazzling opulence around her, Merewyn stared at the beautiful tapestries gracing the walls. Most featured battles. She imagined the sounds that might have accompanied them. The bodies of slain warriors lay on the ground before the victorious. They were the kind of tapestries a bachelor king would display in his hall.

In one corner, minstrels played flutes and a lyre, sending beautiful sounds into the air and providing a soothing background for the boisterous conversations at the tables. All were speaking in Norman French, the language of the court. She understood what they said, having been taught French in her youth. Even though she had not spoken the language much at Talisand or in Wales, she had not forgotten it.

The large chamber was alight with hundreds of candles set into iron rings that hung from the wooden rafters high above. Torches blazed from sconces set into the walls adding to the bright flames of the central hearth fire making the room almost too warm. On the tables, the candlelight was reflected in the silver and golden goblets set before them.

Wonderful smells wafted from trays piled high with meats of all kinds, including roast pig, venison and peafowl. Dishes of vegetables cooked in sauces were set before them, along with bread still warm from the oven. Her stomach rumbled, reminding her she had not eaten since breaking her fast.

Silks and velvet gowns and tunics in bright sapphire, ruby, emerald and yellow were all around her. On the dais, she glimpsed the king in his bejeweled scarlet tunic laughing as he ate with his brother, Robert, and the one called Ranulf. On either side of them sat Earl Hugh and Alex's parents. At the tables, the barons, earls and their ladies adorned in fine raiment and many jewels ate with relish. She was glad for the gown

Lady Serena had given her. At least she was dressed like a lady.

The smells of herbs and spices made her mouth water and she speared a slice of venison from the trencher she shared with Alex. "Do you think we dine on my deer?" she asked him before taking a bite.

"The other hunters took deer also, but 'tis likely one of these is your kill." He bit into a piece of the succulent meat, wiping the juices from his chin with his napkin. "Very good it is, too. I like the wine sauce with cinnamon."

Reaching for her goblet, she sipped her wine and let her gaze wander about the hall, coming to rest on an unusual group. "Alex, who are those three sitting at the other table on the end closest to the dais?"

He let out an exasperated sigh. "I suppose I can no longer delay telling you. Those are the king's courtiers, Gervais, Jocelin and Piers. Guy calls them 'the three graces'."

"The ones in the Roman stories who served Venus?"

"Aye, tis a jest."

"But are they women or men?" Merewyn could not honestly decide. They had the shoulders of young men, but their hair was longer than even the king and his young knights. Their cheeks were rouged and they appeared to be gowned like women.

"Men, the king's own. Were you close enough, you could smell their perfume. 'Tis a heady scent."

"The king is a… a *sodomite*?" she whispered, disbelieving.

"Aye. 'Tis why he has not wed and will never sire a child. By the treaty he signed with his brother, Robert is now his heir."

"I begin to see. 'Twas why you did not want the king to see me dressed as a page." Garbed as an archer with her womanly features, the king could well have thought her one of his courtiers as Alex called them. Her estimation of Alex rose with the realization he had been looking out for her welfare. "You were protecting me."

"I was and I still am."

The intensity of his gaze made her lower her eyes. "I am grateful."

When she raised her eyes it was to watch the king's courtiers. Their feminine appearance, their laughter and their extravagant gestures were more like women than men. Even their earrings spoke of a woman's attire, not a man's. "Why would the king want a man pretending to be a woman when he could have any woman he wants?"

Alex leaned in and lowered his voice. "I cannot say for certain, but young squires are, for the most part, sequestered at a time when their bodies are changing from that of boys to men. When the urge strikes, some find their pleasure in each other. A few of those never grow out of the practice."

"And you?" She could not imagine Alex doing such a thing.

He laughed. "Never think it. I would steal over the wall to a neighboring village, my companions clambering after me. 'Twas worth whatever wrath we incurred from the knights."

At her frown, he took her hand and gave it a squeeze. "You need not worry, Merewyn. Those days are behind me. And were we not in a crowded hall, I would be only too glad to show you why."

Heat suffused her cheeks remembering the afternoon he had wandered into her bedchamber. Did he mean because he could have any woman he wanted he did not have to seek them out or did he mean he wanted only her? Would that it were possible for them to be together, but dwelling on the foolish thought would only bring her sadness.

When the meal was finished, the tables were moved to the walls and the large hall cleared for dancing. A group of minstrels, garbed in bright colors of blue, green and crimson, entered the large chamber and took their place on one side, readying their instruments. Soon they filled the hall with lively music from their lyre, lute, pipes and tabor.

Alex belted on his sword and took her hand, sweeping her into a group of dancers. As before, they danced well together. She was so happy to be with him she paid little attention to the man whose dark countenance stared at her across the circle of dancers. But she had not forgotten the brief introduction to the man named Ranulf.

When the dance ended, Ranulf took his partner's hand and crossed the wooden floor to stand before them.

"Merewyn," he said, bowing. "You might recall we met at the beginning of the evening."

Merewyn nodded. "Of course." She glanced at Alex, who was scowling beneath his black brows.

Ranulf turned to the woman at his side. "Lady Adèle, allow me to present Sir Alexander of Talisand and his father's ward, Merewyn."

Alex bowed over the young woman's hand. "My lady."

Merewyn offered Lady Adèle a smile. "I am honored to meet you, my lady."

The woman gave her a dismissive nod, quickly returning her attention to Alex.

Ranulf continued, "Lady Adèle is the daughter of the comte de Vermandois. She has come to London with her father at the invitation of the king."

Alex stiffened at Merewyn's side. So this is the woman the king desired him to meet and wants him to wed, most likely. Merewyn had always known this day would come but she had not imagined she would be there to witness it. Alex was handsome and his father a powerful earl who had been a favorite knight of the Conqueror. Now his son was taking his place. Was that what stirred this woman's interest? If Merewyn were any judge, it seemed to her Lady Adèle was pleased with the match the king intended.

Adèle of Vermandois was a beauty. With her long dark tresses, she reminded Merewyn of Lora, only her eyes were hazel instead of Lora's dark brown. To Merewyn's mind, the Norman woman seemed fully aware of her effect upon men. She batted her eyes at Alex, not in the amusing way Merewyn had when teasing him, but in a seductive, predatory manner. "*C'est vraiment très agréable de finalement faire votre connaissance,*" said the dark-haired woman. That she found it most agreeable to have met Alex was clear from the gleam in her eyes.

Before Merewyn could say a word, Ranulf took her hand and said to Alex, "The king wished you to meet Lady Adèle, so I leave her with you for this next dance." Then shifting his gaze to Merewyn, "I will see to this lovely one."

Alex sent Ranulf an angry glare, but accepted Lady Adèle's hand when it was offered and Merewyn was swept away to another group of dancers. She and her partner stood on opposite sides of two long lines as a new song began. Facing her, the look in Ranulf's dark eyes was lustful, reminding her of that woodland long ago when she was surrounded by a pack of boys. She wished she were dressed as the archer, her bow at the ready.

As the two lines came together, he said, "My lady, you are the most beautiful woman in the hall. I would you were mine."

She was not flattered. He bore the title of priest yet he wore no priestly garments. Instead, he wore a rich purple tunic that rivaled the king's. On Ranulf's fingers were many rings and around his neck hung a heavy golden necklace. She was certain he was a man of dissolute habits who would seduce her if he could, but for all that, she would remind him of his role in the church.

When next the lines of the dancers came together, she said in a low voice, "You are bold for a priest."

He laughed. "I am many things, my lady. Bold is one of them. As the keeper of the king's seal, I enjoy his favor." His dark eyes narrowed on her like a beast siting its prey. "Were I to ask him, he would give you to me, but I would prefer you come to me of your own free will."

Anger washed over Merewyn at the man's audacity. "It will never happen!" Did he think her some strumpet to come at his call? He was no different than most men, but she resolved not to embarrass Alex by leaving the lecherous chaplain abruptly, as he deserved. When the dance was over, she would find her noble knight.

Fortunately she did not have to worry. When the dance ended, Alex was there to claim her.

"Ranulf," Alex said, inclining his head. "We wish you good eve."

Alex did not give the man time to answer but swept her to the side of the room where wine was being served. Taking a goblet, he thrust it toward her. "From the look of you, you need this."

Her breathing was labored and not from the dancing. "Thank you."

"Are you all right?" he asked, a look of concern on his face.

"Aye, I am now." Alex's very presence made her feel safe. "That man is loathsome, Alex. You cannot imagine what he said to me."

"Oh yea, I can."

With worried eyes, she looked up at him. "He said he could ask the king to give me to him. He would not, would he?"

"He might. But I will not allow it."

"But Alex, what of that woman, Lady Adèle? Is she not intended for you by the king?"

"I care not," he said dismissively. "William can find another noble's son to bind to his lands in Normandy."

Rory and Guy appeared then, casting anxious glances at Alex. "We saw what was happening," said Rory, "but 'twas so fast we could do little and you were there so we did not worry until Ranulf took her off."

"No matter," said Alex. "I doubt anything you could have done would have prevented it."

Suddenly, Duke Robert was at her side. "My lady, would you grant me a dance?"

Merewyn looked to see Alex's reaction. His brows were drawn together in worry but she did not sense the angry storm of emotion he had displayed when Ranulf Flambard had taken her from him.

"Go with the duke," he said, smiling at Robert. "I will reclaim your hand when the dance is finished."

The dark-haired duke, who was twice her age and not much taller than she, flashed her a smile. "I see the young wolf guards you well. Were you mine, I would do the same."

Merewyn did not like being referred to as something to possess, at least not by men she did not even know, but she placed her hand on the duke's arm and allowed him to lead her to the dancing. Casting a glance at Alex over her shoulder, she saw his gray eyes had turned as cold as steel.

★ ★ ★

Alex had endured the dance with Lady Adèle, all the while sneaking glances at Merewyn, wondering how she fared. He missed much of what the young Norman noblewoman said, but he remembered her mentioning that her father, the comte de Vermandois, and Earl Renaud were once young knights together. "My father has great respect for the knight they call the Red Wolf," she had said. "And, I hear his son is much like him."

Alex hoped he never saw the woman again.

Now he watched Merewyn dancing with Duke Robert. "This evening cannot end soon enough for me," he said to Rory and Guy. "Merewyn is assailed from all sides. First Ranulf and his indecent threats and now the king's brother. God only knows who will next appear."

Sharing a concerned glance with Rory, Guy asked, "What would you have us do?"

"Find my father and tell him I am taking Merewyn home."

"Aye, we can do that," said Rory. "Do you need an escort?"

"Nay, my sword will be sufficient."

The moment the song ended, Alex was there to take Merewyn's hand.

Duke Robert bowed to her. "My lady, 'tis been a pleasure. I hope I will yet see you ere we leave London, but a lady guarded by a wolf is not likely to be available for walks along the Strand."

Alex inclined his head but said nothing. As he led her toward the doors, he leaned in close. "We are leaving."

"So soon?"

"Aye. I'd not risk you further this night, not with Ranulf lurking about."

"You are probably right, but the duke was all good manners."

"Robert has a kindly nature, but he, too, has been known to steal a lady's virtue."

"Then 'tis well we go." She looked up at him with trusting eyes. "It has been wonderful, Alex. Thank you for being with me, even if only for a while."

He offered his arm and she took it. Likely she believed he would marry Adèle of Vermandois, but he would not. His father might have been compelled by the Conqueror to marry his mother but from what he had determined in his brief time with the Lady Adèle, she was nothing like the Lady of Talisand—or Merewyn. "If I have my way, my lady, 'twill be for much longer."

Once they had returned to the manor and taken off their cloaks, Alex poured them both a goblet of wine. "Now I can have the wine I would have indulged in at the palace were it not for the need to have all my senses alert to guard you from the circling predators."

She accepted the goblet he offered her, taking a long draw on the rich red liquid. "I think I prefer the hall at Talisand," she said with a smile, setting down her goblet. "It is smaller but more welcome and feels like home."

"Me as well," he said, placing his goblet on the table. "Come, I will see you to your chamber."

As they were ascending the stairs, Nelda came up behind them.

"Mistress, do you require me?"

"Nay, Nelda, do whatever you must to prepare for Lady Serena."

When they arrived at Merewyn's door, Alex stood back and let her enter.

"Will you not come in to bid me goodnight?" she asked.

How he wanted to take her in his arms, kiss her and teach her the ways of love. He wanted to bind her to him forever. "Merewyn, I can protect you from other men but not from myself. I fear I could not act honorably were we to be alone and a bed nearby." Their eyes met and a powerful force flowed between them, like a cable of steel, unbreakable. "I would have you as mine forever," Alex said.

Across her face flitted a look of surprise. A moment passed in which she appeared to hesitate, but then she placed her palm on his chest. "I would have you be mine, also."

"Can it be we have missed what has always been before us?" he asked. "Friendship has, indeed, become something more, has it not? Or, mayhap I only failed to see that you have always been mine."

"You have held my heart since that day in the woods long ago when you rescued me." Smiling, she added, "And still you persist in saving me from danger."

He took her palm from his chest and turned it toward his lips, kissing the soft skin. "I must leave you now, else I would claim tonight what I desire."

CHAPTER 8

In his eyes, Merewyn glimpsed his sincerity. She had come to trust this man. He had never been like the others, like Ranulf Flambard and even Duke Robert, whose desire for her was driven only by lust. Inside, Alex was still the boy who had once rescued her, only now he was so much more.

Taking his hand, she pulled him into her chamber and closed the door.

"Stay," she whispered. With that one word, she knowingly sealed her fate. One day she might lose him to Lady Adèle or some other woman at the king's command, but tonight he could be hers. And she would have the memory to treasure forever.

"Merewyn, do you know what you are saying?"

She turned from him, needing the distance to speak the words she must. The maidservant had lit a candle and Merewyn stared into the flame as she spoke, feeling the heat of his presence behind her. "There has never been another for me, Alex. I had thought with the years passing and you becoming a knight, my feelings for you would change. But they have not."

Turning to face him, she looked into his seductive gray eyes and spoke with the conviction of one who has finally decided. "Whatever happens after this, no matter where your oath to the king leads you or where I go as a consequence, we will always have this night. I will give myself to only you and I will remember this night forever."

"Aye, Merewyn," he said coming closer and putting his hands on her arms, the heat of them robbing her of breath. "You will have your night of love and I vow 'twill not be the last."

Merewyn was aware he spoke the words, believing them to be true, like those he had spoken to her in the king's hall when he vowed to stay by her side. He had meant the words to be true, but others had come between them, as they inevitably must. She would not hold it against him. A knight did not question his king. And she would not allow him to falter in his duty. Not for her.

He gently pulled her to him, holding her close. "Merewyn, Merewyn," he whispered into her hair. "I have long wanted you, wanted this." His words were soothing but there was passion in his voice. "Now you will be mine."

She looked up at him. "And you will forever be the hero of my heart."

He took her face in his hands and lowered his head to kiss her, their lips teasing, tasting, reaching for more. He wanted everything, as he had once told her. Her body seemed to come alive with new sensations. She had experienced his kiss and his body pressed against hers, but never before had she allowed his actions to go where he would lead. Now she did. This man she loved would soon join his body with hers.

His kiss became fevered, insistent, as his tongue mated with hers. She welcomed it, wrapping her arms around his shoulders and pulling him closer. This was Alex, she reminded herself, his masculine smell familiar, the feel of him like coming home.

She threaded her fingers through his long ebony hair as his hands glided over her ribs to her hips. He pulled her into his groin against the hard flesh rising beneath his tunic.

"I would see you," he whispered. To her, it sounded like a question. He wanted her to lead. And so she would.

"Aye, and I would see you, Alex."

He was the one to remove most of their clothing. She was committed, but shy, and her fingers moved awkwardly as she opened his shirt laces. She had never seen a man fully naked. He quickly undid her laces and pulled her gown over her head, laying it on the chest at the foot of her bed.

His deft movements with her clothing reminded her he was an experienced lover whereas she was unknowing, innocent. She was aware of the couplings between animals, but she had never come close to mating with any man, not even Alex.

"I have been with other women, Merewyn, but none were you. Never think you are one of many. You are not. And there will be no other."

She wanted to believe him and, for tonight, she would. So she told herself he was hers and always would be.

Their clothes shed, they looked at each other. "I knew you would be lovely," he said, "but knowing it is you my eyes devour makes it different. You are a treasure I never thought to have."

" 'Tis the same for me, Alex," she said, stealing glances at the hard muscles of his chest and his flat belly. She did not allow her gaze to drop farther.

His knightly pursuits had robbed him of any fat. His arms were thickly muscled; his chest sported a mat of black hair only hinted at when he engaged in sword practice with his tunic open at the neck. She lifted her palm to feel the soft, curly hairs. His muscles flexed beneath her fingers.

He covered her hand. "We must seek our bed for I am anxious to love you."

She swallowed and lowered her gaze to his manhood. It was large and engorged. 'Twould not be long before they were one. It was what she sought, but still, she feared the joining. "There will be pain?"

"For you?" he asked pulling her into the heat of his warm chest, belly and thighs. Smiling, he said, "Mayhap some, but with your galloping pony, it may be that nature has helped you and there will be only a stretching. And I will see you are ready. I tell you the truth; I have never taken a virgin. 'Twas my intent to take only one."

He kissed her once again and every nerve in her body seemed to sing. How she loved this man! She would trust him in this.

"Come," he said. Taking her by the hand, he walked to the bed and pulled back the cover.

She climbed in and lay back on the pillow, fighting the desire to cover herself with her hands. But she did not wrestle long with that desire as he joined her in the bed. He stretched his length beside her and covered her breast with his hand, kissing her, while his palm circled her nipple until it hardened to a bud.

Her woman's center began to ache and she entwined one of her legs with his.

She held him to her as he kissed her everywhere, on her lips, her breasts, her belly. She held his head to her eager flesh, moaning with pleasure. When his lips trailed down her body and licked the folds of her woman's flesh, she raised her hips to meet the thrusts of his tongue, feeling a rising tension overtaking her. "Oh, Alex…"

"Not without me," he said and rose over her, resting his hips between her spread thighs.

His hard manhood nudged against her wet flesh and she opened for him, eager to have him inside her. With a single sharp movement, he granted her wish, filling her, possessing her.

She inhaled sharply. "Ah!" It was not exactly painful, more like an invasion. His hard flesh so filled her she worried he would tear her asunder. She panted out her breath, trying to accept the joining she herself had sought.

He stilled and from his labored breathing she thought he might be holding back for her sake. Her breasts pressed into his chest and she could feel the strong beating of his heart. " 'Tis all right," she whispered.

He let out a sigh and brought his mouth down on hers, his tongue stroking hers as he began to move within her, slowly at first.

She raised her hips to meet him, wanting all of him and relishing the feel of him moving inside her.

"Merewyn," he said, kissing her neck, "you are truly mine."

His voice was soothing, his words sounding sincere. "And you are mine." *At least for tonight.* She would not look for more.

Their bodies were soon slick with sweat. She held on to him, letting him sweep her with him into a swirl of sweet tension, rising within her. When her release came, his followed quickly. He cried out and dropped onto her.

Sometime later, Merewyn awoke with the bells sounding Compline. Alex's arm was draped over her chest, his warm hand cupped her breast and his groin pressed into her bottom. Her nipple hardened beneath his

118

hand at the memory of what they had done.

She had given herself to Alex.

Never again would they be merely friends. Of course, William Rufus had other plans for him. The heir of Talisand was destined for a marriage linking Normandy to England's king. What was she, a bastard, in so much royal scheming? But she would have forever the memory of their lovemaking, for she was certain he had loved her with his whole self.

Even if this were their only night together, she would have no regret.

"Alex," she said, gently prodding him, "You must go, my love, before the others return and Nelda finds you in my chamber."

His lips found the back of her neck where he pressed kisses to her sensitive skin. "You are ever sending me from your bed," he teased. "I will go if I must, but with the greatest reluctance. I want to sleep with you, Merewyn."

She turned to face him. "And I with you. But you know it cannot be."

"Oh, very well," he said, rising to sit upon the bed. Looking back at her, he picked up one long strand of her hair. "I like you all tousled."

"Today is the barons' meeting, is it not?"

"Aye, the king would discuss Scotland. William Rufus rarely consults anyone save his earls and that scoundrel, Ranulf. But today he meets with the barons. My mother will, no doubt, take you to see the wares of London's merchants." At her frown, he reached down to kiss her forehead. "You might even enjoy it."

★   ★   ★

Alex stuffed a piece of bread into his mouth as his father rose from the table and announced, "We had best be on our way."

"Are you certain I am included?" he asked. The king's meeting was for his barons and key advisors. A few senior knights, like Sir Geoffroi, might be summoned, but Alex was not one of those.

"William asked for you by name," said his father. " 'Twas in the second missive the king's messenger handed me at Talisand. His specific words were, 'Bring my other wolf, the cub.'"

119

Alex cringed.

"No matter his name for you, William pays you an honor."

Acknowledging the truth of his father's words with a nod, Alex stood, humbled by the king's faith in him. He could hardly resent the name "cub" when it was bestowed with the king's favor.

Outside the manor, their horses were saddled and waiting. The morning was cool and a wind stirred, blowing his hair. Azor's head perked up as Alex walked to the black stallion and stroked his neck. "Another trip to the palace, boy." He swung into the saddle, noting the gray clouds in the sky and hoped the threatened rain would hold off until that evening. He smiled thinking of the two women he loved most spending the day together.

Rory and Guy, glad for a day free of the king's business, came through the manor door to wish them a good day. Having offered to accompany Merewyn and Lady Serena on their excursion into town, the two knights had a mission that would keep them occupied, one for which Alex was grateful. With more of William's army pouring into London every day, a few knights added to the men-at-arms who would accompany the women were welcome.

As he rode to the palace with his father and Sir Geoffroi, he experienced an unusual contentment as images of Merewyn filled his mind. He had managed to reach his bedchamber just as his parents were returning to the manor. After a deep sleep, he awoke in the morning with the most incredible smile on his face.

What was it about Merewyn that had filled him with the need to claim her? Other women were as beautiful; noble women came with wealth and lands; and he had never wanted for those who willingly came to his bed. But in Merewyn, he recognized strength like his own, a determination to overcome any obstacle and courage to reach the mark she had set for herself. He needed such a woman by his side. His heart filled with the love for her he had not spoken, satisfied in the knowledge he had demonstrated his love in the way he knew best. The passion he had aroused from deep within her was more than he could have asked for. But it was not merely passion that had driven him to claim Merewyn as his own. It had been love, a bond that grew with each day. He wanted to be with her, to have her at his side when he took his father's place.

Now that he had made the lovely brave archer his, he had only to hold her. In time, he would tell his parents and deal with the king's unwanted plans, but for now, 'twould be his secret.

They arrived at the palace along with a large number of nobles and knights who served the king. Inside the hall, men gathered around a table where the king sat with his brother. In addition to Ranulf Flambard, in attendance were Robert fitzHaimo, baron of Gloucester, and Earl Hugh of Chester along with a score of others.

Across from the king sat Duncan, the eldest son of Malcolm, King of Scots. While Alex had not seen him at the feast the evening before, it made sense he would be here now. As a lad, Duncan had been taken hostage by the Conqueror to secure his agreement with Scotland, but upon the Conqueror's death, Duncan was freed and now served William Rufus by choice. Just entering his third decade, the tall, dark-haired knight had shared with Alex his desire to one day take his rightful place as Scotland's king.

"It was my father's wish when he sent me to England that one day I would return to Scotland to govern the people," Duncan had told him.

Alex, his father and Sir Geoffroi approached the king, who gestured to available places around the table.

"Now that all my barons are here," said William, "we will share our royal strategy with you. Our plan is to take the same route my father took years ago following the old Roman road north. My fleet of fifty ships, laden with corn, will meet us on the Tyne River to resupply us before sailing on to Scotland where my army and my ships will corner the wily King of Scots."

Murmurs of agreement echoed around the table.

"Worked well before," said Earl Hugh.

Alex shared a glance with his father and Sir Geoffroi and detected no objection in their eyes. The plan was sound.

He eyed Duncan sitting to the king's right. What did he think of this plan to set upon his father? The knight's face told him nothing. Mayhap he had lived so long among the Normans he was more at home with them than the Scots.

"With the lapse of time," the king continued, "I expect Malcolm has retreated to Lothian and his fortress at Dun Edin. 'Tis where we will find him." He looked around the table at the faces of his barons. "Do any of you disagree?"

Those sitting around the king shook their heads, Alex among them.

Duke Robert stood, goblet in hand. "It appears we are agreed. To the coming encounter with the King of Scots, a battle if it must be!"

All stood, even the king. "To the battle!" they shouted and quaffed their wine. But in his father's eyes, Alex now glimpsed a flicker of doubt.

When the men began to disperse, entering into separate conversations, Alex strode to him. "Father, you have concerns?"

His father shot a glance at Sir Geoffroi, standing next to him. "I remember the Conqueror's meeting with Malcolm in Scotland nearly twenty years ago. The Scottish king was surrounded, William's army before him and the fleet behind him, and yet he bargained for peace and got it. The Conqueror was no fool. A battle on the Scots' territory is not easily fought, nor easily won. He was happy to have Malcolm's oath."

"We were there to see it," said Sir Geoffroi.

"But was not that oath extinguished with the Conqueror's death?" Alex asked.

"Aye," said his father, "but mayhap Malcolm can be persuaded to give it again."

"If the king will agree to take it," said Alex. "I am inclined to believe William will want more."

Their conversation was interrupted when the king came to join them. "Good day to my wolves," he said, "and to you, Sir Geoffroi."

"Good day to you, Sire," replied Alex's father, inclining his head. Alex and Sir Geoffroi dipped their heads, acknowledging the king.

Fixing his eyes on Alex, William said, "You swept the young bowman, Merry, away so fast last eve, I did not have time to inquire of her origins. I would know where such a delightful creature comes from."

Sir Geoffroi answered. "York, My Lord. Her mother was from Yorkshire and she was born there."

"And her father?" asked the king. "Is he also English?"

Sir Geoffroi's expression turned somber. "Nay, he was Norman, a knight."

Alex's father added, "Sir Eude is dead, Sire."

"Hmm…" the king seemed to ponder, then asked, "Killed fighting the Northumbrians?"

"Nay, My Lord," said Sir Geoffroi. "He was killed in York by my own right hand."

The king's reddish brows lifted in surprise at the senior knight towering over him. Alex had known a Norman knight raped Merewyn's mother; he did not know Sir Geoffroi had killed the man responsible.

There was no hint of regret in Sir Geoffroi's eyes. "He was a despicable man, My Lord, unworthy to be a knight. He brutally forced Merewyn's mother, an innocent, and was about to slice the neck of a young orphan under my wife's protection when I stopped him."

The king tossed his mane of yellow hair over one shoulder and rubbed his short red beard with the fingers of one hand. "Some of my father's men were mercenary knights, no doubt ruffians of the worst sort, but that was what he needed at the time." Looking up at Sir Geoffroi, he said, "I cannot find fault with what you did. Mayhap 'twas best my father's army was well rid of him."

"Thank you, My Lord," said the senior knight, looking relieved. "I can assure you we have done right by Merewyn. Earl Renaud and I have assured she was educated as a lady." He glanced at Alex's father. "She is not only a talented archer, but a virtuous young woman."

Having claimed Merewyn's virtue for his own, Alex was pierced by a stab of guilt. But it was not because he had succumbed to temptation. His intentions toward her were honorable. The timing had been hers. He did not believe the church's blessing was necessary, but his mother would have preferred it. He would see Father Bernard when they returned to Talisand to be sure.

The king, who would dictate a different match, knew nothing of his joining with Merewyn. She was not even of noble blood. While it mattered not to Alex, he faced a difficult challenge to make his sovereign accept his choice.

"Where in Normandy was this Eude from?" asked the king, dropping the title "Sir". Mayhap William agreed with Sir Geoffroi that the man did not deserve to be a knight.

"He was Eude de Fourneaux."

The king narrowed his eyes, appearing to ponder this new information. "Ah yes, near Falaise."

"Aye," said Sir Geoffroi.

"Well, no matter." William flicked his hand away from his chin dismissively and looked to Alex's father. "Do you plan to return to the north soon?"

"I do, Sire. My lady is not often away from our youngest son and is anxious to return." Smiling, he added, "The wild child bears watching." Alex's parents were not the only ones eager to return to Talisand. He wanted to leave so he could share the days he had before Scotland with Merewyn.

"By the face of Lucca," remarked the king, "you raise yet another wolf cub for my army."

A grin spread over the face of Talisand's lord. "I just might, Sire."

*   *   *

Shouts of merchants calling attention to their wares filled the air as Merewyn and Lady Serena strolled down Cheapside Street, meandering from one stall to another, delighted with all they found.

The merchants' cries competed with the conversations of the hundreds of people thronging the narrow streets of London. The shops had been opened since the town bell rang at Prime and were now doing a brisk business.

" 'Tis so different from the village at Talisand or the wares to be had in Powys. Even what I saw of Chester tells me this market exceeds what that city offers."

"Aye, London's market is large," replied Lady Serena. "You can find everything here: fine cloth, the craft of the goldsmiths, sword smiths, pottery, spices and all manner of food. Even casks of Normandy's wine are plentiful here. Yet I do not think their wool can match Talisand's. Nor is their salmon so fresh as ours. But there are many things we cannot make that we can buy here. 'Tis why I wanted you to see it."

Merewyn could smell the exotic spices overflowing large, roughly woven sacks stacked in front of the next merchant's stall. "I smell cumin, ginger, cloves and pepper."

They walked to the stall and Lady Serena told the merchant, "We will have some of that saffron you keep on the shelf." She pointed to a carved box behind the merchant.

Merewyn watched as the merchant carefully lifted the box from the shelf and spooned some of the saffron into a small bag. "I have heard it is rare and highly valued for food as well as dye."

"Aye and costly. The red threads of the spice come from a rare purple flower that grows in far-off Persia. A thread of saffron will lend an exotic perfume and savory flavor to a whole kettle of pottage and will dye the dish bright yellow."

Merewyn was amazed at all Lady Serena knew. To be a countess required knowledge in many things. No wonder the king wanted Alex to marry a highborn woman. The reality of how little Merewyn had seen had come to her with their trip to the palace, now even more as the world of the merchants was opened to her.

"The first time I came to London, my eyes were as large as yours," the Lady of Talisand said with a smile as she pointed to other spices she would have. She patted Merewyn's hand, nearly bringing tears to her eyes for the kindness the simple touch represented. "You will learn, as I did." When Lady Serena had made her purchases, the merchant handed her small bags of the spices she had selected.

Rory and Guy walked behind them, their hands on their sword hilts. Behind them strolled two men-at-arms. She was glad for their presence, for the streets were noisy and crowded with men whose rough appearance and leers made her uncomfortable.

Merewyn glanced back to see the two knights gazing longingly at the tavern on the other side of the street. She would have suggested they all stop for some ale, but she was certain a lady did not enter such a place and Rory and Guy would not leave them under penalty of Alex's wrath.

They walked on until they reached the silk merchant. Lady Serena stopped to admire the silk, velvet and wool being sold. "We must have some of this," she said, holding up a length of shimmering blue silk for Merewyn to see. " 'Tis the color of your eyes and would make a fine gown. We could embroider it with golden thread. Oh, look," she said, her attention drawn to the shelf behind the merchant, "he has the thread as well."

The merchant picked up the thread and presented it to Lady Serena for her inspection. " 'Tis fine golden thread, my lady. The nuns use it for altar cloths in the abbey."

Merewyn was humbled by the generosity of Talisand's Lady. After all, Merewyn was not kin to any at Talisand. "You do too much for me."

Lady Serena paid the merchant for the cloth and thread she wanted, then placed her hand on Merewyn's shoulder. "I would do more than this. Emma and I want to see you happy. We loved Inga as we love you."

An hour later, the church bells of St. Peter's sounded Sext as they made their way to Fish Street where the smell of fresh fish was strong. She glanced over to where mackerel, herring, lampreys, eels and cod were neatly stacked in wet, hay-filled crates next to one merchant's stall. On the other side of the stall stood several barrels. "What is in the barrels?"

"Probably crabs and lobsters," said Lady Serena. "Crab would be good for supper. I will ask one of the men to buy some. 'Twill be wonderful cooked with butter, cinnamon, honey and a little vinegar. The cook at the London house has a wonderful way with crab." She handed Rory some silver pennies and gave him instructions on how much to buy.

Listening to Lady Serena's description of the way she would have the cook prepare the shellfish they would have later, Merewyn could almost taste it.

They walked on, passing stalls filled with all manner of summer vegetables, herbs and fruit. A few stops more and Rory and Guy were handing packages from more of Lady Serena's purchases to the two men-at-arms who had resigned themselves to be packhorses for the day as well as their guards.

Suddenly, from out of the crowd, came Alex, smiling broadly.

She could not help but return his smile as she met his gaze, longing to reach out and touch him. But she said only, "The meeting with the king must have gone well."

"Well enough," he said, his eyes never leaving hers.

"You are alone?" his mother asked. "Where is your father? Your horse?"

"A messenger from the king called Father back to discuss some pressing matter. I had a stop to make so Sir Geoffroi went ahead to the manor and took Azor with him."

"Was the meeting of the barons long?" Merewyn asked. Alex had left the manor before she broke her fast, causing her to wonder. Rory and Guy drew close waiting for his answer.

" 'Twas short, but we lingered with the king after." He glanced at her, then at his two friends. "William announced his plans and told me when he would have us meet him in Durham. The barons agreed to his plans. I can explain more when we are not in so public a place." Then, to his mother, "If you are finished, I will walk with you."

"We are ready to leave," said his mother. "What we have now will fill the cart we brought from Talisand."

They turned toward St. Peter's church and the manor beyond.

Merewyn had enjoyed her morning, but with Alex walking beside her, her mood rose higher. Their time might be short but she vowed to enjoy it. As the skirts of her dark blue linen gown glided over the hard-packed earth beneath her feet, it was as if she floated above the ground. Not even the darkening sky could dim her spirits. She laughed at Guy's shameless attempts to amuse them, making fun of the king's "three graces", as he called the courtiers, and their outlandish shoes with long curving toes she had not observed at the king's court.

"However do they walk in them?" she asked.

"Not far, to be sure," said Alex.

"They have only to walk as far as William," offered Rory.

Alex seemed happier than she had ever seen him. He stole glances at her as they walked along. Was he thinking of their time together? She had given him her heart as well as her body. At least for a time, he was hers. She refused to think of Lady Adèle.

That morning when she had dressed for the day, she had spotted her bow leaning against the wall of her chamber. Silently, it had shouted its disapproval.

"Do not stand there rigidly condemning me for my behavior," she had retorted. "Alex is... unlike other men. He is different. And with him, I am different."

Maugris' words had come back to her then. ... *The archer controls the bow and not the bow the archer.*

And so she would.

CHAPTER 9

Alex shared a glance with Merewyn, who rode across from him, resisting the urge to pull her into his lap. They had departed London the next morning before Terce, taking the same route back to Talisand they had coming south.

In the days that followed, Alex was able to share only a few whispers with Merewyn. It was grand torture to be so close to her and yet unable to touch her, except to help her from her pony. At times, he worried his friends, if not his parents and Sir Geoffroi, would sense the new closeness between them and see his gaze drifting often to Merewyn. He did not want the others to know of his intentions concerning her, not yet.

The storms held off making their stop in Shrewsbury pleasant. This time, it was his younger brother, Roger, who lost a game of chess to Merewyn. Alex had watched the game, exchanging occasional, heat-filled looks with Merewyn. That she had been able to keep her mind on the game so as to beat his brother amazed him.

It was a weary group of travelers that rode into the bailey a sennight later. Alex was pleased to be home. He and his men would have only a few days before they would have to leave to meet the king in Durham and he meant to share them with Merewyn when he was not in the practice yard.

Maggie came to meet them as they entered the hall. "My lady, my lord, there is food and drink should ye be wanting it." His parents thanked her and headed for the tables.

Alex turned to Merewyn. "Will you have a drink of ale?" The road had been dusty and his throat was as dry as dirt.

Merewyn looked down at her rust-colored gown, covered in dust. "Ale would be good but what I need is a bath."

He leaned in to whisper. "Would that I could join you."

She blushed and darted a look at the others. " 'Tis most unseemly to say so."

"Aye, I suppose it is."

By the time the weary travelers had drunk their ale and wine and Alex and his companions had hied off to the river to bathe, the afternoon was fair gone. On his way back, he stopped in the stable with Rory and Guy to check on their horses.

As he entered Azor's stall, the stallion was nibbling on oats while the young groom combed briars from his tail.

Alex stroked Azor's neck. "See anything I need to attend?"

The groom stood, one hand on Azor's buttock. "Nay, except he needs a new shoe. I'll see the blacksmith fits him tomorrow."

"And the destrier?" The horse Alex kept for battle was fierce in a fight but too difficult to manage for long rides over the countryside. But he would have his squire bring him to Durham.

"Your squire has seen to him while you were away. The destrier was restless this morning, so I turned him out for a bit of exercise, but you might want to run him through a few paces before you go."

"Aye, I have been remiss," admitted Alex. Unlike Azor, the destrier needed constant training in order to respond in battle to his commands using changing leg pressure. "Tomorrow, I will wear my spurs and bring Rory and Guy. Their warhorses also need the practice. My squire can assist with some distractions."

"Some screeching chickens and straw bales for the horses to jump over are readily available. 'Tis sure your brother, Tibby, will be there to add his shrieks."

Alex laughed. "Just like a battlefield, aye." He patted Azor and thanked the groom.

In the hall, his mother and Merewyn were sitting by the hearth, a bench between them covered with a stack of materials. "Heads bent to stitchery?" he inquired as he strode toward them.

Merewyn's head popped up and she rolled her eyes. "Look closer, Sir Alex. 'Tis not stitchery, but a fletcher's work we are about."

His mother smiled but kept working and did not look up as she carefully fitted part of a feather into the shaft.

"Gray goose feathers?"

"Have I ever used anything else?" his mother asked, finally raising her head. " 'Tis not the first time you have seen me fit a feather into an arrow shaft."

"Have you ever considered using the peacock's feathers?"

"I have used them," Merewyn said. "Sets my arrows apart in a contest."

"A bit bright for me," his mother said, "but Merewyn had need of new arrows so we are making some using the feathers I prefer."

Merewyn kept glancing at his mother's actions, appearing to copy her in the distinctive way she had of placing the feathers.

"Alex," Merewyn said, "can you hold the shaft for me? It keeps slipping."

He took a seat next to her on the bench and reached out his hands. "What do I do?"

"Here," she said, offering the shaft. "Just hold it in the middle while I attach the feather."

He held the shaft still while she worked at the end, biting her lip as she tried to do what his mother had done. He could not take his eyes off her lips. Her delicate scent of flowers wafted to his nostrils and he had to fight the sudden urge to kiss her.

"I have never been very good at this," she said. "Rhodri taught me to make them, but the fletchings he made were always better than mine, more like Lady Serena's. 'Tis why I brought a supply of them from Wales."

"In time, you will be an expert, like my mother," Alex encouraged. "Like many things, it just takes practice." He smiled and she blushed. He was certain she had discerned the kind of practice he had in mind.

"My son speaks the truth," his mother said, setting down her finished arrow. "And it takes patience. I did not have much when I was your age. That, too, comes with time."

"There!" Merewyn said with a look of satisfaction as she took the shaft from him and held it up. " 'Tis done!"

"The best one all afternoon," his mother remarked.

Alex liked that Merewyn took pride in small things, laboring to get something right she cared about, even if it was an archer's arrow and not embroidery. But for his mother's presence, he would have reached out and pulled her into his arms. Ah well, he would see to that this night.

⋆ ⋆ ⋆

Merewyn had just hung her gown on the peg and was about to blow out the candle when there was a soft knock on her chamber door. Wearing only her undertunic, she set down the candle and went to open the door, peeking around the oaken panel.

"Alex!" She opened the door. As he entered, she looked behind him. "Did anyone see you?" she whispered, closing the door.

"Nay, I waited till all was quiet. I could not stand another moment without holding you. Come here." He held out his arms and she went to him eagerly.

His muscled arms closed around her like a safe haven. She wrapped her arms around his waist and laid her head on his chest. "Oh, Alex." She wanted to ask what would become of them but she already knew the answer. Hoping for another was not wise. It was enough to have this part of him for as long as she might.

He turned her face up to meet his lips and with one kiss, swept her mind clean of its many concerns. Lifting her into his arms, he carried her to the bed where he laid her down and crawled in beside her. "Come to me, my passionate archer. I have so much to teach you. Remember, it takes practice."

"I was sure this is what you had in mind when you teased me as I sat with your mother."

"You were right."

When he said such things, and he often did, she asked no more of him than he was willing to give. "Then teach me, my love," she whispered.

And he did, the night becoming sweeter than she could have imagined.

*   *   *

The next day, Alex and his father were standing in the bailey when in through the gate rode the comte de Vermandois with his daughter, Lady Adèle, with their attendants and several men-at-arms.

Alex watched as the new arrivals dismounted. Both the nobleman and his daughter were attired as if they were still at court, but dust now covered Adèle's dark green gown.

"*Bonjour*, Ren" said the comte, extending his hand to Alex's father. "*Veuillez pardonner notre arrivée inattendue.*"

Talisand's lord accepted the comte's hand with a welcoming smile as the Talisand grooms took their horses away. "You are welcome, Herbert, whether expected or not, but I must tell you we speak English at Talisand. I trust 'twill not be an inconvenience?"

"*Ah, bon,*" said the comte. "We speak the English tongue. Again, please forgive our abrupt appearance." The comte glanced at his daughter. " 'Twas the king's wish. William sent us north in all haste shortly after you departed, so that my daughter and your son might have some time to get acquainted before Sir Alex rides to meet William in Durham."

Lady Adèle smiled at Alex. He was certain his face bore a scowl, though he managed to say, "Welcome, my lady," and bow over her hand when offered. William had mentioned naught of this to him at the meeting of the barons. Had the king planned it all along or was this Ranulf's suggestion?

Alex remembered the comte de Vermandois from the evening at court. His face, like Alex's father's, was lined from years in the sun. Both his mustache and short beard were brown, but Herbert's small eyes were blue and his hair, extending only to his nape, was nearly silver. Except when he smiled at Alex's father, the comte's appearance was stern.

"A visit by an old friend is always welcome," his father said to the comte. "Have you met my son, Sir Alex?"

"I have, in London, when he returned Adèle to me after a dance.

Your father and I were young knights together. I was there in Maine when Earl Renaud gained the name 'the Red Wolf.'"

Alex offered his arm to Adèle and suggested their visitors join them for some refreshment after their journey. It felt odd having a woman on his arm who was not Merewyn but he supposed he could play the gracious host for his king. Still, he could not help but wonder, had Adèle's father wanted to travel so far north? Or had the comte chafed at William's command? Some few years ago, the nobleman's allegiance would have been to Duke Robert, but with the signing of the Caen treaty, his lands were now controlled by England's king. Some Norman nobles welcomed the change, for Robert was never a strong leader, but some did not.

Once in the hall, Maggie had servants bring their guests wine, bread and cheese and then sent for Alex's mother.

When she arrived, the Lady of Talisand welcomed their guests and spoke of their lodging. "The castle is quite spacious," she said to the comte, "but if you prefer to avoid the steps, we can provide chambers in the manor, that is if Adèle is willing to share with our ward, Merewyn. Lady Adèle's maidservant can room with mine. Nelda is very accommodating. Alex's younger brother can move into his chamber, which would free a chamber for you and your manservant. Your men are welcome to lodge in the castle's great hall or with our men-at-arms."

"We wish no inconvenience," said the comte. "The manor will be fine and my men can lodge with yours." Alex did not miss Adèle's tight-lipped smile at her father's words. Did she resent having to share a chamber with his father's ward, a commoner?

Alex cared not if Tibby joined him in his chamber, but he was none too sure 'twas a good idea for Merewyn to share a chamber with Adèle, particularly since Merewyn was not of the Norman woman's class.

* * *

Merewyn had just finished her bath and was dressing for the evening meal when Nelda hurried into her chamber, her expression anxious.

"Mistress," she said, breathless, "visitors have arrived from London."

Taken aback, Merewyn sputtered, "Who?"

" 'Tis the comte de Vermandois and his daughter. Lady Serena has made arrangements for the daughter to share your chamber."

"Oh," Merewyn said, turning to show her laces to the maidservant. "Can you help me with these?"

Nelda pulled the laces tight as Merewyn pondered this latest news. "Why are they here? Do you know?" Merewyn remembered the dark beauty from London, the woman the king intended for Alex. Was there to be a betrothal?

"I only caught a bit of their conversation. 'Twas the king who sent them."

The king. Merewyn's heart sunk. So it was to be a betrothal after all. Her laces now tied, Nelda came around to stand in front of her. "Oh, mistress, the woman is here for Sir Alex, I am sure."

Nelda must have observed her affection for Talisand's heir, but Merewyn did not ask what more she knew. Most of the young women had a tendre for Alex and mayhap Nelda was among them and disliked another woman coming to visit him, especially one who was noble born. "Well," said Merewyn, speaking the truth, "there is little we can do about that."

"But mistress—" Nelda began as if in protest.

Merewyn held up a hand, stiffening her resolve and ignoring the pain that suddenly gripped her heart. "We must make Lady Adèle feel welcome." Looking around her chamber, Merewyn said, "She can have the large bed and I will take the small one."

"But that is *your* bed, mistress."

"Surely it will be for only a short while," Merewyn assured the concerned maidservant. "I do not mind." Truth be told, Merewyn did mind, not that she had to share the chamber, but that the woman who would claim Alex had come to Talisand, invading the one place Merewyn believed was hers alone to share with him. Mayhap they would have less time together than she had thought.

*   *   *

Alex had never felt so uncomfortable sitting on the dais with his parents and their guests. The meal that evening was bound to be awkward. Lady Adèle sat on his left next to her father. On his right were his parents and then Maugris, Sir Geoffroi and Lady Emma. As soon as he sat down, his gaze reached out to the trestle tables where Merewyn ate next to Lora and Jamie. Across from her sat Rory and Guy. Their faces, when lifted to Alex, were marked by curious stares. He had not had time to tell them of William's sly move in sending the comte and his daughter north to Talisand.

His father stood to introduce their guests. Goblets were raised in welcome. Alex drank heartily, but seeing Rory attempting to charm Merewyn, his mood darkened.

"The salmon is very good," remarked Adèle, running her tongue over her bottom lip, a gesture he was certain was meant for him. She was younger than Merewyn but seemed older, wiser in the ways of the world. Her teasing, sensual gestures were familiar to Alex, having known other women at William's court much like her.

"Do you hunt, my lady?" he asked her.

"With the men?" she asked, aghast. When he nodded, she shook her head. "Never. A lady would not do so." Alex refrained from telling her his lady mother had once hunted game for Talisand's kitchens.

"Might you play chess?"

"A bit," she said, "but I am not proficient like my father. Do you play?"

"Aye, I do. 'Tis a game knights learn in the evening when a candle's light is available."

She took a drink of her wine, licked the last drops from her bottom lip and smiled. "We could play... together this eve. There are many candles in your father's hall."

He supposed it was expected of him to entertain her, but he much preferred to play chess with Merewyn. Still, he would do what was required of him. Thus, at the end of the meal, when there was music and games of chess organized, he led Adèle to the trestle table where the games would be played.

His father sat opposite the comte, just setting up their board. Next to them, Sir Geoffroi smiled across a board at his wife, Lady Emma, known to be an intelligent chess player.

Unable to resist, Alex's eyes often drifted to Merewyn, who sat talking with his friends a short distance away.

"That woman," said Adèle, "the fair-haired one I met in London, she is your father's ward, *non?*"

"Aye. Ranulf introduced you to Merewyn at William's court. You will be sharing her chamber."

"Oh, yes," she said with a decided lack of enthusiasm. "She was not there when I went to the room. Is it true what they say, that she hunts with the men?"

"Aye, she does," he said, resisting the smile forming on his lips.

Her hazel eyes widened. "I had heard she went to the king's hunt disguised as your page, but I could not believe it. 'Tis hardly the action of a lady."

Alex laughed. "Some of the women of Talisand tend to be unusual in that way." He did not mention his mother was one of them.

"Does she also play chess?"

"Yea and well." Where was the woman going with this? "Many women play chess."

She gave Merewyn a perusing look, her eyes narrowing slightly.

He set up the board and they began to play. In between moves, he stole glances to where Rory was now playing against Merewyn. The knight was enjoying himself, a bit too much to Alex's mind. His red-haired companion was fair good at chess and the two were having a rousing game. Not so with he and Lady Adèle, whose awkward moves were ensuring their game would be over soon.

Adèle's gaze followed his to where the other two were now playing a second game, Merewyn having won the first. Alex chuckled to hear Rory sighing deeply.

Alex's game with Adèle continued. Mercifully, he finished it, uttering the word "Checkmate." The comte's daughter did not seem at all disappointed. "Come," he said offering his hand, "I will introduce you to my friends."

They moved down the table and joined Rory and Merewyn. Guy, sitting nearby, expressed his desire to play against Merewyn since her game with Rory was just ending.

"See if you can do better," Rory said to Guy. "She has twice checked my king. 'Tis enough victory for her at my expense."

Merewyn smiled encouragingly. "You put up a valiant fight, Sir Rory."

"Valiance alone is not enough to win a fight against an opponent with foresight and strategy," he answered.

"I thank you for the compliment," said Merewyn, winking at the redhead. "You lose with good grace."

A servant refilled their goblets as Guy set up the board for his game with Merewyn.

"Want to play, Alex?" asked Rory.

"Do you mind?" Alex asked Adèle.

"*Non.* I will watch."

Alex took a seat next to Guy across the table from Rory. Lady Adèle sat next to Merewyn, which seemed odd to Alex. What was the young Norman woman thinking? Did she sense the admiration in his voice when he spoke of Merewyn hunting with the men?

While Rory contemplated his next move, Alex's gaze drifted to the game next to him. Intent upon the board before her, Merewyn reached for her goblet.

Maugris, who was just passing the table, leaned in to speak to her, accidentally knocking the wine from her hand. The liquid splashed onto the board. Merewyn brushed the few drops from her gown that had reached that far. Guy dabbed the wine from the board.

"Please forgive me," said the seer, lifting the goblet, now empty.

"No matter," said Merewyn. "There is more wine and you did no harm."

"Allow me to pour you another," offered Maugris. He lifted the nearby pitcher and filled Merewyn's goblet.

" 'Tis kind of you, Maugris, but I think I have had enough for to-night."

The speaking glance the wise one gave Alex suggested his knocking the goblet from Merewyn's hand had been no accident. Why would he intentionally spill the wine and want Alex to know he had done so?

He would not... unless the wine was... poisoned.

With Alex's mind on Maugris' "accident", he managed to lose his game to Rory.

"Finally, I have defeated you, Alex!" Rory beamed from across the table.

"Aye, you have, and well played. My congratulations."

Merewyn fingered the stem of her goblet, looked up and smiled at Alex, then bent her head to the game before her. Guy was playing well tonight.

When Maugris left the hall, Alex made his excuses to Adèle and followed after the seer.

There was no one in the bailey and the guards at the gate were far enough away they could not hear them. "You did that a purpose," he said to the old man.

"I did," Maugris confessed, a gleam in his eyes reflecting the light spilling from the hall windows. "The young woman from Vermandois placed something into Merewyn's goblet. Even now, I cannot be certain she would not do it again. She was quick. Best to watch her closely. She is aware your eyes are often on the fair archer."

Alex let out a long breath. "You have my thanks, Maugris."

"Go now," the wise one urged. "Before the night is done, warn Merewyn not to take food or drink from Lady Adèle."

★   ★   ★

Merewyn looked askance at Alex. "But why would she, a noblewoman, give me aught to eat or drink?" They stood in the bailey where he had led her when the games were over and Lady Adèle had gone to the bedchamber she would share with Merewyn. " 'Twould be more likely I would serve her. She is our guest." *An unwanted one, but a guest nonetheless.*

He pulled her into the shadows and kissed her on her forehead. "Do not doubt me, little one. Maugris warned me the woman means you ill."

"Oh."

"I must go, but promise me you will be careful."

"I promise," she said and watched him enter the manor. Above her, the stars glistened in the night sky. She decided to look in on Ceinder before seeking her bed. As she walked to the stables, she worried over her predicament. It was not good she was coming between Alex and his future. Mayhap it would be best if she returned to Wales when Alex left to meet the king. Already, she may have lingered too long, for she was becoming accustomed to seeing his face each day and sharing his kisses at night.

Ceinder was glad to see her, nickering softly at her approach. Before she left the stable, she looked in on Azor, thinking of his master.

She opened the door of her chamber to see Lady Adèle sitting on the edge of the large bed combing out her long dark tresses.

After greeting the young Norman woman, Merewyn began to remove her outer tunic, turning toward the wall as she did. Her body was slim, modest in feminine achievement, whereas Lady Adèle possessed an ample bosom. A man like Alex could not help but notice the difference with approval.

"How long have you known Sir Alex?" the woman asked.

"All my life," Merewyn said without turning. "But he was away much and so was I. I have only recently returned to Talisand."

"Your parents are here?"

To Merewyn, the questions were asked in a manner so as to sound hostile, as if she were being judged and found wanting. She answered in the shortest way she could. "Both are dead."

"Were they both English? With your fair coloring, I would have—"

"Nay, only one, like Sir Alex." Merewyn did not like where the woman's inquiries were leading. She would not discuss her sire, especially not with one who meant her ill. Merewyn spared one glance for Lady Adèle and then blew out the candle on the small table next to her bed and slipped beneath the cover.

The room was still bathed in a faint flickering light, for another candle burned next to the larger bed where Adèle sat plaiting her hair.

Merewyn stared at the ceiling.

"I assume you know," Lady Adèle said, "the king means for Sir Alex and me to wed." The words sounded like a warning.

"Yea," said Merewyn, her voice trembling. "I think all of Talisand knows that." She turned her back to the woman and faced the wall, tears silently falling to her pillow.

★　★　★

Alex was just coming off the practice yard when Lady Adèle walked up to meet him. "Good day, my lady."

"And to you, Sir Alex." When he headed toward the palisade gate, she said, "I was hoping we might walk a bit."

"Of course." He gestured toward the river, but away from the village. He did not need his people to see him walking with the woman and wonder.

The waters of the River Lune were tranquil, only a few ducks leaving ripples in the water as they swam along.

" 'Tis very peaceful here," she said as they walked along the riverbank, "but not as beautiful, I think, as my father's lands in Normandy."

"I have seen Normandy on many occasions. Its rolling green hills and pasturelands are, indeed, beautiful to the eye, but England is my home and always will be." He hoped he had put to rest the woman's ambition concerning him, but the set of her jaw and her lips pressed tightly together spoke of her resolve to proceed.

"I suppose one could spend some part of the year here and the rest of it in Normandy," she ventured.

"If one had a mind to do so, yea," he said with indifference. How long would she talk around the real purpose of her seeking his company? He was certain it had not been in her mind to admire the beauty of harvest time in Talisand.

She stopped walking and turned to face him, her countenance no longer as sweetly pleasant as before. "Surely you must know, Sir Alex, William wants my father's lands tied to a Norman noble who is loyal to England's king. He means to see us wed and what the king wants, he will have."

"Aye, my lady. William will certainly tie your father's lands to a Norman loyal to him. But I would prefer that Norman not be me, for another lady holds my heart and Talisand will be my home forever."

"Another *lady*?" She emphasized the last word and anger welled up inside him for he knew her intention to slight Merewyn for her commoner status.

"Yea, a lady." He would say no more. "I must take my leave of you now, for I have a meeting I must attend to." He did not say the meeting was with his horses. Bowing, he left her frowning. So be it. He cared little if she was not smiling. He only hoped Merewyn remembered his caution based upon Maugris' warning.

★   ★   ★

Merewyn was gathering her new arrows with the gray feather fletchings when the door of her chamber opened. Lady Adèle entered, shutting the door behind her with a loud "thump". On her otherwise lovely face was an angry frown.

"Is something wrong, my lady?"

"Indeed!" she exclaimed, eying Merewyn as if she were a piece of discarded clothing. Her manner was haughty and disdainful as she said, "Have you given Sir Alex the impression he has aught to say about the king's intention to see us wed?"

Merewyn straightened from where she had been bent over the arrows, pausing to stare at the furious woman before her. "Whatever made you think I have done so? Nay, I have always encouraged Sir Alex to abide by the king's wishes."

"Well, it is best he do in this matter of our marriage or some ill may befall you both. When a king orders a wedding, a wedding there shall be!"

Tired of the woman's ill-tempered speech, Merewyn asked, "Has the king ordered a wedding?"

With that, the woman turned on her heels and quit the chamber. Merewyn stood looking at the closed door. Sill angry, she remembered the woman's threat of harm and trembled. Would she hurt Alex?

★   ★   ★

Days later, Alex stood with his parents by the open gate, watching as the guests from Normandy disappeared over the hill. The comte and his daughter had stayed for several days and were only now taking their leave. It was not soon enough for Alex.

"Well?" his father asked, "What say you to William's choice?"

"He is scowling," Alex's mother put in. "I told you he would. Alex likes her not."

"Herbert's daughter is comely enough," his father offered. "And her father is enthusiastic about the match and his lands in Vermandois are extensive."

Alex's scowl deepened. In his mind, he saw only the woman he had come to love: Merewyn racing through the forest on her white pony as she raised her bow to shoot; Merewyn smiling at him over the chess-board; Merewyn walking along Fish Street in London, laughing with his mother. "I would choose my own wife. And you are correct, Mother, 'twould not be Lady Adèle."

"There, you see," said his mother, giving his father a knowing look.

"A king's knight does his sire's bidding," his father calmly reminded her.

His mother pursed her lips, but said nothing.

They began to walk back to the manor.

"What about Sir Geoffroi?" Alex asked, raising the one exception he knew of, a knight respected by his father for his defiance of the Conqueror. "He defied his king."

His father's brow furrowed. "I admit there are times when honor requires a man to take his own path. But is this a question of honor? You could be more than the heir of Talisand. You could have lands in Normandy and the favor of your king."

The words Maugris had spoken came to him. *Honor is revealed in the face of temptation.* "It is a matter of honor to me." He had claimed the woman he wanted and would do right by her. The temptation for more lands or a woman of noble birth would not lure him from his intended course.

His father shrugged. "Then it falls to you to find a way to appease your sire if you are one day to choose your own bride."

They arrived at the door of the manor and his mother asked, "Do you go to the practice yard?"

"I have no choice. Our visitors took up my time when I should have been preparing the men to meet Malcolm's warriors. I have heard the Scots are fierce and fight like wild men and there are but a few days to prepare before we must leave."

"You distress your mother by such talk, Son."

Indeed, his mother's face was full of worry.

"Forgive me. I would not have you anxious for my sake. But I would have your prayers while I am gone."

"You will have them," his mother replied. "Father Bernard has agreed to say prayers each day for your return and a peaceful outcome."

He smiled at his mother and nodded to his father, then left them as he headed toward the armory where he was to meet Rory and Guy.

Ahead loomed William's plans to deal with the Scots and after, Alex's future with Merewyn. He must step carefully.

★   ★   ★

Merewyn retrieved her arrows from the target with the help of Cecily and her two companions. Behind the round disk, the leaves in the woods were rapidly changing color from summer's green to September's yellow, gold and crimson. Soon, Alex would leave for Durham.

Fighting back the tears that suddenly filled her eyes, she turned to her young shadows. "My practice is done for today."

"Can I shoot, Merewyn?" pleaded Cecily. The redheaded vixen was adorable in the boy's clothing she donned whenever she followed Merewyn to the archery field.

"Not unless we can shoot, too," insisted Alex's youngest brother, Tibby. "Else 'tis unfair." There were times—and this was one of them—when the boy's frown reminded her of Alex, making her smile.

"Me, too!" shouted Ancel. Only eight summers, Lora's young brother had a head of brown curls that made him appear even younger. But somehow, he always managed to keep up with the other two.

"I will agree to this," Merewyn said, looking into the three young faces staring back at her with eager anticipation. "First, each of you must gain the approval of your parents. If Father Bernard assures me you are doing your lessons, I will begin your training. At Sir Geoffroi's manor, I have the bow I trained with." She held up her bow. " 'Tis smaller than this one. If your parents approve, you can use it and I will make you arrows with wooden tips until you are ready for metal-tipped ones. 'Twill serve for your lessons like the wooden swords the pages use in practice."

The three grinned widely, nodding their heads. Cecily jumped up and down.

"But I will not begin your training without Lady Serena's approval and only after Sir Alex and the men have gone to meet the king. There will still be archers at Talisand who can assist me with your training."

The three ran off and Merewyn watched them, reminded of their youth. They had begged her all summer to teach them the way of the bow. Reluctant at first, she had finally decided that if their parents and Lady Serena agreed, she would do it. To help the children realize their dream of learning archery would bring her great pleasure. And she would need something to do after Alex was gone.

But she still thought about returning to Wales. It would make it easier for Alex if he did not have to face the choice of acting honorably toward her or obeying his king. To shun the marriage the king intended would gain Alex the wrath of his sovereign and the disdain of his people. She could not allow that to happen.

Another glimpse of the changing leaves convinced her the time was short if she were to teach the children before she had to travel to Wales.

CHAPTER 10

The crisp edge to the wind Alex encountered as he stepped into the bailey reminded him autumn would soon be upon them. Already the winter wheat and rye had been harvested in the fields beyond the village and his father's villeins would soon turn to the crops of peas and beans.

The bailey was crowded with villagers who had come to see him and his men off, knowing they might be going to war against the Scots. Jamie and some of the house knights stood near the gate.

He walked to where Azor waited, saddled and ready, his squire holding the reins. The stallion's intelligent eyes bore an alert expression as he raised his head and pricked his ears toward his master. Alex tightened the girth. "I know you are anxious to leave, boy."

Azor was not the only impatient one. Alex, too, wanted the business with the Scots behind him and he hoped if William Rufus' dealings with Malcolm were successful, the king would be in a mood to grant him his desire.

Alex and Merewyn had said their goodbyes the night before, the last moments still clear in his mind.

"I know you must go," she had said with stiff resolve. " 'Tis your duty." But the tears she fought to hide had spoken more loudly.

Kissing her forehead, he had assured her he would return. He had not told her of his intention to speak to the king. He had plans, too, if William Rufus did not agree to the match, but he would not have her worry over them now. He did not like to think he might not return but every warrior had to consider the possibility. The letter he had left for his parents, hidden in his chamber, would be discovered if he died and Merewyn would be provided for with the accord due her.

Azor snorted, bringing Alex's attention back to his stallion. He accepted the reins from his squire, who went about securing Alex's shield and helm to the saddle.

Rory rode up beaming his pleasure. "See what your lady mother has given me!"

Alex tilted his head back to see the long, narrow banner affixed to a wooden pole Rory carried. Stretched the length of the crimson silk was a rampant black wolf, its bright red tongue thrust out from its open jaws. Alex smiled. His father had seen to this. "My mother might have made it but this is a gift from my father and, with it, he gives me his blessing."

"Aye, your mother said as much." The wind blew Rory's red hair across his forehead. "And, if you are willing, I would be your bannerman, as Sir Alain carries the banner for the Red Wolf. What say you?"

"So be it! I can think of no better knight to have at my side or at my back."

Maugris ambled up to Alex and tipped his silver head back to take in the tall banner. "Ah the wolf rampant rises," he said in his mysterious way of speaking. "Soon 'twill fly above the red hart. I have seen it."

Alex and Rory stared at the wise one, who promptly turned and meandered away.

"I do wonder if Maugris knows the meaning of his visions," said Alex.

" 'Tis that prophecy again," said Rory, watching the old seer disappear into the crowd.

"Aye, and I know no more now than the last time he spoke of it, save a wolf rampant flies on my banner."

"Whenever he speaks like that," said Rory, "it brings up bumps on my skin. 'Tis eerie the way he sees things."

"Aye." But Alex had no more time to think on it. His men were mounting their horses. "If we are to arrive in Durham before the king, we had best be going. 'Tis at least two days' ride even with favorable weather."

Alex slipped his foot in the stirrup, launched himself into the saddle and walked the black stallion to the head of the column. Rory, holding the banner in the leather sheath affixed to his saddle, rode behind him. Alex's squire, leading the destrier, rode with the other men.

Beneath him, Azor was restless, but Alex could not leave until he bid his parents goodbye and glimpsed the face of the woman he would miss the most.

His parents stood together at the door of the hall, along with his friends' fathers, Sir Geoffroi and Sir Maurin and their wives, Lady Emma and the redheaded Cassie. Jamie had come from the gate to stand next to Lora. As captain of the house knights, however reluctant he was to remain behind, his priority was to guard the demesne.

Alex raised his hand to acknowledge his parents.

Not far away, Merewyn stood in the shadows of the manor, her cheeks glistening with tears. It tore at him to see her so. He wanted with all his heart to call her to him for a last kiss, but he could not allow the others to think she was more than a friend. Not for her sake. Not yet.

With his shouted command, the score of men followed him out the gate.

⋆   ⋆   ⋆

Merewyn hastily looked down at her feet, brushing away the tears, unwilling for any to see the pain she kept hidden in her heart. When she looked up, Alex was already through the palisade gate. Would she ever see him again? She vowed to remember always the way he sat so erect upon his great stallion, his long raven hair flowing over his mail-clad shoulders and the long sword sheathed at his hip.

There was no banter, no teasing, with his men this time, only the somber faces of knights going to war, determined to face the king's enemies without fear.

Behind Alex, Rory carried proudly the new banner, proclaiming to all the Black Wolf now rode in his own right. No longer merely the son of a legend, Alex was becoming a legend himself.

She choked back the tears.

Every step he took away from Talisand was a step away from her.

How long might he be gone? Would it be months, as Jamie expected? Would he survive the coming battle? In that instant, cold fear lashed at her insides. Losing him to death would be far worse than losing him to a wife chosen by the king. At least with the latter, he would still live.

He had to survive. A legend could not die before his time. Comforted with the thought, her mind raced to what would happen when the fight with the Scots was over. Would the king Alex so loyally served betroth him to Lady Adèle? The Norman woman had been so sure she would wed Alex. Mayhap it would be so. Merewyn could not bear to see again the smug smile on the woman's face were that to happen. Nay, she must be gone before that day arrived.

She turned and slipped into the manor to change her clothes. In her chamber, she donned the archer's tunic, hosen and leather jerkin that cloaked her femininity. Her bow spoke a word of rebuke for her past sins. She ignored it. Picking up the bow and quiver, she set her course for the stables. This time, she would practice her shooting with Ceinder.

As she would in her new home—in Wales.

★   ★   ★

Night was falling as Alex stared into the fire his squire had built and thought of Merewyn's tears. Once this campaign was over, he vowed never to see Merewyn cry again. He would fill her life with laughter and her belly with their sons and daughters.

Above him the sky was as dark as his mood. The night air was cold, making the fire welcome. He held out his palms to warm them in the heat of the flames. Thus far, they had been spared rain, for which he was grateful. Rain made a knight's travel miserable.

He and his friends had caught three hares now roasting on a spit stretched over the fire between two forked branches thrust into the ground. His stomach rumbled at the smell of the meat. "Are the men settled in?" he asked Rory who sank onto the log beside him.

"Aye, and cooking their own suppers. Your squire and mine are seeing to the horses."

Guy approached with a leather flask he thrust at Alex. "Here, warm your bones with some of Normandy's wine." Alex accepted it gratefully and took a drink before passing it to Rory. The red wine was welcome after a hard day of guiding his men across vast open spaces, then picking his way through rocky outcroppings and sparse vegetation.

"Tomorrow should see us in Durham," he told his companions, "well before the king is expected to arrive."

" 'Tis best we arrive afore him," said Rory. "William waits for no man."

* * *

Alex held his fist in the air to halt his men as they emerged from the woods a short distance from Durham. The countryside spread out before him, golden fields dotted with scattered woodlands. But that was not what had sent a chill crawling up his spine.

"What is it, Alex?" asked Rory coming alongside him on his right at the same time Guy appeared on his left.

"Something is amiss," he said. "See the fields of ripe flax in the distance?"

"Aye, what of it?" asked Guy.

"They lie half-harvested yet there are no villeins, no carts nor any cattle to be seen. 'Tis as if the whole city has drawn into itself, hiding behind Durham's walls."

"Could word have reached them of William's army marching north?" asked Rory.

"Possibly," Alex said, considering what might have happened. "Or, it could be the Scots frightened the people into abandoning their fields and hiding their cattle."

"I was always taught the Northumbrians like neither the Scots nor the Normans," said Guy.

"Your mother, Lady Emma, would know," Alex said, casting a glance at the younger knight. "In York, she saw the worst of the Conqueror's wrath and after, Malcolm was known to raid even before this."

"Aye," said Rory, "we will find no welcome here."

Turning Azor, Alex faced his other men and gestured to the woods. "We will camp here for the night. Be vigilant on your watches for we do not know who yet roams the woods or if all the Scots have departed." He then made assignments as to who would hunt and forage and who would take the first watch. The squires would gather wood and build the fires.

Alex reserved for himself the work of spying out the land to see what might be learned.

Turning back to his friends, he said, "Leave the banner, Rory. Let us water the horses and then see what lies beyond these woods."

By the time the three of them left the camp, the sun was low in the sky but still provided ample light for the mission Alex had in mind.

Not knowing what they might find, they had donned their helms and carried their shields, their weapons at the ready.

The land they scouted bore the marks of the season, spring crops ready to harvest, winter seed not yet sewn. Sloping, gorse-covered hills and scattered leaf-strewn woodlands surrounded all.

Rocky outcroppings sometimes slowed their progress, but eventually they crested a hill to look down upon the city of Durham to the east. Around the elevated walled city meandered the River Wear. Dense vegetation grew tall on either side of its banks.

They were just heading down the slope when Alex spotted a large group of mounted warriors to the north, as many as two hundred. The riders wore mail, but then, both Normans and Scots did. Narrowing his eyes and scanning the group, he spotted the familiar banner of Nigel d'Aubigny, a white lion rampant on a bright red field.

"'Tis Sir Nigel," he said, urging Azor down the hill to where the baron sat on his horse surrounded by his knights.

Alex and his friends posed no threat to the large group of knights but they were closely watched all the same, heads turning at their approach. Since he carried no banner, neither his father's nor his own, they were not recognized until they drew close.

Sir Nigel rode out to meet him. "I'd know that stallion anywhere. Greetings, son of the Red Wolf! How is your father?"

Alex grinned, pleased to find a friend when he could have so easily encountered an enemy. "He is well at Talisand and sends his regards and his eldest son to carry the message."

Sir Nigel chuckled, took off his helm and extended his arm to Alex. His gray-streaked brown hair was still thick and framed a lined face.

Alex doffed his helm and accepted the arm of friendship. "Cainhoe and Bedfordshire are a long way from Durham. Do you ride with William's army?"

"Aye, the king asked me to take a strong force ahead to chase the Scots north. Word of our arrival had its effect. Malcolm must have mistaken us for William's full army. When we got here, the city was caught between the remnants of the Scots fleeing north and our knights advancing from the south."

"And the people of Durham? We've seen none."

"Holed up in the city," Sir Nigel said, looking over Alex and his two companions. "How many of you are there?"

"A score of knights and men-at-arms camped in nearby woods. We only just arrived. Do you expect William soon?"

"Tomorrow, I should think. He rides with his brother and Duncan, King Malcolm's son. Even Ranulf has come. The man's no warrior but mayhap William feels in the need of a priest."

Alex laughed. They both knew Ranulf had few, if any, duties as the king's priest.

"Tonight you and your men must join my camp," insisted Sir Nigel. "Many of the knights with me are of an age with you and the conversations around the cook fires will no doubt have them telling outrageous tales of their valor."

"Thank you," said Alex. "My men might enjoy that."

* * *

Merewyn stood behind Cecily, helping her student to square her stance. "Keep your feet apart the distance between your hips."

Cecily dutifully adjusted her legs. The morning sun filtered through the trees to fall on the leaves that had drifted to the ground forming a cinnamon-colored carpet beneath the girl's feet.

The two boys, ever with her, watched from a nearby rock as the lesson proceeded. It was not her first and the boys were slowly losing their interest.

"It feels awkward to stand this way," Cecily protested.

"I know. It did for me as well, but you will get used to it. And once you find the right stance, you must do it every time the same way."

Cecily squared her shoulders in a determined manner and placed her toes so they just touched the arrow Merewyn had laid across the ground as a guide. "When do I get the bow?"

Merewyn reached for the small bow that had been the one she used for her own training. "How about now?"

Without moving her feet, Cecily beamed up at Merewyn. A year younger than Tibby, Alex's brother, at nine summers, Cecily already had a will of iron.

The lesson continued as Merewyn showed Cecily how to hold the bow, how to keep her arm almost straight and how to hook the bowstring with her fingers and pull it back to her chin. "You must practice every day until it is as natural as breathing and the bow becomes an extension of your arm."

Several minutes of practice later, Merewyn called a halt when she detected Cecily was tiring. "Tomorrow we shall begin again."

"When do I get to shoot an arrow?" the young redhead asked.

Merewyn smiled, remembering when she had been just as impatient. "In a day or two. The better your form, the more likely your arrow will hit the target."

The young girl sighed. "All right."

"Come on, Cecily!" shouted Tibby, who had been shifting about on the rock, apparently desirous of playing another game. Once the boys had seen how much work learning to be an archer required, they had decided to wait to see what their friend's lessons produced. So far, Cecily was doing well, but the lessons had only begun.

Cecily ran off to join her companions.

Snatching up the girl's practice bow and her own, larger bow, Merewyn headed back to the manor. Before she had gone very far, her stomach lurched and her mouth filled with saliva. A sudden urge to spew up the meal she had eaten an hour before took hold of her. Ducking behind a tree, she leaned over and heaved. Wiping her mouth with the back of her sleeve, she leaned against the tree, feeling weak.

She was never ill, but mayhap there had been a touch of mold in the grain used in the gruel.

A moment later, feeling better, she pushed away from the tree. By the time she got back to the manor, it was as if it had not happened. *How strange.*

The next morning after Cecily's lesson, Merewyn went to see Ceinder and the same thing happened. Only this time, she was in the stable when the urge to spew came over her.

Jamie, who had been in the stable, hearing her retch into the straw, came to her aid. "Merewyn, what is it?"

" 'Tis nothing," she said. " 'Twill pass."

"You are ill?" His concern was evident.

"Nay. It happened yesterday, too. Mayhap my gruel of late does not suit my stomach."

"Come, sit on this stool." He gestured to a stool in the corner and she sat. "Your face has no color."

"Thank you," she said with a half-hearted smirk. A few moments later, she began to feel better. Jamie still stood beside her. "See," she said, rising from the stool, "I am now hale and, I trust, no longer without color."

"Merewyn, I am no stripling lad, nor even a young knight. I have observed many women act as you have and always the cause is the same. Forgive me for asking, but could you be with child?"

Merewyn stared at the beam of light falling onto the straw. *Yes, I could.* They had come together only a few times but in her mother's case, it had taken only once. Merewyn's flow was often irregular, but it had not come this last month. Yes, she could well be with child. Alex's babe! Excitement for the babe and fear for her future warred within her.

Turning her face to Jamie, she nodded. "Promise me you will say nothing."

"I will say nothing, but I must know, 'tis Alex's child?"

"If I am with child, Jamie, it could only be his, for I have known no other."

"I thought as much. You two were very close before he left to meet the king. I have long suspected there was more than friendship between you. You need have no fear. Alex will wed you, I am certain."

She shook her head vigorously. "You know as well as I that Alex must wed a noblewoman, most likely the daughter of the comte de Vermandois. Lady Adèle is the king's choice for Alex, not a woman like me."

"But he cares for you, I know it," insisted the blond knight. "He

155

would never have allowed this to happen otherwise. He is honorable."

"Oh, Jamie, I know that. But you must understand, I cannot let Alex take me as his wife. Do you not see what would happen if I did? The king would be very angry with him and, in time, Alex would hate me for robbing him of his king's favor and the lands a marriage to a noblewoman of Normandy would bring. Even Talisand might suffer."

Jamie let out a sigh. "You care for him, I see."

"I do, too much to see him give up his future for me."

"Well, if not Alex, you must wed another." Raising his chest, he declared, "I would be your husband, Merewyn, should you have me."

His blue eyes were earnest, his words true. He would do it and she loved him for his noble offer. But she could never allow him to marry her when he loved another, as she did. She smiled at him, grateful for the man he was. "Nay, I will not have you, dear Jamie."

He returned her a puzzled look.

"You love Lora, Jamie, I have always known it. It is Lora you should wed, not me."

His gaze suddenly shifted to the straw at his feet, confirming her assumption.

"But what about you?" he asked, raising his head to meet her gaze.

"Do not worry about me, Jamie. My mother bore me alone and I can bear this child the same way if I must. I am not without friends. In Wales, I have many."

His brow furrowed. "Alex will not like it."

She picked up her bow and quiver of arrows. "Alex will never know."

CHAPTER 11

Alex sat atop Azor next to Sir Nigel watching the thousands of mail-clad knights and men-at-arms coming toward them from the south. They swarmed over the land like locusts, their silvered helms reflecting the afternoon sun. Impatient to be about the king's business, Alex was pleased William's army had finally arrived.

Without turning, he said to Sir Nigel, "Now, at last, we can pursue the Scots."

As the army drew closer, Alex saw the king and his brother, Robert, riding ahead of the barons and the army.

Behind the king to one side walked his archers, hundreds strong. Their green and brown clothing was not unlike the bowman's garb Merewyn wore, but not one rode a horse. Merewyn would love to have seen it. His chest tightened as he imagined her smiling at him from her Welsh pony, her bow slung over her shoulder. She was brave enough to ride with William's army, he had no doubt.

The sooner they dealt with the Scots, the sooner he could go home—and return to Merewyn.

The king rode forward to meet them, on his head a conical helm circled by a golden crown. Beneath his helm, Alex could see William's red beard, now trimmed. His long blond hair was splayed out on his mail-clad shoulders.

Alex bowed from his saddle. Sir Nigel did the same.

"Sir Nigel, Sir Alex," said the king, "I am glad you ride together.

What news of the Scots?"

"Malcolm's army fled north as we arrived, My Lord," said Sir Nigel.

"Fie!" The king's face grew flushed with anger and the bejeweled fingers of his right hand clenched around the pommel of his saddle. "By the holy face of Lucca, we shall pursue the rabble to the very door of Malcolm's pile of stones in Dun Edin. I will have an end to his excursions into Northumbria!"

The king's chestnut stallion stamped his hoof and snorted, no doubt sensing his master's anger. William's moods were not unknown to his men. Alex had seen his anger flare before, often just as he ordered some torture for a defiant prisoner.

"We expected no less, My Lord," said Sir Nigel.

Alex wanted to deflect the king's attention to other, more urgent needs. "Sire, would you have the army camp here tonight or go on?"

The king looked across at his brother. "What say you, Robert? Do we camp?"

Alex did not have to wonder what the answer would be. Robert, who had always been tenderhearted to suppliants, turned to survey the king's barons and senior knights, their weariness apparent. Robert fitzHaimo, baron of Gloucester, the ponderous Earl of Chester, Roger Bigot, Sheriff of Norfolk, Ranulf Flambard, the king's advisor, and Sir Duncan were among them. "Aye," said Duke Robert, " 'tis been a long day and the men and horses need rest. We would not get very far else we do."

William appeared to accept the answer. "Have you sufficient food?" he asked Sir Nigel.

"My men have taken deer and game, My Lord, but you may need more for the army."

"*Parfait*," said William. "We have some provisions and the men and archers can hunt. It will serve until we meet my ships on the Tyne. What of Durham?"

"From what we can tell, My Lord," said Alex, "the people have fled to the woods or are now behind the city's closed doors. There are no villeins to be seen in the fields."

"The city was caught between Malcolm's army and the men I brought with me," added Sir Nigel.

The king's brows drew together. "We have no time to deal with the Northumbrians. They can remain behind their city walls for now. On the morrow, we will chase the Scots north."

The men made camp, erecting a tent for the king. The horses were watered and allowed to forage. And soon, cook fires dotted the countryside as the men prepared their supper before bedding down for the night.

Alex returned to his men. After a meal of roast venison, he and his companions shared a conversation around the fire, speculating about the fight to come.

" 'Tis unseasonably cold," said Guy, clenching his cloak to his chest, "and we have yet to enter Scotland."

"Aye," said Rory, "These are not the pastures of Normandy."

Alex, too, felt the damp cold seep into his cloak and was glad for their fire. At least it had not rained. He laid his pallet on the ground and stretched out to stare up at the stars, remembering the conversation he'd had with Merewyn as they had looked up at the radiant circle of stars the night he'd first kissed her. He would never again see the stars without thinking of her.

★   ★   ★

"I wonder where she learned to do it." Jamie muttered under his breath as he watched Merewyn fire another shot from her pony to hit the target's center. He had counseled her against riding in the weeks since he'd learned she was with child but she insisted both she and her babe enjoyed it. Her body showed no signs of the child growing within her—Alex's child, he reminded himself—and the sickness she had once displayed no longer troubled her.

"Iorwerth issued her a challenge and she accepted," said a voice from behind him.

Jamie whipped around to see a tall young man wearing the brown and green clothing of a Welsh bowman, except that beneath his leather jerkin he wore mail. *Not just any bowman, but a warrior.*

The dark-haired man was nearly Jamie's own height though younger by several years. Added to the archer's clothing were leather gauntlets and guards over his shins. From his belt hung a wicked-

159

looking axe and in his hand he carried a longbow. Slung over his right shoulder was a quiver of arrows, the brown-tipped fletchings unlike any Jamie had ever seen. Circling the top of the quiver was a band of metal with an ornate Celtic design.

"Who might you be?" Jamie asked, his hand itching to reach for his sword. The young Welshman was unknown to him, but the voice carried the same accent as Rhodri's, the prince of Powys whose true name among his people was Iorwerth.

"I am Owain ap Cadwgan," he said in his accented English, looking behind Jamie to where Merewyn was watching them from her pony. "I see she has not forgotten all she learned from me."

"You knew Merewyn in Wales?"

"I did."

He expected the Welshman to say more but he only dipped his head respectfully and walked around him, heading toward Merewyn. He had not even asked Jamie his name.

Jamie was suddenly anxious, yet he did not know the reason. Since his conversation with Merewyn about her condition, he'd been very protective of her, for he knew Alex would expect it no matter that she spoke of leaving. He did not like this new person coming to Talisand, a warrior bearing serious weapons who seemed to know much about her. He had said he had taught her. *What was he to her? And with war threatening with Wales, why had he come to England now?*

* * *

Merewyn watched Owain walking toward her, his dark brown eyes intense as he approached. Despite his serious demeanor, it cheered her immensely to see him again.

"Merry," he said, drawing near, "*fy golau*." "My light" was the name he had given her for her fair hair, unusual among the Welsh.

"Owain!" She dismounted and, with her bow and quiver slung over her shoulder, led Ceinder to meet him. "What brings you here?"

He took her hand and pressed a light kiss to her fingers, his lips warm on her skin. Never before could she recall his acting so much the gallant. "I had a desire to see this place you spoke of, this Talisand," he said looking around. Reaching out to stroke her pony's neck, he added,

"I see you and Ceinder are still a pair."

"We do well together," she said, wondering why Owain had come now at a time when his warrior skills were so needed by his people.

He continued to stroke the pony's neck but his eyes stayed on her.

"It is wonderful to see you," she said. In truth, she had missed her friends in Wales and had been thinking much of Rhodri and Fia as she contemplated returning. "You must share some wine with me in the hall and tell me about all that has happened since I left."

"Nothing would please me more," he said with a subtle smile. Owain was a prince, Rhodri's nephew. Still in his second decade, he was already a respected warrior among his people. She knew he lived a turbulent life, raiding, plundering and defending his family. Yet for all that, he spoke poetry around the hearth fire and he had taken the time to teach her to shoot from her pony.

Owain had been there for her transformation from a frightened girl to a woman secure in her ability to protect herself.

She walked beside him toward Talisand's captain. "You met Sir Jamie?"

"Briefly."

"Jamie," she said, as they reached him, "a friend has come from Wales."

Jamie inclined his head. "Owain introduced himself."

Merewyn smiled at the two men, each studying the other like two roosters facing off with their hackles raised. "You two should get to know each other. Owain is a prince of Powys," she said for Jamie's benefit, "and Rhodri's nephew. And Jamie is the captain of Talisand's house knights," she told Owain. "Both of you are respected commanders of men."

Jamie offered his hand and Owain took it. Merewyn was happy the two roosters had declared a truce. Together, the three of them walked from the archery field.

"Where is your horse?" she asked Owain.

"I left him with the stable boy."

"He will be welltended," said Jamie.

Unable to contain her curiosity any longer, she asked Owain, "How is Rhodri? And Fia? And the children? I have missed them."

He grinned at her show of enthusiasm. "Rhodri and Fia and their children are all well. And, if I am included in the ones you have missed, it makes me glad to hear it."

Jamie frowned and Merewyn wondered at the cause. She considered both Owain and Jamie her friends. But since Jamie had learned she was carrying Alex's child, he had become very watchful of her.

They passed through the palisade gate and she handed Ceinder's reins to a waiting stable boy. Crossing the bailey, the three of them entered the hall. Merewyn set down her bow and quiver and asked a servant to bring wine and cheese for their guest.

When the servant appeared with a tray bearing a pitcher, three goblets and a plate of cheese and bread, Merewyn offered to pour the wine.

She handed Owain a goblet and he lifted it to his lips and drank deeply.

Jamie took a sip of his wine and, turning to Owain, said, "You come to England at a time when the king's men fight the Welsh." To Merewyn, it sounded like a challenge.

"A difficult time, yea," Owain answered, "but I did not come because of the fighting between our countries. I came for Merry."

Jamie frowned at the Welshman's words. "I am sure she appreciates the visit."

The captain stayed only long enough to finish his wine, all the while his eyes stayed on the Welsh prince. After she and Owain began to share stories, Jamie excused himself and left the hall.

When he was gone, Owain said, "You have grown lovelier. Your face seems to glow."

Merewyn did not feel lovely. Dressed in her bowman's clothing, she was dusty and her brow damp with the exertion of her practice. From where it sat on the table, her bow scolded her for her shabby appearance in the presence of a Welsh prince. Ignoring it, she said, "Mayhap you remember me as only a novice archer in need of training."

"Nay, I remember you well. One day you were there, like the sun, and the next day, Rhodri had taken you back to England. Every day thereafter was full of clouds."

"So somber! What happened to my demanding teacher of the bow?"

"I have never been far."

*   *   *

Alex drew his woolen cloak tightly around him, glad for his mail and helm as a sharp gust of wind knifed through his clothing. Azor bent his head to the wind but continued on.

It had been stormy and cold as they left Durham. Alex was only vaguely aware of Rory and Guy riding beside him, their heads tucked into their hooded cloaks. His mind was not on the dark clouds that promised more rain, the brown and green hills that seemed to go on forever, nor on the heather trodden down by their horses. He took it all in but his mind was focused on the golden-haired archer he had left behind.

He imagined Merewyn warming herself with a cup of wine in front of Talisand's hearth fire as she and his mother fashioned fletchings for their arrows. He saw her as she looked the night before he left when he had kissed her goodbye.

He had not seen her for a month. Did she think of him often as he did her?

"Does my wolf brood over the cold?" asked the king as he rode up beside Alex. Guy pulled back on his reins, dropping behind to make room for William's chestnut stallion.

"Nay, Sire, though 'tis a brutal autumn. But I do worry about feeding the men. We could have used the corn and other food the ships would have brought us."

William's face grew red with his increasing anger. "By the face of Lucca, I will have an explanation for their delay!"

When they had reached the River Tyne, the fifty ships William had expected were nowhere to be seen. The king had waited two days and then, cursing and red-faced, ordered his army to push on.

Since then, they had passed the crumbling stone wall built by the Emperor Hadrian to separate the Romans from the barbarians, a symbol of the Romans' might much as the Conqueror's timber castles were a symbol of the Normans' military strength. As they'd pressed on toward Lothian, Alex could not help but think of the Roman legions of a thousand years before. The Scots William would face were no less formidable than the Picts the Romans faced then.

Later that day in the king's tent, William shouted to his senior knights and nobles. "Our seamen had best be there when we reach the Firth of Forth!"

Alex hoped William was right but he had his doubts. Moreover, William, too, was worried. Judging by his ruddy cheeks and the sparks shooting from his eyes, his anger was replacing his concern.

Alex and his men made camp to the sounds of the red deer rutting. The loud bellowing of the stags echoed through the glens, sometimes broken by the sharp clash of antlers, as the males fought each other for control over the hinds. With their food stores running low and the few people they had encountered hostile, Alex knew they must hunt.

After he had watered and rested his horse, Alex had approached the king to seek his guidance. In response, the king sent his best archers into the woods to search for grouse, hares and small game. But to feed the army, they would need to set upon larger prey. The king called for three hunts for the red deer. William proposed to lead one group himself and the other two would be led by his barons, each setting off in a different direction.

At the king's request, Alex and his men joined William. As they cantered behind the king, Alex's thoughts turned to the days ahead. They would soon cross into Scotland. Would Malcolm's army be waiting for them or, as the king had suggested, must they lay siege to Malcolm's fortress at Dun Edin?

$\star \quad \star \quad \star$

Merewyn and Owain rode their horses along the bank of the River Lune, the trees' autumn colors of yellow, gold and red reflected in the waters. Gentle breezes rustled the leaves, causing some to fall.

A golden leaf drifted down to the water, hovered for a moment on the surface, and then was carried away downstream. Soon, all the colored leaves would fall, the trees would be bare and winter would be upon them. She could be like that leaf and allow the flow of her life to carry her and her babe back to Wales.

Owain might take her.

Would Rhodri and Fia welcome her? Or might they rebuke her for the predicament she had gotten herself into? If she were to bear a child with no father to raise it, she would know her mother's shame. Yet she would have Alex's child to love, mayhap a son that looked like him, and that would be reward enough for loving a man she had known from the beginning could never be hers.

The air was colder than she would have expected for this time of year, but she had worn her woolen cloak and it warmed her.

Owain broke the silence. "When I first arrived, you said you missed Wales."

"Aye. I was many years among your people and I made friends. I could hardly leave and not miss them."

"Do you ever think to return?"

"Yea and recently."

"Your captain, Sir Jamie, thinks me a spy for the Welsh who would throw off the Norman yoke. I have seen it in his eyes. 'Tis true, we wish them gone and, in time, my father, Cadwgan, will see to it. But that is not my purpose in coming. I was speaking the truth when I told your captain I came for you, Merry."

"For me?"

"Yea, I came to bring you back to Wales. Does that surprise you?"

"I suppose it does." She had wanted to leave so that Alex would be free to pursue the future his king intended for him. Here was her chance. She shut her eyes tightly against the painful thought of leaving the father of her child, the man she loved. But it had to be done.

Owain glanced at her from where he sat on his Welsh pony. "I had begun to think of you as always being with us. Your absence did not sit well."

She looked into his dark eyes. What she saw there was different from what she remembered from their time together in Wales.

"There are things you do not know about me, Owain. My beginnings, for one thing. Then, too, much has happened since I left Wales."

"I have known you for many years, Merry. Your beginnings, whatever they were, do not matter to me. I doubt they would matter to my father or Rhodri, should they learn of them." He chuckled. "Even knowing you were English did not matter when Rhodri invited you to train with his archers. You were family to my uncle and you are more to me."

He paused, then continued, looking intently into her eyes. "Whatever may have happened since you left us has not changed you. You are still *fy golau*, my light, and I would take you back to Wales. Should you be willing, I would make you my wife."

His words came as a shock and they changed everything. She had never considered Owain had such feelings for her. Would it be fair to him to allow him to see her to Wales? After all, she loved another and carried that man's child. Mayhap if Owain knew, he might not want to marry her. A prince of Powys must have sons of his own, not those of another. But if he knew the truth and was still willing to take her to Wales, she and her babe might find a new life there. She needed to think of what she could say, how to tell him.

"I must have time, Owain."

"You shall have it," he said. "I will stay until the coming winter forces me to leave. After that, the snow in the mountain passes will make the journey unwise."

"We will talk again before then," she assured him. "But not today."

Her head swiveled toward the river at the sound of beating wings. Hundreds of pink-footed geese rushed through the air to descend on the water. The beating of their wings and the incessant, high-pitched shrieks made conversation impossible.

Drawn from the serious discussion they had been pursuing to the glorious sight, she stared in wonder. The coming of the gray and brown geese with their unusual pink feet was always a magnificent sight. And it reminded her winter would soon be upon them.

"I do love the geese," she shouted over their honking.

"We have them in Wales," he shouted back.

She laughed as they turned to go. Once the geese had settled on the water and quieted, she said, "You may yet persuade me to return to Wales."

That evening, with so many knights and men-at-arms away, Owain was the object of every young woman's attention. The tall Welsh archer with his noble bearing and unusual clothing looked very much the prince he was, handsome in both form and face, but also a warrior. Many at Talisand knew Rhodri and this nephew of his was much talked about.

Lady Serena had been thrilled to welcome Owain to her hall. "You must sit on the dais with my husband and me tonight," she urged. "Rhodri would expect it." It did not matter to their lady that Wales warred with England's Norman king. The bond Serena had forged with the Welsh bard had been a strong one. For Merewyn, too, Wales was a source of happy memories.

Lady Serena waited for Owain's answer and he looked at Merewyn.

" 'Tis an honor to sit with the Lord and Lady of Talisand," she told him. "Go."

Reluctantly, it seemed to Merewyn, Owain took his place beside Alex's father and she returned to the trestle table to sit with Jamie and Lora. Merewyn was glad she had refused Jamie's noble offer to marry her for the sake of the babe. The affection she now saw in Lora's eyes for the captain was its own reward.

"Your Welsh friend is drawing many admiring glances," said Lora, leaning in to speak in a low voice.

"Aye, Owain is a handsome one."

"And?" Lora raised her brows, waiting for Merewyn to say more. "Why has he come so far?"

"He said he wanted to see Talisand." She could never tell her friends that Owain had come for her, but Lora was perceptive.

"More like, he wanted to see *you*," her friend said, nudging her in the ribs.

"We are merely friends," Merewyn insisted. "He was the one who taught me how to shoot from my pony."

Lora answered her with a suspicious grin. "He does not look at you the way a man looks at a 'mere friend'."

Merewyn let out a sigh and reached for the bread next to their shared trencher. From his seat on the other side of Lora, Jamie shot her a sidelong glance. Merewyn was certain he had overheard the last of Lora's comments and was thankful for his silence. Jamie was the only one at Talisand who knew of the babe and she meant to keep it that way for as long as she could.

★   ★   ★

The messenger's grim expression spoke loudly to Alex, telling him the news was not good. Having already endured a shortage of food and many storm-filled days, the king's army, camped on muddy ground south of Lothian, needed their spirits raised, not lowered.

The king, his brother and the barons had been discussing strategy in William's tent when the man stepped through the opening, removed his hat and bent his knee before the king. Alex, invited to join the discussion, looked on with interest.

"My Lord," the man said with bowed head.

"Rise," said William, his eyes narrowing on the man.

The poor wretch trembled in the face of his monarch, who was obviously impatient. Slowly, the man got to his feet, worrying his hat in his hands. His clothing was ragged and salt-crusted and his jerkin was smeared with mud nearly the same color as his mussed hair.

"Out with it man! What news have you brought us?" Next to the king stood Duke Robert with furrowed brow. Behind William was his chancellor, Robert Bloet, his advisor, Ranulf Flambard, Earl Hugh and Sir Duncan. All bore worried expressions.

"I am one of your seaman, Milord. We was sailin' north of the Tyne when the ships ran aground on the rocks of Coquet Island. 'Twas over so quick, I can still scarce believe it."

"By the face of Lucca!" the king stormed, glaring at the shaking seaman. "Was there foul weather? What cause?"

"Nay, My Lord," the man humbly answered, uncomfortable with the truth he had to convey. "The weather was fair, but the waves were like great mountains, swampin' the ships and forcin' them into each other. The hulls split open and the cargo washed away."

The king's face turned a dark red as he erupted in rage. "My... my ships lost? All... all of them? By God's face, man, how... how can that be? And what of the men?"

The seaman hung his head. "All lost, Milord, save the few of us able to swim ashore."

For a moment, Alex thought the king might draw his sword and sever the man's neck, but Duke Robert interceded, placing a hand on his brother's arm. "William."

Alex watched the king take a deep breath, apparently managing to control his anger before shouting at the seaman, "Go!"

The man scampered out and William turned to face his men. The loss of the ships put a hole in the king's strategy to encircle the Scots as the Conqueror had done. And it meant there would be no supplies. "So," said the king, "we mu... must make do with our army and wha... what food we have with us."

One baron opened his mouth as if to protest.

The king's chin took on a stubborn tilt, his nostrils flared and the sparks in his eyes turned to flint. "We go on!"

It said much for William's determination that he would push on in the face of such dire circumstances. And, at that moment, Alex was proud to be one of his knights.

★　★　★

"Thwack!" The arrow hit the target, but not in the center. Still, it was close enough to be a winning shot for Merewyn's young novice.

Cecily beamed her joy.

"Very good," said Merewyn. "I can see you have been practicing."

Cecily nodded enthusiastically. "I have."

"By the time she is your age," said Owain from where he leaned against a tree, "she will be able to compete well with those of greater experience who also use the shorter bow."

Like most of the Welsh archers she knew, Owain was a master of the longbow. But neither Lady Serena nor Merewyn used the bow that took a strong man's arm to pull the string. She was pleased that Cecily had done so well with her child's weapon. The girl's two friends, envious of her new skill, had recently expressed a renewed desire to begin their own lessons.

"I will win, too!" shouted Cecily.

Owain pulled away from the tree and walked to where the small redhead nocked her next arrow. "Your arm is not in the correct position, imp. I can show you how to improve your form so you will hit the target every time."

Cecily gazed at the Welsh prince in adoration. "I would like that."

Merewyn stifled a laugh. Owain had won the affection of Rory's youngest sister. And, truth be told, he had conquered the hearts of several younger women at Talisand, including Bea and Alice, who vied for his attention each night in the hall.

Watching Owain and Cecily together reminded Merewyn of her first year in Wales. Lady Serena had taught her much, but in Wales, she had come to see she knew little compared to Rhodri's archers. While they also wielded the lance, the Welsh took their archery most seriously. Their longbows were crafted with careful skill, their arrows beautifully made. And they were deadly. Rhodri had over one hundred archers in his personal guard and hundreds more at his command.

If she were to return to Wales, he would have another.

She would have to decide soon. There had been no news from Alex, but she had not expected any. Not until he and his men faced the Scots and sent word of victory or defeat.

Each day, she prayed for his safe return. But even if her prayers were answered, her decision would be the same. She had less than a month to leave, for the child growing within her would make itself known by November when winter would descend with its fury and blanket the mountains with snow.

★   ★   ★

William's army proceeded north, crossing the River Tweed, finally stopping to camp in a Lothian glen. Hunger gnawed at Alex's stomach as he stood on a crest looking north, the wind blowing his hair and cloak behind him. Vast untamed hills stretched before him in all directions. In the distance, brooding gray storm clouds dropped curtains of rain. He could almost smell the scent of the torrent that would soon be upon them.

The Scottish terrain, like its people, warned intruders not to venture forth. He felt the threat in his bones and shuddered. Not just a warrior's fear before a battle that he had experienced many times. This was the Scots and their wild land challenging William Rufus and his knights as they had the Conqueror.

Having lost the supply ships to the sea and with the unexpectedly harsh weather descending upon them, William's men often huddled around the night fires still hungry. The king's stubborn determination had brought them this far. But what now?

Alex wanted to put the battle behind him so he could go home, but he knew it would not be so easy as that. The time it had taken William to raise his army had given Malcolm months to prepare. And they would now be fighting the Scots on their own land.

The next morning, Sir Nigel came to Alex's tent. "Would you take a few of your men and go with me to scout out the land? William wants to know if Malcolm's army draws nigh."

Alex nodded and mounted Azor as Rory and Guy swung into their saddles. The three of them followed Sir Nigel and two of his men north toward Dun Edin. Cresting one hill, they looked into the distance beyond the valley below and saw thousands of mounted warriors riding in their direction, covering the ground like a cloud of dust.

"We have what we came for, lads," said Sir Nigel. Turning his horse, he shouted, "Make haste to the king!"

They galloped toward the glen where William's army was holed up. Soon, they were inside the king's tent, where the tension hung thick in the air.

"Well?" demanded William of Sir Nigel. "Did you see Malcolm's army?"

"Aye, My Lord. He leads an army to match ours, possibly more numerous, and they are not far."

"Since we know of them," offered Alex, "we must assume they are aware of us."

Duke Robert, his dark eyes and hair a contrast to his younger brother, stepped forward. "Our father agreed to terms with the Scottish king and Malcolm once swore loyalty to me as well. We could seek terms now. Should you agree, William, I would ride to meet him and ask for his fealty on your behalf."

"What terms?" demanded William.

"The same terms he gave our father."

William huffed his displeasure. Clearly unhappy to be considering a negotiation rather than a battle, his hand moved to his sword hilt, and his fingers flexed over it, itching for action. "I will give you leave to try. Take Duncan, Malcolm's son, and Sir Alex with you." Then to Alex, he said, "Your uncle is one of Malcolm's chiefs, is he not?"

"Aye," said Alex. "Steinar is Mormaer of the Vale of Leven."

Duncan came forward and nodded his willingness to try to convince his father to agree to terms. "I, too, met Steinar long ago. He is a good man, a Northumbrian, loyal to my father."

And so it was that Alex, along with Duke Robert, who had known Malcolm for years, and Sir Duncan, Malcolm's son, rode out alone to meet the King of Scots and his army.

CHAPTER 12

Merewyn glanced at the yellow leaf blowing in the wind, adjusted her aim accordingly, and pulled back the string, focusing her eyes on the distant target, before loosing the arrow. It flew across the field to land with a resounding "thwack" in the center of the target.

Cecily and her two companions, watching from where they sat on their favorite rock, clapped their hands with glee. Merewyn paused to give them some advice on shooting when the wind was up and how difficult it could be to hit the target if they did not account for it.

Owain tossed Merewyn a smirk, stepped to the line and carefully took aim. With his greater strength, he brought the string of his longbow back to his chin and released his arrow in one smooth stroke. In a "whoosh", it flew through the air and split her arrow.

The three children stared in wonder.

"Now you are making a show of it," chided Merewyn, but she tossed him a smile. She had seen him split an arrow once before in Wales. Not many archers could match the feat.

"For your benefit, aye," Owain said, his smirk back.

He had taken to spending his afternoons with her on the archery field. The archers that remained behind when Alex had gone to meet the king seemed to accept her Welsh friend, often admiring his skill. But Merewyn had observed them watching Owain closely whenever he went off by himself. She suspected one of them followed, mayhap on the orders of Talisand's lord.

Owain was never without his weapons. Even when he shot arrows from his horse, his wicked axe hung from his hip, an intimidating sight.

October was nearly gone when Owain began pressing Merewyn to leave Talisand. He was right in thinking they could delay no longer. And why should she not go? Would it not be best if she were gone when Alex returned? She had not yet felt the child moving in her belly, but she was keenly aware it was growing. Her body was changing, her breasts swelling. She often thought of the babe's father. Her mother had to bear alone the child of a man she abhorred and, while Merewyn might be alone, she would bear the child of the man she loved.

With her palm on her belly, she would sometimes speak to their child as she lay in bed or was alone in her chamber. This afternoon as she changed into a gown for supper, she told the babe, "Your father will live, do not doubt it, young wolf."

That evening, after supper, she and Owain played chess in one corner of the hall. With Alex and his men gone and no news from Northumbria, most evenings the mood of those gathered was somber. Everyone waited for news. Maugris had told Lady Serena her son would return, but he did not say he would be without a wound.

This night, a minstrel played his lute softly as the candles burned and men played games on the trestle tables. Lady Serena and Lora stitched by the hearth fire. Bea and Alice had returned to their homes with their parents. There had been no dancing. Any celebrations would have to await the return of Talisand's men.

She looked at Owain across the board as she considered her next move. He was a good chess player, though not as good as Rhodri or Alex. Still, his skillful moves sometimes required her to consider carefully what she would do next. She returned her attention to the board and reached for one of her knights when he said, "'Tis time, Merewyn."

She met his dark gaze. "Have I delayed my move overly long?"

"I do not speak of chess. We must be on our way."

"Tomorrow, Owain. I will give you my answer tomorrow."

He dipped his head. "As you wish, but I believe you will be going with me, so prepare."

The next morning, Merewyn rose early, dressed warmly and walked through the village, heading toward the stone church. There was a chapel in the castle, but she rarely went there. She preferred the stone church set amidst the oak trees with its weather-beaten doors and small arched windows. It was the only stone structure in Talisand and Lady Serena had told her it had given the old thegn much pride to build it.

As she entered through one open door, her attention was drawn to the walls, painted in bright red, blue and yellow, depicting scenes from the Bible that reminded the people of their faith. One wall depicted the seven deadly sins she had been warned about as a child.

"Did you come to see me, my child?"

She turned to see Father Bernard standing behind her, his white hair and well-trimmed beard rising above his gray cowl robe. "I was hoping you might pray with me... for Sir Alex and his men."

"Of course. We will kneel together."

The priest's words comforted her as he asked God to protect Talisand's warriors who rode with the king. And he prayed for peace in the land that had known so much war.

When she got to her feet, she felt much relieved. "Thank you, Father."

"I am always here, my child."

Outside, she pulled her cloak tightly around her against the wind and tugged her hood over her head. Hunched down as she walked, she nearly ran into Maugris.

"Oh!" She gave a start, looking up. "Please forgive me."

"It is nothing, Mistress Merewyn. You come from the chapel?"

"Yea."

"That is good. You do well to seek direction from the Master of the Heavens."

"I was praying for protection for Sir Alex and his men. We have heard nothing."

"Ah," he said, nodding. "That, too, is needful. Few wounds are as painful as those of the heart."

"Is Alex wounded?" she asked, concerned.

"Should he return and find you gone, I have no doubt he will be," the old man said. "Your future is here, Merewyn. I have seen it." Without another word, he bowed and took his leave.

175

Merewyn watched the old man go, his dark gray cloak blowing out behind him. He did not try and stop her from leaving. But the stab of sorrow she experienced at the prospect of causing Alex pain was enough to give her pause. Mayhap she had been wrong to consider returning to Wales and wrong about the depth of Alex's feelings for her. Should she stay no matter the consequences?

★   ★   ★

Alex peered into the distance of the Lothian countryside, a mélange of colors, wide swaths of green bordered by stands of trees still bearing the autumn colors of gold and yellow. He rode with Duke Robert and Sir Duncan, heading north toward the Firth of Forth.

King Malcolm must have been warned of their approach because three riders emerged from a copse of trees to appear before them.

Alex had never met the King of Scots, but there was no doubt the imposing figure riding the white charger with his scarlet cloak thrown back from his broad, mail-clad shoulders and his dark hair and beard beneath his helm encircled by a gold crown was the man they had come to see.

Two other men flanked the King of Scots, both warriors by their appearance, garbed in mail and helm and wearing both swords and long knives at their belts.

As the three drew close, Alex could see Malcolm was no longer young, but his weathered face bore the proud look of the warrior king Alex had heard so much about. He had led his people for decades, outliving the Conqueror. He had the air of a man confident in his abilities, a king worthy of being followed.

Malcolm's long legs suggested he possessed a height not shared by either Duke Robert or England's king, both of whom were men of small stature. When standing, the Scottish king would tower over them.

On King Malcolm's right, rode a man Alex had never met, but who had to be his Uncle Steinar from his resemblance to Alex's mother. Once they arrived in front of him, Alex glimpsed his mother's violet eyes. Forced to flee England as a rebel, fighting against the Conqueror, Steinar had been welcomed in Scotland where his fortunes had risen. He now appeared more a Scot than an Englishman, his blond hair long with small plaits on the sides. On his face, both a mustache and a small beard.

On the king's other side rode Edgar Ætheling, the fair-haired brother of Malcolm's Saxon queen, who Alex knew from his time in Normandy. He had been correct in thinking Edgar had gone home to Scotland.

"Robert, my old friend," said Malcolm, his gaze briefly resting on the duke and then Alex before alighting on Duncan. "You bring my son to me?"

Robert smiled graciously and Alex understood the wisdom of sending the duke to bargain with Malcolm. "The King of Scots knows well why I am here. It is true your son, Duncan, has come with me. I also bring the nephew of your chief, Steinar." He gestured to Alex. "Sir Alexander of Talisand. For what we have to discuss, 'tis best we are among those we trust, no?"

Steinar dipped his head to Alex, acknowledging his presence, and Alex nodded in return.

"Welcome to Scotland, nephew of my mormaer," said Malcolm to Alex. Then facing Duncan, the king smiled. "It has been long since my eyes have seen you, my son. I trust you have remembered all we spoke of when last we parted."

"I have, Father." Duncan's words brought to Alex's mind his conversation with Duncan in which he had said his father expected him one day to reign over the Scots.

"Well," said Robert, "now that we have made the necessary introductions, is there somewhere we can share a cup of wine and talk? My mission is to avoid war, if 'tis possible."

"My tent is not far," said Malcolm. "We can talk there. You have my word you will be unharmed."

Duke Robert rode beside King Malcolm and Duncan paired with Edgar, who he apparently knew, leaving Alex to ride beside his uncle.

They followed the others until they came to a wide glen. Well protected on a rise, Malcolm's army stretched as far as the eye could see. Alex took in the field of white tents and many horses. As they rode into the Scots' camp, fierce-looking mail-clad warriors with long hair and beards stared at them with narrowed eyes. At their waists were belted swords but many knives and a few axes were visible, as well.

The threat of violence lay thick in the air.

One of the Scots, a rough bearded warrior, wore across his chest two thick leather straps bearing two knives. He waited until his king passed, then he spit on the ground as Alex crossed in front of him as if the very dirt was tainted by a Norman's presence. Others jutted out their chests, as if begging for a fight. Alex had been right in thinking the Scots had time to prepare. They were armed, confident and, no doubt, well-fed, whereas William's men were weary and hungry.

Alex did not shy from their hostile looks but turned his face ahead. Unlike William, Malcolm was a man of his word. They would not be attacked in the Scots' camp.

"You have the look of your father," said Steinar, drawing his attention from the warriors around him.

"I have been told that since I was young," Alex replied.

Steinar chuckled. "You are still young."

Alex gave his uncle a sidelong glance. By now, Steinar was in his fourth decade, a proven warrior trusted by the Scottish king and a member of the Scottish nobility, the rank of mormaer being the same as an English earl.

"Scotland has been good to you," Alex remarked.

"Aye, it has. My sister, Serena, how does she fare?"

"She is well, the Lady of Talisand, mother of four sons and loved by her Norman husband."

"I saw that for myself before I left. You were just a wee babe then. Rhodri has brought me news over the years so I knew of my other nephews. Do you know the Welshman I call friend?"

"Aye, but since the trouble between England and Wales, Rhodri comes less often to Talisand."

Steinar stared off into the distance as if contemplating the past.

"Do you miss your home?" Alex asked him.

"I miss my sister and the people I knew there, but I no longer think of Talisand as home. Scotland has been my home for more than a score of years. It was here I gained lands of my own, here I met my wife, Catriona, and here my children were born."

"Do I have many cousins?"

He laughed. "Aye. We adopted an orphan to begin. Then, like my sister, we lost a girl child at birth, but after that, God gave us five sons."

"A large family. I wish I could meet them." In truth, Alex would never know them, at least not as long as their kings chose war over peace.

They reached the center of the Scots' camp. Malcolm's army bowed their heads as their king passed. Reining in his white charger in front of the largest tent, Malcolm dismounted and handed the reins to a squire. A guard held open the tent flap for the king to enter.

Once inside, Alex was struck by how sparsely it was furnished: two pallets on one side of the tent and a table with benches on each of its four sides in the center. But then, a warrior king prepared for battle would not indulge in opulence.

Malcolm removed his helm and cloak and handed them to a waiting servant. Then he beckoned Duke Robert to sit. The king and the duke faced each other across the table. The servant, who had been awaiting his master's signal, came forward and poured the two men cups of red wine. Alex and Duncan stood behind the duke and Steinar and Edgar behind Malcolm.

"Your king is not here," Malcolm observed, taking a drink of his wine.

"I act for my brother in this," affirmed Duke Robert, lifting his cup to his mouth.

Malcolm set down his cup. "He is no fool to send you, the only man to whom I am obligated. I owe William nothing and since he expelled Edgar from Normandy, I hold him in no high regard."

"That was unfortunate."

Alex glanced at Edgar, standing behind his brother-in-law, the King of Scots. The Conqueror had robbed Edgar of England's crown and, fearing the Ætheling's popularity, forced him to leave Scotland where his brother-in-law could aid his cause. Then the Conqueror's son had taken from Edgar the lands in Normandy granted by Robert. Edgar was a man wronged by two Norman kings, unable to gain a foothold anywhere. And yet, he still had the look of a Saxon prince.

Robert took a deep breath, mayhap preparing for what would be a difficult negotiation. "You once agreed to terms with my father," the duke reminded the Scottish king, "pledging your fealty to him for your lands in England. Will you not do so again, to the king who is the

Conqueror's son?"

"Why should I?" questioned Malcolm. "You have seen my army and you stand on Scotland's soil. I am aware William's ships were lost off Northumbria. And, besides all that, England's current king is not known to be a man of his word."

Robert ignored the criticism of his brother. All knew William disregarded his vows when it suited him, even his vows to the church. "I cannot find fault with anything you say, but consider this: It would spare both Scotland and England a war. And your pledge need not be unconditional."

Malcolm leaned forward, his dark gaze penetrating. "Explain."

"It need only concern your lands in England. William likes not your intrusions into Northumbria—"

"Northumbria is Scotland's!" Malcolm insisted, his fist pounding the table.

"At the least," Robert calmly replied, "it is disputed. Were you to agree to cease from taunting William by raiding Northumbria, my brother would assure you of all that you held under our father: twelve villages in England. And to that he would add twelve marks of gold a year."

Knowing William as he did, Alex doubted Malcolm would ever see that gold, but he was pleased the discussion continued. Despite Malcolm's strong words, Alex believed neither side wanted a battle.

In the end, after much blustering and back-and-forth, once Robert agreed to reconcile William and Edgar and see that Edgar's lands in Normandy were restored to him, an agreement was reached.

The next day, the King of Scots appeared before William, giving the same promises he had made to the Conqueror and confirming the obligation with an oath. Alex could see by Malcolm's expression, it was a distasteful thing to bind himself to a Norman king. And, by his dark glare whenever he glanced at William, it was clear Malcolm mistrusted William in particular.

Before the Scots left the meeting place to head north, Steinar handed Alex a sealed parchment. "For Serena."

Alex nodded and placed the message beneath his mail, relieved the negotiations had been successful and he did not have to fight his way out of the Scots' camp. "I am glad to have finally met you, Uncle. Mayhap one day I will see those cousins of mine."

"And one day I might see my other nephews," returned Steinar.

Alex turned Azor south, riding with William Rufus and accompanied by both Edgar and Duncan. Edgar, now hopeful of regaining his lands in Normandy, rode beside Duke Robert.

Duncan had told Alex he must return to England for he would one day need William's support to claim Malcolm's throne. What King Malcolm thought of the choices of his brother-in-law and his eldest son, Alex could only guess.

"He will understand," Edgar assured Alex.

Alex had not had the chance to wield his sword against the Scots, but he was not disappointed. He could return to Talisand with good news for his mother about her brother. And he would be home before winter. The only fire he wanted to sit beside this winter was one he shared with Merewyn.

★ ★ ★

"I cannot go with you," Merewyn told a disgruntled Owain. She had thought and prayed about it and considered Maugris' words. Even if it brought her shame, she could not let Alex return and find her gone. Maugris had said it would cause him pain. And so she had agreed to meet Owain at the river's edge to try and make him understand.

"Why not? Why would you want to stay when I have sensed you are unhappy here?"

His mood had turned angry. Owain did not understand the source of her unhappiness. She was not unhappy with Talisand only with the truth that she loved Alex but could not call him hers. Because she had hurt Owain by refusing him, she owed him an explanation. "I said we would talk and now the time has come."

They were standing on the bank of the river some distance from the palisade and the village. The afternoon was chill as it had been this morning when she'd gone to see Father Bernard. Drawing her woolen cloak around her, she took a seat on a fallen log and Owain dropped down beside her, his long legs stretched out before him, his gaze intent upon her.

"Owain, I cannot go with you because I love another."

His brows furrowed. "Who? I have seen you with no other."

" 'Tis the son of the Red Wolf, Sir Alex."

He paused to consider for only a moment. "The eldest son who is away on the Norman king's business?"

"Aye."

"Do you expect he will wed you?"

"He has said... Nay, it can never be. The king has chosen another woman he would have Alex marry. But it does not seem right to leave now. I carry Alex's child and only learned of it after he had gone. He knows naught of it."

His cheeks reddened and his brows drew together, his nostrils flaring in anger. "This knight has seduced you?"

She did not want to discuss what happened between her and Alex but she could not allow Owain to think the worst of him. "Nay, Owain," she said, meeting his disquieting gaze. "He did not."

"I see. You carry his child but he will not have you for your lowborn status. Can you really be that foolish to love such a man? I care not that you may have agreed to lie with him, Merewyn. You were innocent and he took advantage. How can you stay to face the shame of a fallen woman when in Wales you could be the wife of a prince?"

She remembered the seven sins vividly portrayed on the walls of the stone church. Which had been hers? Surely not lust. Nay, it was love. And that was no sin. The vow she had spoken to Alex had been sincere. *I would have you be mine.*

Owain believed he was doing right by her, but a marriage should be based upon more. If she could not have the man she loved, she would have no one.

He leapt to his feet and grabbed her arm, wrapping his fingers tightly around her sleeve. "Come, we are leaving."

"But Owain, I told you I would not go!"

His jaw was set, his eyes dark pools. "I know what you said, but in time, you will see, I am the one who cares for you. I am the one who is looking out for your welfare. Not him."

He pulled her along behind him toward a copse of oak trees. For the sake of the babe, she did not struggle. Owain was so much stronger than she was it would have availed her little.

They arrived in the copse where Ceinder stood saddled next to his pony. "You were planning to take me to Wales were I willing or no?"

"I did not intend to leave without you," he said, quickly tying her wrists together and lifting her to the pony's back. Gathering up Ceinder's reins, he mounted his own horse and headed south, leading Merewyn's pony behind him. "I will go slowly for the sake of the babe."

"What about my clothes?" She had worn a simple gown of dark green wool and her heavy cloak to meet him, but she had nothing else.

"I have your archer's clothing. You can change whenever you will."

"And my bow?"

"That, too." And then she saw it, tied to the back of his horse. Her bow and her quiver of arrows tied with his. Owain had planned this well. He had spoken truly when he said he had come for her. He had always meant to take her with him when he returned to Wales.

★   ★   ★

"It was probably best William settled on terms," Alex told Rory and Guy when he returned to camp and they were gathered around the fire, chewing on what remained of their dried venison. "The Scots were ready for us. Malcolm's army appeared strong and eager for a fight."

"And William without his ships," said Rory.

"Aye, and little food for his men," Guy put in. Alex shot him a glance, thinking the youngest knight among them was looking rather wane. They had not had a good meal in weeks.

"We leave at dawn for Durham," encouraged Alex. "Mayhap the townspeople will see fit to sell us some of their winter food stores this time."

The king drove his army hard, but none of Alex's men complained as it meant returning sooner to better weather and, hopefully, better provisions.

The barons had not been unhappy to turn away from war. Sir Nigel had told Alex his men were as cold and hungry as the rest of the army.

When they arrived in Durham three days later, the king supped with William de Saint Calais, Bishop of Durham, who had returned to the city in September, the day after William had marched his army north.

Alex had been invited by the king to join Sir Nigel and the barons to hear the old bishop's explanation as to what had happened to the king's ships.

Alex was impressed by the simple manner of Bishop William's attire, his long green robe over white linen and his brown tonsured hair threaded with gray. He was obviously aged but his dark eyes reflected a keen intelligence.

As the men around the table grew quiet, all eyes focused on the bishop. "My understanding," he began, "is that your ships arrived at the mouth of the Tyne a fortnight after you left Durham. With you gone, My Lord, the seamen decided to plunder Tynemouth." The bishop cast a disapproving glance at the king. "They took many goods and precious items. They even robbed an old woman of a cloth she was weaving."

William listened half-heartedly. Alex could tell from the king's restless stirrings that he was growing impatient.

The bishop continued. "The woman appealed to St. Oswin, whose shrine, I suppose you know, is in Tynemouth Priory. The next day the ships ran aground on the rocks of Coquet Island."

"We know the ships ran aground, good bishop," said the king, tapping his fingers on the table.

"What you may not know," said the bishop, "is that the bodies of the seamen and the pilfered goods washed ashore around Tynemouth, the same town your seamen plundered. The people emerged from their hiding places and reclaimed their stolen property. They believe St. Oswin answered the old woman's prayer, granting a miracle and rendering judgment upon your ships. I, for one, cannot disagree."

William's countenance grew troubled, his face turning ruddy as his brows drew together.

Sir Nigel cast a glance at Alex, who took it as a warning that the king's temper was about to loose itself on the bishop. While the king was not a man who accorded much weight to the teachings of the church, he was superstitious.

"By the face of Lucca!" William swore. "The saints dare oppose me?"

The men of the church sitting around the bishop began murmuring to each other. Even Ranulf Flambard expressed concern. He was, after all, a priest, though he seldom acted the part.

Duke Robert shook his head. "A very regrettable incident, but the seamen paid for their rash acts with their lives."

"And I have lost my ships!" William pounded the table and sent a stern glower at the bishop. Then his face turned bright red, making his blond hair appear even lighter, as he rose and stomped from the chamber.

War had been averted and the Scots reined in for the moment, but it was a somber evening in Durham as the barons planned to take their leave.

The king was still in a dour mood the next day, his every word sharp and accompanied by a frown, barking at his barons and his guards for the smallest thing.

Alex waited for a lull in the king's shouted orders in which he could broach the subject of his intention to formally make Merewyn his wife. But given William's current state of mind, he decided to tread carefully, speaking only of his dislike of the choice of Lady Adèle.

"My Lord, might I have a moment of your time?"

Still brooding, William gestured Alex to the side of the large chamber where he had been attending his barons. "What is it?" he snapped.

"Sire, I know you had in mind a match between Vermandois' daughter and me, but I would prefer another."

"Another? You would risk my displeasure by rejecting a Norman bride I have proffered?"

Alex opened his mouth to speak but the king cut him off.

"I must have my lands in Normandy tied to England, sir wolf. Remember that. If you care not for the Lady Adèle, I will find another. But I will see you wed to Normandy. Doubt it not! Now, leave my sight lest I consider you out of favor."

Alex bowed and turned away from the king's wrath. It had not been a good time to try and gain William's approval. Finding Sir Nigel, Earl Hugh and the other barons speaking together, he bid them goodbye. "My men and I are departing for Talisand."

Ranulf Flambard inquired about Merewyn. Alex shrugged him off with a scowl.

"So, the Black Wolf disdains my interest in the girl? You cannot keep them all for yourself, Sir Alex."

"And you cannot have that one at all, Ranulf!"

In reply, Ranulf just laughed.

Relieved to see the back of the king's advisor, Alex and his men turned their horses toward home. A few hours later, they were free of the black mood of the king and sharing the laughter of men who are glad to be alive and returning from the brink of war to the people they love.

Only one face lingered in Alex's mind as he led his men home: A slender archer whose blue-hazel eyes beckoned. To have her by his side, he would find a way to defy his king.

CHAPTER 13

"Where is she?" Alex asked Lora. He had searched the archery field, Merewyn's chamber and the stable. Finally, more than a little annoyed, he had come to the hall. Though it would be hours before the evening meal, he was nearly frenetic.

Lora returned his gaze. In her eyes, he detected unease. "Welcome home, Sir Alex." Then, lowering her eyes, in a soft voice she said, "Merewyn is not here."

His blood began to boil. "What do you mean, 'not here'? Where is she?" he demanded.

She raised her head, her dark eyes full of regret. "She left Talisand yesterday, we believe with Owain. I did not see her go."

It was not a name Alex knew, but it sounded Welsh. "Who is this Owain and why would Merewyn leave Talisand with him?"

Lora's attention shifted to the few servants who were cleaning the tables.

"Come," he said, "we can speak outside." In the bailey, he urged Lora to a more secluded place, scattering chickens as he strode across the hard earth. "Now, tell me who Owain is and what happened."

Brushing a strand of dark hair from her face, Lora took a deep breath and let it out before responding. "While you and the others were gone, a man from Wales came to see Merewyn. Owain is a prince of Powys and nephew to Rhodri. She and Owain were friends in Wales."

"She left with this Owain?"

Lora nodded.

How could she leave me? Did my love mean nothing? He had promised to return, assuming he survived. Why would she not wait for him? Given what they had shared, what they had vowed, he could not understand how she would leave and with another man.

"Tell me about this Welshman. I would know more."

As he and Lora left the bailey and walked toward the river, the wind stirred the dry leaves that had fallen to the path. The days of autumn were dwindling.

He listened as Merewyn's friend described the archer, Rhodri's nephew, who had taught her to shoot from her pony.

"Did she have tender feelings for him?" He had to know but he dreaded the answer.

"As far as I could tell, she considered him only a friend. But I think he would have her be more. I could see it in the way he looked at her. Some of the men believed him a spy for the Welsh, but he asked no questions about the men, where you had gone or the king's plans. He spent all of his time with Merewyn, even helping her teach the children archery."

"She said nothing to you about leaving?"

Lora shook her head. "Nay."

"But you are her good friend!"

"I do not understand it myself, Alex. It came as a complete surprise. You might ask Jamie about Owain. I think they had a conversation or two. In your absence, Jamie was very protective of Merewyn. He was not pleased when he discovered she was gone."

Alex took his mail to the armory and washed the dirt from his face. He'd been covered with more dirt than he realized. Donning a fresh tunic, he went looking for his father's captain. He found him in the practice yard sparring with one of the house knights. When the match ended, Alex signaled to Jamie, who sheathed his sword and came toward him.

Jamie ran his fingers through his curly hair and wiped the sweat from his brow. "I had heard you and the men were back and the king has made peace with the Scots. A good result."

" 'Tis true, but not why I have sought you out." Alex was impatient to glean as much information as he could about the woman he had thought of every day he was gone. "Lora said Merewyn has left with some Welshman. Do you know anything of it?"

He hesitated before answering. "A bit." Folding his arms over his chest, Jamie said, "He arrived one day about a fortnight after you left. I am certain Merewyn did not expect him, but she seemed quite happy to see him. She knew him from her time in Wales."

"That much I have already ascertained."

Jamie's blue eyes were in earnest. "He said he came for her. Told me that when I questioned his purpose in being here."

"And while he was among you… What passed between them?"

The captain uncrossed his arms and again ran his hand through his hair. "They practiced archery in the afternoons, played chess in the evenings and I occasionally saw them riding their ponies together. He has one much like hers, only gray."

"Did she say anything about leaving with him?"

"I do not think so. Certainly not to me. Last night at the evening meal, your lady mother noted Merewyn's absence and asked about her. No one knew where Merewyn was and a search disclosed she was not among us. Then we realized Owain was gone, too, and both their ponies were missing from the stable."

Alex frowned, speaking his thoughts aloud. "I cannot believe she would leave without saying goodbye to my mother and her friend, Lora." *Or to me.* "Merewyn has made a life here. Why would she go back to Wales?"

"I doubt she would want me to tell you, but I believe she left for you."

"For me?" he asked, incredulous. "Why, when I want her to stay?"

"Because she believed you might be tempted to disobey King William if she stayed. The affection between you two was clear to all who had seen you together."

"I will not wed the woman William has chosen for me," Alex said forcefully.

"Would you defy your king to wed Merewyn, a Norman's bastard?"

"Do not call her that! She had no choice in the matter of her birth. And, yes, I would defy William to have her." *I have defied my king to have her.*

Jamie smiled. "The wolf defends his chosen mate. I am glad to see it."

Alex scowled, impatient to be going. "I must find her." The wind stirred in the trees, drawing his attention to the branches half-bared of leaves. Soon the coming winter would prevent him from crossing the mountains of Wales to find her.

"Take Rory and Guy with you," Jamie counseled. "Wales has many archers."

★ ★ ★

Jamie watched as Alex strode back to the hall, his long legs eating up the ground. It was at such moments the son reminded him of the father. He had no doubt Alex had gone to advise Talisand's lord of his plans and would soon be summoning his two friends.

He had provoked Alex enough to reveal his possessive feelings toward Merewyn and yet preserved unbroken his promise to her to say nothing about the babe.

Alex was a strong knight who handled himself well in battle. Mayhap he could reclaim Merewyn without killing the Welsh prince. 'Twould be a good thing because to kill Rhodri's nephew would be messy and neither Lady Serena nor Merewyn would like it.

Merewyn's leaving without saying goodbye had dismayed Lora and concerned Lady Serena. Both were women close to Jamie's heart. One was like an older sister, having raised him after he'd lost both his parents. And the other he intended to make his wife. Merewyn loved both of them. Leaving Talisand without saying a word was not something she would have done, which caused him to wonder, had she gone willingly?

★ ★ ★

The day grew colder. The sky turned a pale gray, hovering, it seemed, just above her head as Merewyn reached up with both hands, her wrists still tied together, and pulled her hood down farther over her head. She huddled beneath the woolen cloak, a gift from Lady Serena. Made from the wool of Talisand's sheep, it would keep her warm even in the snow

190

she believed would fall before they arrived in Wales.

It was not unknown for snow to fall at the end of October. She remembered once when it had descended on Talisand at that time. The sheep had stood in the meadow looking perplexed, blinking the white flakes from their eyes, as she and Lora, then young girls, had erupted in laughter.

What must Lora think of her sudden departure? And Lady Serena? Surely they knew her well enough to believe she would never leave without some word of explanation. But they had seen her with Owain and must be wondering. She did not want them to worry. And what would Alex think? Had he returned by now? Was he hale and whole? She had once thought to leave before he returned but now she saw how wrong that would have been.

She peeked out of her hood to see Owain riding in front of her on his gray pony. He, too, had donned a cloak, brown like his hair and most of his clothing.

She was relieved that he had not pressed her to ride long days or at a great pace. She did not fear for the babe. Serena had always ridden into the early months of carrying a child, but in the afternoons, Merewyn sometimes felt queasy until she had nibbled on some bread. The frequent stops Owain made had allowed her the time she needed to eat and relieve herself and, for that, she was grateful.

"You have been kind, Owain."

He looked at her over his shoulder. "And why would I not be kind to the woman I expect to marry?"

"Owain..."

"I know what you have said, but the passage of time may change your thinking on the matter."

When the path widened, he pulled Ceinder's reins, drawing her nearer so that they rode abreast.

"We would do well together, you and I," he said. "Rhodri and Fia would be pleased were I to take you as my wife. I would raise the child as my own, of that you need have no concern."

She inclined her head to glimpse his mouth, twitching up in a grin.

"In time," he said, "you might even learn to love me."

Merewyn was not at all convinced one could "learn to love" someone, particularly when she had given her heart to another, but she was comforted in the knowledge that Owain did not mean her ill. He might have forced her to leave Talisand, but she did not think he would force her to his bed. He had not even tried to kiss her. But his long lingering looks told her he wanted to.

"Where will we seek shelter this night?" she asked. They had made camp in the woods the night before but the weather had been more favorable then.

"I know a place. 'Tis not far."

★   ★   ★

By the time the horses were rested and fed and Alex had packed a few things he would need, Rory and Guy had returned to the hall and people were gathering for the evening meal. He had told his mother of his plan to go after Merewyn and thus any feast should be delayed. Maggie had urged them to eat, even ordering the servants to bring their food to the table early.

Alex was anxious to be going. Only a few hours of daylight re-mained.

When he told his father of his intention to bring Merewyn back, the reply had been terse. "I see. Well, best be about it then."

The meal was served and, having been nearly starved for a month, Alex and his fellow knights dove into their trenchers piled high with salmon and roast duck.

"Eat hearty, lads," said Maggie coming to their table. "Ye look like half o' yerselves."

Alex smiled up at her. The kindhearted housekeeper worried over them like a mother hen. Rory might be her grandson, but she had coddled the three of them since the day they were born.

He was enjoying the taste of home and the enticing smells of the roast duck and the herbs rising from the salmon, but all the while he ate, he kept thinking of Merewyn suffering the cold night as she traveled the same road they had taken to Chester. What did she have to eat and where did she stay? He hoped this Owain was a noble sort, else Alex would carve out his heart, no matter he was Rhodri's nephew.

Alex had wanted to depart after they finished the meal but in between bites, Rory argued they should leave on the morrow. "They will stop for the night and so must we."

"Aye," Alex conceded. " 'Tis probably best to ride with the dawn when we can see the path before us."

"I agree," put in Guy, washing the last of his duck down with his wine. "I like not riding over rough ground when 'tis dark. We did enough of that with William and the only result was some lame horses."

Alex was glad his companions had been willing to go to Wales, given they had only just returned home and there was great risk because of the animosity between the two countries. He wanted Merewyn back, safe in his arms. If they rode fast, he might be able to catch up with Owain before he took Merewyn over the Welsh Marches. Once in Wales, three Norman knights would be an easy target, dead before he could say his family was friend to Rhodri. Facing one skilled longbowman was enough. He had no desire to face hundreds.

"All right," he reluctantly agreed, "but we leave at first light."

★   ★   ★

They were not far from Chester when Owain pulled rein and turned to face her. "We will stop here. There's a stream just over there where we can water the horses." He came and lifted her down from her pony and untied her hands, which he always did when she needed to drink, eat or relieve herself. She had changed to her archer's clothing the first night because the clothing was more comfortable and less unwieldy.

It was the same trip Merewyn had made in the summer with Lady Serena, Alex and the others, but now the days seemed much longer. She was weary and cold. Owain had told her they would not enter Chester but would cross *Afon Dyfrdwy*, the Welsh name for the River Dee, at a point west of the city.

Determined to wash the dirt from her face, she walked with Owain to the stream where he led the horses. As Ceinder drank, Merewyn bent down on one knee, threw back her hood and scooped water in her hands, splashing it onto her face. The water refreshed her. She lifted another handful to her mouth to drink.

Her mind raced with thoughts of what was to come. They would soon be in Wales. Would Rhodri bring her back to Talisand if she asked?

He had done so once before when war threatened. Mayhap he would do so again. At the very least, she could send Alex a message.

She rose from the ground, brushed the loose dirt from her cloak and walked to Ceinder. Stroking the pony's neck, she said, "You have done well, my friend." The mare raised her head and nuzzled Merewyn's hand. "I've no oats for you, but soon."

Owain stood nearby watching his pony drink, one hand on his bow tied to his saddle next to hers. "Come here and I will retie your hands. It won't be long until we leave the road for Wales and then 'tis just a few days to my home."

"You are taking me to your home, not Rhodri's?" she asked, startled by the news.

Before he could answer, a familiar voice caused her to whip her head around to peer into the dense growth of alder trees some distance away. "You take what is mine, Welshman! Let her go."

Alex! She thrilled to hear his voice, to know he was here, but how had he found her?

Owain grabbed his bow and two arrows and shoved her behind him. "Who speaks?" he asked, his eyes narrowed on the woods as he nocked the first arrow.

Alex stepped from the trees. "Alexander of Talisand. I come for Merewyn."

Merewyn's heart leapt to her throat. He was here! He was alive and, to all appearances, whole. *Oh, Alex.*

"Ah, the Red Wolf's cub," Owain said, holding his bow before him, his fingers on the string. "You shall not have her. You do not deserve her. I am taking her to Wales where she will become my wife."

"That would be rather difficult," Alex said, tossing Merewyn one of his rare smiles. "I may not deserve her, but she is already my wife and what I claim, I keep. She will never be yours."

Merewyn inhaled sharply, shocked by his words. Did he say them to convince Owain to let her go?

"You lie, Norman!" Owain spit out.

Alex drew his sword, the sound of the steel sliding from the sheath loud in her ears. He stepped forward, his sword grasped firmly in his hand. He must look this way in battle as he confronted the enemy, his stance sure, his sword raised and his dark presence threatening.

Owain did not wait for him to lunge. He pulled back the string and loosed the arrow. It hissed through the air and sank into the calf of Alex's right leg. Alex stumbled back but did not fall.

"Alex!" she screamed, starting toward him.

Owain held her back with his arm.

She pushed at him. "You shot him!"

Alex staggered. From his mouth came a feral snarl, a sound more like an animal than a man. His gray eyes became like shards of granite as he glared at Owain. "Have you never heard, Welshman, a wounded wolf is more dangerous? I asked you to give me what is mine. Now I will kill you before I take her."

While the men faced each other, Merewyn sped the few feet to Owain's pony and reclaimed her bow.

Owain nocked another arrow and took aim.

Merewyn, too, nocked an arrow and swiftly drew alongside the two men, separated by a dozen feet, lifted her bow and pulled back the string. "Both of you stop!"

The two men turned their harsh looks from each other to her.

"Owain, you will not loose another arrow. Alex, you will let Owain go. He meant me no harm."

Alex gave her an angry, incredulous look, but he held his sword still. Blood dripped from his leg. Her chest heaved for the panic she experienced. The arrow could mean his death.

"Owain, go!" she shouted.

Owain looked at her with disdain. "You would choose to stay with this Norman dog, who would plant a babe in your belly yet offer you no ring for your finger?"

"It is my decision to make, Owain. Wales is not far. Leave us." When he failed to move, she added, "Please!" Her unwavering gaze met Owain's angry brown eyes. "Go!"

Owain slung his bow over his shoulder and swung onto the back of his pony. "Only because you ask it of me, Merewyn. But should you change your mind, you have only to send for me and I will come." With that, he shot another glare at Alex, turned his pony and galloped away.

She ran to Alex and kissed him. With his free arm he drew her to his side. She looked down to see the arrow had gone through his leg, the tip sticking out the back of his calf. "You must have care. Let me help you." She placed her shoulder under his left arm and leaning on her, he was able to sheathe his sword.

"What was that about a babe in your belly?" he gritted out, wincing with the pain, as he tilted his head toward her.

"Can we come out now?" said a voice she recognized as Rory's. The redheaded knight stepped out of the trees. Beside him stood Guy. Both were wearing mail, their swords drawn.

Alex's gaze shifted to his companions. "Aye. Might as well join us. You can see I have managed to get myself shot and the Welshman got away."

"But you did rescue the fair damsel," said Guy, his mouth twitching up in a grin.

"Aye," said Alex. "My errant wife."

"We need to talk about that, Alex," she whispered. He might have claimed she was his wife for Owain's benefit, but why did he persist in doing so now that Owain was gone?

"You two can talk in Chester," said Rory, sheathing his sword as he walked to where they stood. "Let Guy and me help you to your horse." Bracing Alex under his right shoulder, he said, "It seems we must impose, once again, on Earl Hugh's hospitality."

Guy sheathed his sword and came alongside Alex. Merewyn relinquished her hold.

"First," said Alex, "break off the fletching and pull the arrow through. I would have it out sooner rather than later."

"If you insist," said Rory. "Hold him steady."

With Guy and Merewyn holding him, Rory tore open Alex's hosen and broke off the fletching.

Merewyn kept her eyes on Alex's face. He clenched his jaw and closed his eyes, bracing for what was coming.

Rory pulled the arrow through. Alex grunted, bearing the pain.

"Hold him for a moment while I fetch the horses," said Guy.

Merewyn took Guy's place.

Guy returned with their horses and accepted the weight of Alex from her shoulder.

"We can take him," Rory said to Merewyn and the two of them began to help Alex toward the horses.

"Wait!" They stopped and she tore a strip from the hem of her undertunic and bent to Alex's leg. Placing a wad of cloth against the wound, she wrapped a long length around his leg and tied it tightly. "Mayhap it will staunch the blood."

"My thanks, my lady," said Alex in a weak voice.

With Alex between them, Rory and Guy helped Alex into his saddle, his face contorting with pain as they did. He was growing weaker with the loss of blood. The bandage she had made for him was already leaking the crimson fluid.

Rory helped her mount Ceinder and then he and Guy swung into their saddles and flanked Alex as they rode toward Chester. She thanked God it was only a few miles away.

"Owain was kind," she said to their backs.

"What do you mean?" asked Rory. "He shot Alex. I would hardly call that kind."

"Owain never misses. Had he meant to kill you, Alex, you would be dead. He only wanted to slow your advance."

Alex huffed. " 'Twould have done him no good."

CHAPTER 14

Still in her archer's clothing, Merewyn paced in front of the door to Alex's chamber, chewing nervously on her knuckle, while Countess Ermentrude patiently waited beside her. On the other side of the door, the earl's physic was tending to Alex's leg, which was still bleeding when they arrived at the castle.

Rory and Guy were allowed to stay with Alex, but Merewyn was escorted to the corridor. "I would go in," said Merewyn to the older woman who had been gracious in admitting them to the castle a short time before.

" 'Tis not fitting that you should be in Sir Alex's chamber while the physic examines his wound."

"My friend, Lora, tends all manner of wounds," she argued. "She is more knowledgeable about herbs than anyone at Talisand, save only her mother. Lora often gives the wounded a mixture of hemlock, wormwood and henbane in wine for the pain and to help them sleep."

Lady Ermentrude patted her arm. "Our physic also uses such herbs. Cease your worry. It will not be long now."

A few moments later, the door opened and the physic emerged to speak to the countess. "I have cleaned and bandaged the wound and given him a potion for the pain. He may not long be awake, but you may go in."

"Will he be all right?" Merewyn inquired anxiously.

"Yea, but he needs rest," said the older man. "The wound must not be allowed to mortify."

Merewyn thanked him and hastened through the door with the countess following. Alex's two friends looked at her from where they stood on the far side of the bed. Her eyes were drawn to Alex, who lay with his right leg on top of the cover, his calf wrapped in bandages.

As soon as he saw her, he gave her a faint smile. It was clear he was already feeling the effects of the potion.

She went to sit on the edge of the bed and took his hand. "You look pale. How do you feel?"

"I am told I will survive. 'Tis only a scratch." She knew better, of course, and a quick glance at Rory's troubled countenance confirmed the wound could prove dangerous.

She squeezed Alex's hand. "I do not imagine you will like it, but you are to rest."

Alex shrugged off her counsel and his gaze met that of Lady Ermentrude standing behind her. "Thank you, my lady, for your hospitality."

Lady Ermentrude stepped forward. "I am just glad you were close enough that we could help. Besides, to have three handsome knights and a young woman who plays chess as my guests is an unexpected delight. My children are all on their own and with the earl and his senior knights away, the castle seems empty. Who was it, by the way, who shot you with that arrow?"

"A Welshman, alone in the woods," Alex said, shooting a glance at Merewyn. "I should have been more wary."

On the other side of the bed, Rory and Guy looked down at the floor, saying nothing. Merewyn was relieved Alex and his friends had not named Owain as the one who had wounded Alex, for it would only make him a target of the earl's wrath, already kindled against the Welsh.

"They are not usually so close to Chester," said the countess. "Even now the earl and his cousin are chasing the Welsh deeper into their mountains."

Merewyn despaired at the news that her Welsh friends might be in danger, but she took heart that they were worthy warriors who had successfully fought back the Normans more than once. Mayhap they would again.

"Might I see Merewyn alone for a moment?" Alex asked from his pillow where his eyes had begun to droop.

"Of course," said Ermentrude, promptly shuffling Rory and Guy from the room as she left the chamber.

When they were alone, Alex squeezed her hand. "Is it true? You carry my babe?"

"Aye," she said, suddenly shy. "I only learned of it after you left to meet the king. And then I did not want you to know."

"Why?" he asked, his brows drawing together in a frown, his gray eyes turning flinty.

"Because you might be tempted to defy your king and marry me."

"Ah," he said, laying his head back on the pillow and closing his eyes for a moment. "Jamie said as much."

"Jamie told you?"

He opened his eyes. "He said nothing of a child, only of your concern for my relationship with the king."

"I did think of returning to Wales—"

"I would have come for you just as I did."

"In the end, as Owain made to leave, I realized I could not do it. But he gave me no choice."

"Did he touch you?"

"Nay."

"If he had, I would hunt him down. I was very angry with you until I realized you were his prisoner. Then my anger kindled toward him. Had you not stopped me, I would have killed him."

"I am glad you did not," she said with a small smile. "He wanted to marry me. It was only after I refused to go with him he took me. We have long been friends. To him, you were the villain."

Alex appeared to be succumbing to the potion as his eyes drifted closed. " 'Tis good we are wed," he murmured.

"Nay," she said, shaking her head, "we are not! Why do you say that we are?"

He opened his eyes. They were suddenly serious. "When we returned from London, I consulted Father Bernard to confirm I was right. He told me that we needed only to say it was our desire to belong to each and once the bond was consummated, the marriage was complete."

Merewyn felt her cheeks heat.

"We said the words, Merewyn, and I meant them. Did you?" His black brow was raised in challenge.

She nodded. Nothing could make her deny the truth of what she had told Alex that night in London.

He smiled. "Since you carry my babe, it will be clear to all the marriage has been consummated."

Tears filled her eyes. She wanted it to be true more than all else in the world, but she could not let him do it. "But what of the king? He has already chosen the woman he would have you wed."

"Lady Adèle?"

Reluctantly, she nodded.

"I will not wed her." He smiled, his eyes closing. "I have already wed the woman I want."

"I cannot let you defy your king, Alex. You would only come to hate me if I did."

Alex did not open his eyes. His speech was now slurred. "We will speak of this more when I wake." With that, his hold on her hand loosened and a moment later, he was fast asleep.

★   ★   ★

They did speak of it the next day and much to Alex's increasing frustration, Merewyn did not budge. "What did you think the words we spoke in London meant?" he asked her from his mound of pillows where he lay with his lower leg wrapped in bandages. "I vowed to have you as mine forever and you replied with similar words. I ask you again, did you not mean them?"

She paced in front of him, quite adorable in the gown the countess had given her. "Of course I meant them," she insisted. "But wanting something does not mean you can have it. I have never believed I was worthy of Talisand's heir."

"Now there, you would be wrong. I want no simpering Norman woman with poison in her wine cups."

Merewyn looked at him, shocked. *Poison?* Had the woman really meant to kill her?

202

"Aye, poison. Nay, I prefer a fierce English archer who wears a bowman's clothing."

"You jest."

"A bit, mayhap, but not in my intention toward you, Merewyn. You are mine; I have claimed you in all ways recognized on earth and by God above."

"What of your parents? Even if you do not want Lady Adèle, the king may have another."

"I have done all William has asked of me, yet I never requested a favor. I know him to be generous. Once his anger from the loss of his ships has cooled, he will grant me my heart's desire. And my parents have three other sons to give him for his lands in Normandy. Raoul is off on some quest. Mayhap a boon for his efforts can be a Norman bride."

She gazed down at him, her brows drawn together in apparent frustration. "I cannot persuade you of the folly of wedding a bastard?"

"Never have I liked that byname, though the Conqueror himself bore it for a lifetime. And it will not stop me from making known to all that I have taken you as my wife."

She pressed her lips tightly together as if in protest.

"To prove I am serious," he ventured, "I ask you to bring me my cloak."

"Your cloak?" she asked, confused.

He pointed to the dark blue garment lying across the chest at the foot of the bed.

She picked it up and handed it to him.

He dug into the pouch he'd had a seamstress sew into the cloak in London, his fingers closing on the gold ring. Lifting it from the garment, he reached for her left hand.

Pulling it toward him, he slid the ring on her finger. "I chose this ring for the sapphire that reminds me of your eyes."

She sat down on the bed and stared down at the rounded blue stone set in the band of gold. When she raised her eyes to his, they were filled with tears. "But when?"

"Remember that morning when I came upon you visiting the merchants of London with my mother? Buying fish, as I recall."

"You purchased a ring for me in London?"

"Aye, as soon as the barons' meeting ended, I was off to the gold-smith's stall. When I saw this one, I knew it had to be yours."

"Oh, Alex!" She flung her arms around him and kissed him.

He kissed her back, wrapping his arms around her, pulling her on top of him. He deepened the kiss and slid his hands over her gown, her hips, her buttocks, all the sweet curves he remembered. His groin swelled in response. It had been too long since he had lain with her. Wanting more, he broke the kiss and looked into her beautiful blue-hazel eyes. "Shall we seal our vows once more?"

She smiled up at him from where he cradled her head in the crook of his arm. "What about your leg?"

He brushed the tears from her face. "I am certain, with your help, I can manage."

★　★　★

Two days later, Merewyn had just finished a game of chess with Lady Ermentrude when the countess stifled a yawn. It was late and dinner long concluded. Merewyn sat back, waiting to see if her hostess would play another game. She had replaced her archer's clothing with a lovely rose silk gown, one that had belonged to the countess' daughter. Around her neck on a riband tucked into her gown was Alex's ring. She did not wear it on her finger because she did not wish to explain its sudden appearance to Lady Ermentrude. But knowing she belonged to Alex, that he had decided to make her his wife, was a happy truth that settled deep within her. She only hoped his parents agreed with his decision.

" 'Tis time I retire," said the countess. "Will you stay awhile by the hearth fire or is it time you looked in on your patient?"

"I will bide here for a bit. Rory and Guy are keeping Alex company, each trying to beat him at chess. He claims I only defeated him because of his weakened condition."

"Humph! Even he does not believe that. You are a fine chess player, Merewyn. Sir Alex has always been an arrogant young pup. And his handsome face keeps him so. To lose a game of chess to a beautiful young woman will keep him humble."

Merewyn laughed. She did not think it was possible to keep Alex humble for long. "I thank you for the compliment, my lady. I will check on him before I seek my bed. He wants to leave on the morrow."

"Whenever you think it prudent, my dear." The countess pressed her palms on the table to assist her to stand. " 'Tis late and I am not one for late nights." Ermentrude bid Merewyn a good night and went to the stairs, ascending them slowly.

Merewyn picked up a candle from the table and wandered about the hall, retracing the path the countess had taken when she had shown Merewyn around the castle the day after they arrived.

Peeking into the alcoves behind the tapestries that adorned the castle's main hall, Merewyn made her way around the cavernous room. The weavings displayed beautiful scenes of gardens and animals, likely reflecting the countess' taste. They were so unlike those that hung in the king's hall in London.

Each alcove was sparsely appointed with a small table and bench seats. One held two narrow beds.

As she neared the far corner of the hall, she spotted stairs leading down. She had not noticed them before as they were partially hidden by a wall that extended part way into the room.

On either side of the stairs were copper lanterns hung on sconces. In each lantern burned a small candle. Curious, she decided to see where the stairs led. Still holding her candle, she followed them down to the floor below where she encountered a corridor with many doors. Each door had an iron grate at the top that allowed one to look inside. Before she could look into the first one, she heard the sound of men's voices ahead.

From a door halfway down the corridor came a gruff voice. "Have another cup of wine, Marcel. The castle's asleep and the prisoner is locked away. Why should we stay sober all night guarding an old man in fetters?"

An old man in fetters? The King of Gwynedd?

"Well, mayhap just one more before I leave you to your watch. 'Twill be a cold night."

She must hide! Holding her candle to the grate of the door closest to her and standing on her toes, she peered into the chamber. Sacks of grain and spices filled the room. The smell of cinnamon and cloves was distinct in the air. Quickly she tried the handle and it gave way. Blowing out the candle, she entered and crouched behind one sack, glad for the strong smell of spices that masked the smoke from her snuffed candle.

She waited until she heard the men's heavy footfalls on the stone floor.

"I will see you to the hall as I must pay a trip to the privy before I stand watch for the next hours," spoke the gruff voice.

"With all that wine in my belly, I will join you," said Marcel.

Their voices faded as they ascended the stairs. She took her candle and left the small room. Continuing down the corridor, she found a large chamber some distance from the others. Peering through the grate, she glimpsed a man chained to the wall. Straw had been loosely strewn about the floor.

She no longer had the light of the candle, but the moonlight falling into what she realized was a prisoner's cell revealed a man clothed in a frayed red tunic, chained to the wall. Tall, blond and bearded, he sat on a bench leaning against the stones, his eyes closed. He may have been sleeping, she could not tell.

"Are you Gruffydd ap Cynan?"

The prisoner opened his eyes. "I am." He seemed to study her face for a moment. "Have you come to peer at the earl's prisoner, my lady?"

"Nay, King of Gwynedd. *Fi yw ffrind i ffrind.* I come as the friend of a friend."

He sat up, giving her his full attention. "And who might your friend be?"

"Iorwerth ap Bleddyn, My Lord, though I call him Rhodri."

He struggled to rise from the bench, his chains rattled and he strained against them. In a tone that spoke of hope, he said, "He and his brother, Cadwgan, are my allies."

"I know Cadwgan's son, Owain." She did not tell Gwynedd's king that she had just sent Owain away, rejecting his suit.

"Are you their messenger? Are they here to free me?" the Welsh king inquired.

"Nay. I am alone but if I can, I will free you." Trying the door, she found it locked, a bar across it held firmly in place. "The guard will soon return to his post. What can I do?"

"In the years I have been here," the blond Welshman said, "I have heard the guards speak of keys kept on a hook behind a tapestry in the hall."

"I will find them." She started to go and he called her back. "Beware the guard and the earl's men."

"There is only one guard and he is in the privy. The earl and his men, or most of them, are away."

"Then hurry, for the guard will certainly return."

She set down the candle, turned and ran, racing up the stairs, glad for the lanterns that lit her way. As she neared the top, she slowed, listening. Hearing nothing, she peeked around the corner, her heart pounding. But the guard had not yet returned.

Behind the tapestry closest to the stairs, she found a ring of iron keys she had not noticed before. Carefully, she lifted them from the peg and pressed them close to her body so they would not jingle.

When she returned to the King of Gwynedd's cell, she fumbled in the dim light of the corridor, trying three keys before she was able to locate the one that freed the crossbar. Lifting it, the door opened.

Gruffydd stepped as far away from the wall as his chains allowed. "Good lady, you have done it!"

She hurried to his side and handed him the ring of keys.

In short order he had the fetters unlocked. "Go quickly and I will follow. Speak loudly of the weather should you encounter the guard."

Merewyn picked up the snuffed candle and slowly retraced her steps. As she climbed the stairs, she listened for any sound. But for whatever the reason, the guard did not appear. Then she thought of the hounds she would have expected to see lying about. The earl must have taken them with him. And for that, she was grateful. She was certain the Welsh king would kill any guard or hound that got in his way. After years as the earl's prisoner, she could hardly blame him.

Behind her she heard his faint footfalls.

She froze, seeing someone moving in the hall. A servant woman swept across the large room blowing out candles.

Merewyn stepped into the light. " 'Tis a gloomy night with snow on the way. Might you leave some candles lit?"

The woman of middle years, judging by the face beneath the head cloth, started. "Oh, my lady! Ye gave me a fright. I did not see ye. Are ye alone?"

"Yea, the countess retired. I was just admiring a tapestry, but I am on my way to my chamber now."

"Here," said the servant, lighting Merewyn's candle with one of her own. "Yer candle has gone out. I will return later to snuff the ones we do not keep lit for the night."

Merewyn waited until the woman left the room before turning to face the Welsh king. "There will be guards at the gate and men in the bailey," she whispered. "How will you get past them?"

"Leave that to me. You have done the impossible. What is your name, my lady?"

When she told him, he said, "You have risked much to free me, Merewyn. Be certain Iorwerth will know of this."

Merewyn moved aside, allowing him to go before her. He moved like a shadow, skirting the edge of the hall, before disappearing through the door that led to the kitchens.

Never would she have believed she could free Gwynedd's king imprisoned for so long. She was both excited for what she had done and afraid. What would Alex think of her treachery against Earl Hugh and England's king? But after all Rhodri had done for her, how could she have done otherwise?

*   *   *

Alex had just defeated Guy in a second game of chess when Merewyn opened his chamber door. "Still playing?" she asked.

Her face was flushed as if she'd been running, making her unusual eyes all the more striking. When he looked at her more closely, she averted her eyes. *Now what has she been up to?*

"Alex is having a good night of it," said Guy, beginning to gather the chess pieces off the board. "Took my queen with his rook."

"I was able to beat him once," said Rory, who had been watching their game.

"Want to play?" Alex asked her.

"Nay. I just finished two games with the countess," she said, closing the chamber door. Again, Alex wondered what had left her ivory skin so flushed. Her breathing was more rapid than normal, her chest heaving slightly.

Guy put away the chessboard and set the pieces in their velvet-lined box. Rory rose from the bench he'd been sitting on and stabbed at the coals in the brazier.

"We will come for you at dawn's light," said Rory. "I will make sure the horses are saddled."

"We cannot leave soon enough for me," said Alex. "I am tired of lying about. Besides, I want to be gone before the earl returns. He would only pester us with questions we do not want to answer."

As his friends departed, Merewyn walked to the window. "Do they leave us alone because they believe we are wed?"

"Possibly. I have told them it is so. Or, they might have done it because they know I would wish to be alone with you." The rose gown fit her well, reminding him of the curves beneath the silk that were now his. Her breasts were fuller with the child. He longed to have her join him in the bed, but he sensed she was pondering something.

She opened the shutters, letting a blast of cold air into the room. The fire in the brazier flickered.

"Tell me what you see," he said.

Her face lit like a small child's. "Snow is falling," she said excitedly. "The white flakes make the village appear like a fairy land. It seems lit from within, even though it is night. The last of the castle's servants are leaving through the gate, no doubt heading for their hearth fires." Raising her head, she gazed outward. "The woodland in the distance looks like a sack of flour has been shaken over it."

He studied her profile, the upturned nose, the lips that never failed to entice him and the proud but delicate jaw. There was not another woman in England he would have chosen above her.

She closed the shutters and turned to face him. " 'Tis an early first snow."

"Mayhap the sun will rise tomorrow and melt what remains." He hoped it would be so. "Our travel north will be muddy in any case, but we must go, no matter. I do not care to spend the winter here."

"Nor I," she said.

He held out his hand.

She walked to the bed and took his hand. He pulled her down where he could reach the rest of her. She was chilled from her time at the window. "You are shivering."

"And you are like a great brazier, a warm fire on a cold night," she said, a subtle smile spreading across her face.

He circled her with his arms. "Then let me warm you." He did what he had wanted to do since she entered his chamber and pulled her into his lap. His heart thundered in his chest as he held back the desire to take her hard and fast. She was new to this and there was the child to consider. His child. The thought pleased him greatly.

Gently cupping her face in his hands, he brought her mouth to his and savored the taste of her. Raising his head, he looked into her passion-glazed eyes. "I would take you over and over until you are fevered," he said.

"But your leg!" she softly protested.

"I am certain the pleasure will outweigh the pain."

He turned her so he could unlace her gown. Soon they were naked beneath the cover.

"Loving you is unlike anything I have ever done," he whispered, feeling her breasts against his chest. He pulled her hips against his swelling groin. "Can you feel my body's need to have you?"

She responded by running her hands through his hair, then over his shoulders. "Aye."

He slid his hand between them to the soft nest of hair at the juncture of her thighs. "And can you feel your body is ready for me?"

"Oh, yes, sir knight."

★   ★   ★

The next morning, Merewyn descended the stairs to the sound of men's raised voices. When she reached the bottom of the stairs, she saw guards clustered around the countess.

"Escaped?" Ermentrude asked.

Merewyn cringed. This had been her doing. She had not told Alex the night before that when she looked out the window of his chamber into the snow, she had seen the King of Gwynedd slipping past the guards with the villagers on their way home. She fretted for the concerned countess, but she was glad Gruffydd had got away.

"I do not understand," the countess continued. "How can that be? Was the prisoner not guarded at all times?"

"He was, my lady," insisted a swarthy mail-clad knight. She recognized the voice as the one called Marcel. "But sometime during the night, Sir Drew fell ill and spent some time in the privy. When he was able to return to his post, all seemed well. The prisoner's absence was not discovered until this morning when a servant brought him food."

Merewyn wondered if the man had truly been ill or if this was a story to cover their drinking while serving guard duty.

"The keys?" asked the countess.

"Still on the peg where they are always kept, my lady" said Marcel.

"My husband will not be pleased to hear of it," said Ermentrude. "The man could not simply vanish. He was chained! Do you think someone intentionally made Sir Drew ill?"

"I cannot say, my lady. He will be disciplined for leaving his post, of course."

"You can hardly punish a man for being ill."

Merewyn saw a flicker of relief in the man's eyes. He, too, knew the countess to be kindhearted.

The countess looked up just then and saw Merewyn, who was trying very hard to keep her face calm.

Ermentrude gave some order to the swarthy knight and then came toward her. "I see you wear again the archer's clothing."

Knowing Alex intended to leave, Merewyn had changed her clothing and her hair was confined to one long plait down her back. Over her bowman's attire, she wore her warm winter cloak. She carried her bow and quiver of arrows and the gown she had been wearing when she was taken from Talisand. "You have been kind to us," she said, her guilt niggling at the back of her mind. But she had no regret for freeing King Gruffydd. By treachery he had been captured and by treachery he had been freed.

"It was my pleasure to have you," said the countess. "If you are seeking your companions, they are helping Sir Alex in the bailey. They want to leave before more snow descends upon Chester. I have had the kitchen wrap some food for your travels. The package lies on the table there."

Merewyn retrieved the package of food and walked with the countess to the bailey where Ceinder waited.

Alex was already mounted on his great black stallion and the countess went to stand next to him. "Will you be all right?"

"Fortunately, I am not walking," Alex said. "I am well enough to ride and the pain will keep me awake. I thank you for your kindness."

Merewyn secured the package and her bow and arrows to Ceinder's saddle and mounted.

The countess looked at them with anxious eyes, her face full of worry. "Have a care in the woods. The earl's prisoner escaped last night."

Alex thanked her and soon they were riding out of Chester's gate and crossing the River Dee.

The sun glistened on the newly fallen snow. Where the bright rays fell on the white patches, it had begun to melt. Only the snow lying in the shade of the trees was still unaffected. The horses found their way through the thin white coating left on the path well enough, but it was cold and she drew her cloak around her.

Flicking her plait to her back and pulling her hood over her head, Merewyn eyed Alex, watching his face for signs of pain. He winced whenever his stallion's hooves encountered a rough patch of ground requiring him to brace his right foot in the stirrup, but otherwise, he voiced no complaint. She expected none from a knight who had survived many battles. She had observed the scars on his naked body which, by this time, she was beginning to know well. The wound in his leg was not the first one he had suffered.

They had traveled for what seemed like an hour, riding through the dense conifers in Chester's hunting forest, when suddenly the canopy of trees exploded with the sound of hissing arrows shooting across their path and thudding into the bark of the large trees.

Ambush! Merewyn's heart fled to her throat as she reached out to calm Ceinder. Should they seek to run from the outlaws? She looked to Alex for guidance but he was settling his great stallion as his eyes searched the woods. He drew his sword.

Merewyn pulled her bow from the back of her saddle and nocked an arrow.

Ahead of them, Rory and Guy tightened the reins of their horses to halt them from running. The horses tossed their heads and then stilled under the practiced hands of the knights.

A voice came from a tree in a Welsh accent. "Do not think to charge forward, Normans, or you will find our arrows in your backs. We are many and some of us are ahead of you."

A man's head emerged from the branches above them. His shoulders and arms were attired in the green and brown of a Welsh bowman. "Look lads!" he shouted. "Norman fruit, ripe for the picking!"

From the trees around them she heard other Welshmen respond to their leader. From their voices and what she could see, she guessed there might be a dozen.

Alex moved his stallion close to Ceinder but, surrounded on all sides, there was no way he would be able to shield her. "We only wish to pass," he said to the place where the first bowman had appeared. "We are not among those who fight the Welsh."

"Shall I kill them now?" One of the Welshmen flung the question at an older archer.

"Mayhap," he replied. "A few of Chester's men might be a fitting present for the king's homecoming."

"We do not serve Chester!" insisted Rory.

The first man pulled back his bowstring and took aim at Rory. "But you came from the castle in Chester."

Rory said defiantly, "Welsh dogs!"

Another bowman pulled back the string of his bow.

"*Aros!*" Merewyn screamed. "*Peidiwch â saethu. Yr ydym yn ffrindiau!*" In Welsh, she had told them to wait, that they were friends.

The one with the arrow aimed at Rory paused.

"Friends?" asked the older man in accented English, tossing her a smirk. "That one," pointing to Rory, "calls us 'dogs'. What would you know of our friends, small archer who speaks our tongue?"

"Merewyn, do not—" Alex began, but she cut him off.

"We are from Talisand to the north and friends of Iorwerth ap Bleddyn," she said loudly, not knowing which of them was in charge.

The first bowman stuck his head out of the thick branches overhead, his eyes examining Ceinder and then roving over her tunic and leather jerkin. "You are a woman, yet you ride a Welsh pony and dress like one of us. Who are you?"

"My name is Merewyn," she said. "If you serve the King of Gwynedd, I am known to him."

The leader returned her a disbelieving stare. After a moment, he said, "I know the name." A hasty conversation ensued among the Welsh bowmen in their tongue. She understood they were discussing her and their king, but she did not catch all their words.

With a grand gesture, sweeping his arm down the road, the older one said, "You may go, Merewyn." Then he shouted to the trees ahead, "Allow them to pass!"

Slowly, they rode forward, Merewyn expecting an arrow in her back at any moment, but none came. The archers in the trees did not question their leader's change of attitude but their eyes never left her as she passed in front of them.

Once they were clear of the Welshmen and some distance away, Alex pulled rein and turned to her. "Would you like to explain what exactly happened back there?"

Rory and Guy turned in their saddles waiting for her response.

"Last night I freed Gruffydd ap Cynan, the King of Gwynedd, from a cell in Earl Hugh's castle. Before he took his leave, he asked me for my name."

Alex glared at her, the shock of what she had done clear on his face. "*You* are the cause of all the excitement this morning? *You* set the enemy free?"

"I did. After all, Gruffydd was captured by treachery. Why should he not be freed in the same manner? Besides, he was not my enemy. Given all the Welsh have done for me... and what Rhodri means to Lady Serena and Talisand, it seemed the right thing to do."

Rory and Guy stared at her, open mouthed.

Alex pursed his lips and let out a breath. "Well, we shall say no more of it, for your deed, good or bad, saved our lives. And frankly, I would not put either treachery or cruelty past Earl Hugh."

"We have you to thank for our lives, Merewyn," said Guy, finding his voice. His smile told her he did not hold her action to free the Welsh king against her.

"You continue to surprise me, wife," said Alex. "I suspect with you, life will never be dull."

They rode on in comfortable silence. At Wigan, the priest was welcoming and again provided them with lodging. Merewyn was glad to be out of the cold. When Alex told the priest they were wed, he was happy to show them to a chamber they could share. Alex did not make love to her that night but wrapped his body around her and, with one hand possessively on her breast, told her, "Get some rest."

CHAPTER 15

Two days later, on a dreary afternoon, Alex and his companions rode through Talisand's gate. He had accomplished his purpose and rescued Merewyn from the clutches of the Welshman, but none save Rory and Guy knew he had rescued his wife. Even Merewyn refused to agree they were wed. She still kept the ring he had given her on a riband around her neck, hidden beneath her clothing.

He felt a scowl building as he recalled their last conversation.

"You will wear my ring. I will not have the likes of Owain or Ranulf thinking you are available for their pursuit."

"Nay, I will not! Not until I know your parents have accepted the idea of our marriage. They may yet expect you to wed a noble born woman. And then there is the king. Oh, and Alex, please say nothing of the babe until you have their answer."

He knew she was resisting for his benefit but he liked it not. In his mind, they were well and truly wed and there was no way she would be slipping out of it. She was the only woman he wanted to be mother to his sons. The only woman he would have in his bed. The only woman he loved with a passion.

He cast a sharp glance at her belly before raising his gaze to her face. "Already you swell with my child," he whispered, leaning in close so only she could hear. "You cannot hide the truth of it for long."

She turned her head forward, stubborn as always, and said nothing.

He would see an end to her defiance. Tonight, he would raise the issue of their marriage with his father.

★   ★   ★

Jamie was in the bailey talking with Lora when Alex and Merewyn passed through the palisade gate, followed by Rory and Guy. "By all the saints, he has brought her back," Jamie muttered under his breath.

"I am not surprised," said Lora. "When you told me Alex had gone after her, I did not doubt he would bring Merewyn back. He can be very determined."

Jamie turned to the dark-haired woman at his side, aware she had once harbored a tendre for Talisand's heir. "Alex has decided on the woman he wants. Does his choice concern you?"

Lora watched Alex and Merewyn dismount. "If what you suggest is true, I am happy for them. They make a fine couple, he so dark and she so fair. Alex needs a strong woman like Merewyn and I think she has always cared more for him than she was willing to say."

"And you? Did you not find Sir Alex a handsome knight?"

She turned to face him. Nearly as tall as he, she had only to tilt her chin slightly to meet his gaze. "Once, like many of the girls at Talisand, I might have allowed myself to dream of Sir Alex, but I am no longer a girl. I have seen the man I would call husband, a knight who is much admired. And he is not Alex."

The sparkle in her brown eyes brought a smile to his face. "If that be so, Mistress Lora, with your permission, I would speak to Sir Alain when he returns. Should your father agree, you and I will be wed."

"Aye, Jamie," she said, "you have my permission."

He was so intent on Lora, so thrilled with her answer, he had not detected Alex's approach, but the familiar voice drew his attention. "Will you stare at each other all afternoon or will you join us for some ale?"

Jamie turned to see Alex supported by Rory on one side and Merewyn on the other. "Of course, we will join you." Then looking down, he noticed Alex stood on only one leg, the other bent at the knee as if injured. "What has happened?"

Alex let out an exasperated sigh. "I caught an arrow from a Welsh bow."

"Well, no matter whose arrow it was, we had best get you off your one good leg," Jamie said. Replacing Merewyn on one side, Jamie helped Alex into the hall.

Lora took Merewyn's arm and followed closely behind them.

"It is so good to have you home. Jamie thought you did not go willingly with Owain. Is it true?"

"Aye. Poor Owain. He believed he was doing right by me."

"Was it Owain who shot Alex?"

"Aye and Alex meant to take his head but I persuaded him to let Owain go. Imagine how Rhodri would react to Alex's killing one of Powys' princes."

Jamie smiled to himself hearing the women's conversation. Merewyn would make an interesting Lady of Talisand.

When the six of them were in the hall and Alex was seated, Jamie drew Merewyn aside. "I have said nothing to Alex of the child."

"I thank you for keeping my secret, Jamie, but Alex knows and I suspect, very soon, all of Talisand will know as well."

* * *

After Jamie left her, Merewyn went looking for Lady Serena, to let her know they had returned and that Alex had taken an arrow in his leg. She found her in the kitchen with Maggie.

Before she could open her mouth to speak, Lady Serena rushed toward her. "Merewyn! You are back!"

"We thought ye'd run off with that Welshman," said Maggie with an expression that spoke of her disapproval.

"Nay, I did not. I was taken, but Alex rescued me."

After she told them about all that had happened, well, except for the nights she shared his bed and her freeing the Welsh king, she assured them Alex was on the mend. "The earl's physic said he will recover. The wound still pains him, but 'tis healing well."

"Where is he?" asked Lady Serena, wiping off her hands on a cloth.

"In the hall, drinking with Sir Jamie and the others."

"Go to yer son, milady," Maggie urged her mistress. "I will see if I can find the crutch Earl Renaud used when he injured his leg. 'Tis around here somewhere."

★   ★   ★

Alex did not intend to ask his father about Merewyn becoming his wife. He preferred to announce it as an accomplished fact. Because of the importance of what he was about, he had asked Merewyn to wear the blue velvet gown she had worn that first night in Chester when she had defeated him in chess, for he would have all of Talisand see their new lady. He dressed in the midnight blue tunic his mother had given him.

When supper ended and the minstrels finished their songs, he rose and, with the crutch Maggie had given him supporting his wounded leg, he took Merewyn's hand to walk the short distance to the dais. "Come!"

Merewyn was none too pleased. "You know I do not want to be with you when you speak to your parents," she whispered as he limped forward with her in tow. "It will make them feel awkward."

"You must be with me," he hissed back. He loved her with all his heart but, at times, his fierce archer could be stubborn. "I do not intend to ask, but to tell."

When they arrived before the dais where his parents sat with Sir Geoffroi, his wife, Lady Emma, and Maugris, Alex said, "I have a declaration to make."

A hushed silence followed as everyone in the hall turned to listen. He felt the eyes upon him and stiffened his resolve.

"First," nodding to Sir Geoffroi and Lady Emma and then to his parents, since all four might claim Merewyn as their ward, "I must ask your forgiveness for not having sought your permission, but I have taken Merewyn as my wife."

Gasps of surprise echoed around the hall. Alex kept his eyes on the five people before him.

Maugris and his mother smiled in what he hoped was evidence of their approval.

Sir Geoffroi frowned. "When?"

"In London," he said, squeezing Merewyn's hand. Giving her a sidelong glance, he saw the fear in her eyes.

"But there was no ceremony, no blessing. I was there!" insisted Sir Geoffroi.

"Since there would be no dowry and thus no contract, it seemed a simple exchange of our intent sufficed. Our love made us eager to bind ourselves to each other."

Merewyn's hand moved to her belly where the babe was just beginning to make itself known beneath her velvet gown.

Alex did not fail to note the move nor, apparently, did his mother.

"You are with child, Merewyn?" the Lady of Talisand asked.

Merewyn flushed and nodded.

"You have dishonored my ward?" protested Sir Geoffroi. His wife, Lady Emma, patted his hand. "Perhaps not, my love."

"We exchanged the required words. Only then was the marriage consummated. Father Bernard has assured me such is sufficient to see us wed."

Father Bernard rose from his seat. "If I might, my lord, my lady…"

The lord of Talisand gestured the priest to approach the dais.

"Sir Alex speaks the truth. All that is required is for the two of them to make present statements of their intent. When followed by their physical union, the bond is completed. No witnesses need be present and a formal blessing, though not required, can follow."

Behind Alex, he heard the voice of his mother's maidservant. "My lady, I overheard their vows spoken in London."

Alex's mother acknowledged Nelda's statement with a nod. "Well, and 'tis obvious the bond has been sealed."

Alex snuck a look at his bride. Merewyn's cheeks were flaming, her lips tightly pressed together and her eyes lowered.

All this time Alex's father had remained silent, his expression inscrutable. Now he spoke. "What about the king? Does he know of this?"

"I have yet to speak to William about Merewyn. When I left him in Durham, he was in no mood to hear it."

"Well, first let me say, you are wrong on several counts, my son, which in this case is to the good. First, Merewyn will have a dowry. Geoff and I spoke of it before we left for London, thinking she might find an acceptable suitor there, which apparently she did."

His stern look passed from Alex to Merewyn, who lowered her eyes.

His father continued. "Geoff and I will see she brings coin to her marriage. We had even thought of land, but that will no longer be necessary. It seems you will have plenty. And perhaps I can help you with the king."

Alex's spirits rose. His father would not oppose their marriage. He shot a glance at Merewyn. She, too, appeared hopeful.

"It seems both the king and his brother were taken with the young page who shot the deer," said his father. "Duke Robert, in particular, was delighted when the page turned into a lovely young woman. After we left the barons' meeting, William and Robert inquired about Merewyn's sire. Eude de Fourneaux was the only son of a nobleman, who recently passed. His lands in Fourneaux are among those William now controls by virtue of the treaty in Caen. When William called me back to the palace that morning it was to tell me he wished me to betroth Merewyn to one of my sons. Whichever son I chose would be given the Fourneaux lands near Falaise."

Beside him, Merewyn's right hand flew to her throat. "Lands in Normandy?"

"I have no doubt William expected me to wed Merewyn to Raoul, but since he failed to dictate my choice, I will advise him I have given Merewyn to you. With the lands in Normandy she brings you, he should find the match acceptable."

Alex pulled Merewyn into his arms and kissed her.

The hall erupted in loud shouts of congratulations.

When he ended the kiss, her eyes were glistening with tears. "Now will you wear my ring, my lady?"

"Oh, yea, I will!"

Alex held out his palm. She lifted the riband from her neck and removed the ring, placing it in his hand. He slid it on her finger and looked into her teary eyes. "With this ring, I proclaim you mine for always."

"Well done, Alex!" cried Rory.

Cheers erupted from the people behind them.

When the hall quieted, at the head table, Maugris leaned across Alex's mother to speak to Talisand's lord. "My lord, do you know the animal on Fourneaux's banner?"

Alex's father shrugged and turned to Sir Geoffroi. "Do you know, Geoff?"

"As I recall from Eude's shield, Ren, 'tis a red hart bearing many prongs on its antlers."

A broad smile spread across the wise one's face and his pale blue eyes twinkled with mirth. "All is well," he pronounced. "Did I not say it would be so?"

CHAPTER 16

Merewyn loved the end of autumn when wheat seeding was completed and everyone was busy with preparations for winter. The air was brisk, gusts whipping leaves to the floor of the woodland. The old stock and swine were slaughtered and salted to supply meat, villeins cut reeds and sedges for thatching so no roofs would leak when the rains came in full force and herdsmen gathered bracken for the cattle's winter bedding.

Added to that was the candle making that the women did together to assure Talisand had a goodly supply of light for the short winter days.

But this year, an excitement filled the air beyond the normal preparations for the Martinmas feast because they were to celebrate the marriage of Talisand's heir. Father Bernard had agreed to bless their marriage on St. Martin's Day and Maggie assured Lady Serena they would have enough roast goose to feed all of Talisand.

Alex had joined the men hunting geese for the feast and Merewyn was helping Lady Serena and Lady Emma with the candle making. Cecily and her two ever-present companions were gathering wood with the other children.

By now, the half-dozen women making candles just outside the kitchens had filled many racks of the long tapers. Merewyn had just dipped her candles into the hot tallow mixture for the third time when the babe quickened within her. The flicker of movement made her start. She brought her hand to her slightly rounded belly waiting for the next movement.

"The babe?" Lady Serena asked holding up a rack with a half-dozen candles she had just dipped. The honey-colored candles were nearly done.

Merewyn smiled at her mother-in-law. "Aye. 'Tis the first time I have felt the babe move."

Lady Emma left the candles she was dipping and came to join Merewyn. Like Serena, Emma, who was also in her fourth decade, barely showed her years. Her skin was smooth and her blue-green eyes clear and beautiful. "I feel as if this child will be my first grandchild as well as yours, Serena."

Lady Serena shook her head. "Two grandmothers and Maggie to dote on him."

Hearing her name, Maggie raised her head from where she was working. "And why not?"

Merewyn was delighted to have so many she cared for look forward to the birth of her child. "I think he will be much loved," she said.

Lady Serena wiped her hands on her linen apron. "You said 'he'. Do you believe the babe will be a male child?" Emma and Serena paused in what they were doing to wait for her answer.

Merewyn smiled remembering her encounter with the wise one after morning prayers. "Maugris told me this first child will be a boy, one with a will to match his father's and his grandfather's."

Maggie looked up from where she was inspecting the candles drying on the long rack. "Another wolf?" she asked, resignedly. "As if the pack we have is not enough. May the Good Lord save us."

"Mayhap this one will encourage my Tibby to be responsible," said Lady Serena. "After all, he will be the babe's uncle."

"Your daughter, Bea," Merewyn said to Lady Emma, "has already offered to help me with the babe."

"Aye, she would. Bea loves children."

Lora, who had just dipped her candles in the hot mixture, laughed. "She will have a time of it fending off Cecily. I expect the imp will take charge and command her two swains and everyone else concerning the babe. My brother, Ancel, will not question her dictates."

Merewyn laughed with the women. Surrounded by so many she loved made her feel like she really had come home. Maugris had been right. Her future was at Talisand.

Maggie issued instructions to the servant women, then walked to where Merewyn stood with Serena and Emma. "I'd best see how Cassie is coming with the feast preparations. Tomorrow will be a busy day."

"Maggie reminds me that time is short," said Lady Serena to Merewyn. "I would show you the gown I have for you to wear tomorrow. Would you like to come?" she asked Lady Emma and Lora.

The faces of the two women lit with interest. "Oh, yes!" said Lora.

Wiping off her hands, Lady Emma said, "Indeed, I want to see it."

The four women walked to the chamber in the manor Merewyn now shared with Alex, the one that had once been her own. Lying across the large bed was a shimmering blue silk gown, the neck and sleeves embroidered with golden thread.

"Oh…" Lady Emma and Lora exclaimed together.

"It is the most beautiful gown I have ever seen!" said Merewyn.

Lady Serena smiled. "I do not wonder but that I was thinking of this day when I purchased the silk and thread in London. I could not be more pleased with Alex's choice for a bride."

As Emma and Lora stood admiring the gown, Lady Serena reached for a circlet of silver intertwined with intricate gold leaves. Presenting it to Merewyn, she said, "This was a gift from my father. I wore it on the day I wed the Red Wolf many years ago. And I would have you wear it tomorrow."

"I have never seen that circlet," said Lady Emma. " 'Tis beautiful."

Lora just stared at the beautiful circlet.

Merewyn took the delicate piece in her hands, tears filling her eyes. "You have been so good to me, my lady. To let me wear your own circlet is a gift I would never have expected."

" 'Tis yours, Merewyn. You are the only daughter I will ever have. And now you are my daughter-in-law as well. Mayhap one day, it will grace the head of your own daughter."

"Do not forget, I count Merewyn as my own, too," said Lady Emma. "You will be lovely in the gown and circlet, Merewyn. I hope you will wear the gold necklace I gave you."

"I will," Merewyn said, kissing Lady Emma's cheek. "I treasure it."

"Alex will be all agog when he sees you," offered Lora with a grin.

Merewyn set the circlet down and hugged the women. She had been blessed with two mothers and a wonderful friend. "I love you all."

"And we love you," said Lady Serena.

★   ★   ★

Alex entered the hall the next day to the enticing smells of roasting goose wafting through the air. His leg still bothered him but he needed no crutch to walk. His father had teased him that they were now a matched pair of limping wolves, but Alex hoped in time he would have no limp.

He had left his bride tousled in bed where he had made love to her for most of the morning. It was the first time he had told her that he loved her. Mayhap his love began to grow from the first moment he looked at her in her archer's clothing.

Father Bernard's blessing was to be given just before the feast so he had time to share a goblet of wine with his father and his closest friends while Merewyn prepared. When he had left their chamber, his mother, Lady Emma and Lora and had just arrived to assist her.

"Hail the bridegroom!" shouted Guy from where he sat with the others. "You look fit for William's court."

Alex bowed. "I am honored you should wait for me to begin." Around the table gathered with his father were Sir Geoffroi, Maugris, Jamie, Rory and Guy, all attired in their best tunics for the day. Sir Alain and Alex's brothers, save for little Tibby, would miss the Martinmas blessing and the feast that followed, but the babe coming could not wait the months that might pass before they were home.

"Well, 'tis only now that Maggie has come to tend our thirst and since this is for you, we thought to wait," said his father who looked every bit the Lord of Talisand this day with his chestnut hair combed back from his face and a tunic of dark green wool stretched over his broad shoulders. He was not a man given to jewels but he needed none with his noble bearing.

Maggie was directing the many servants bustling about the hall as they prepared for the feast, but she managed to see the men supplied with wine.

Once each man had been served, his father stood and lifted his goblet. "To a happy life and many sons!"

They all stood and drank.

"To lands in Normandy for Talisand's heir!" said Sir Geoffroi.

They drank again.

"To the Black Wolf who has finally claimed his mate," said Jamie with a wink.

Before they could drink to that, Rory added, "To the worthy bride!"

Another swallow followed.

"To Rhodri, who taught Merewyn to speak the Welsh tongue that saved our hides," said Guy.

They laughed and imbibed more of the rich wine of Normandy.

Alex raised his goblet. "To Talisand!" His father and his friends echoed his shout and downed their wine.

*　　*　　*

Merewyn had waited, giving Lady Serena, Lady Emma and Lora time to get to the church. Now, she slowly descended the stairs, attired in the blue silk gown, her head covering graced with the silver and gold circlet Lady Serena had given her. Around her neck was the golden necklace Lady Emma had brought from York. And on her finger was Alex's ring with the blue stone. She smiled to herself thinking Owain had been wrong about Alex not giving her a ring.

At the bottom of the stairs, Alex waited, his hand extended to her. "You look like a queen."

"And you, my love, are not only the handsome favored knight of the king, but my champion for always."

He took her hand and kissed it. She felt her cheeks heat. He had made love to her many times and still he could make her feel the shy innocent.

"Come, my own," he said, "walk with me to the church where Father Bernard awaits."

As they stepped out of the manor, a great crowd greeted them, parting like the flood waters in Moses' time to allow them to walk the path through the village to the church. Cheers went up from the villagers who lined the way.

As they neared the church, on one side of the path she saw Lady

Serena waiting with Earl Renaud, Lady Emma and Sir Geoffroi. On the other side stood Rory and Guy. Next to them was Lora with Jamie. Rory's sister, Alice, held the hand of her younger sister, Cecily. Next to Cecily stood Tibby and Ancel. All them were smiling, their faces filled with joy.

Father Bernard waited in front of the door to the stone church. "My children," he said, reaching out to take their hands. He crossed them over each other and then placed his hand over theirs. "May your days be long, your love strong, your children many. And may God lead you all of your days. In the name of the Father, Son and Spirit, I ask God's blessing upon your union."

When the good father was finished, Alex kissed her. Shouts erupted behind them. Then, taking her hand, he turned her to face their friends and the villagers gathered around them.

"I give you Lady Merewyn of Talisand and Fourneaux," he said in a loud voice.

Cheers and good wishes surrounded them as they returned to the hall for the great feast that was to follow. Merewyn's heart overflowed with love. She supposed she was a lady now, for the lands she brought to her husband had bestowed upon her that status. And this day, she would dance with the hero of her heart.

"Come, my love," he whispered. "First we feast on duck and then I feast on you!"

EPILOGUE

Talisand, December 1092

Merewyn kissed the fine hair on the head of her young son. The babe already had Alex's gray eyes and she assumed he would eventually have his father's raven locks. Alex had named him "William Renaud", after the king and his grandfather, but everyone called him "Rennie". Born in the last days of May, Alex made sure all of Talisand had glimpsed the babe at least once. The memory of her proud warrior carrying his infant son through the village brought a smile to her face.

"Can I hold him?" Lora asked, reaching out for the babe. Rennie gave Lora a huge smile and lifted his little hands toward the woman who had become like a second mother to him.

"Aye, take the little rascal. He is getting sleepy and should give you no trouble. I must seek the privy. This second child I carry has me seeking the chamber pot often."

When she returned, Lora asked, "Where is Jamie? I did not see him when I came in."

"Showing Alex the King of Gwynedd's gift, I think."

Lora bounced Rennie on her knees and the babe grinned with glee. " 'Tis not every child who is given a Welsh pony in his first year."

The grateful King of Gwynedd had managed to deliver the pony to Talisand despite his country was immersed in a war with King William. With the pony, the king had sent a missive expressing his gratitude for "the extraordinary gesture of kindness" she had shown him. He added a note telling her the pony had been named Dyfodol, which means "Future" in Welsh. Rennie was the future, to be sure, but mayhap the king had hoped their two countries could, in the future, be at peace. It was her fervent wish, as well.

"Then there is the wolf dog," said Merewyn, looking down at the sleeping whelp lying next to the hearth, already bigger than his young master. Sir Geoffroi and Lady Emma had given Rennie a pup from their female hound's last litter and suggested they name him "Magnus" after her beloved hound that had died many years ago. "Already, Rennie and Magnus are inseparable. The pup sleeps by his cradle each night."

The fire crackled invitingly and Merewyn lifted the cup from the small table next to her and sipped the warm spiced cider. Holding the cup between her palms, she watched the flames of the fire, her mind going over all that had happened in the last year. December was a time for reflection.

The month Rennie was born, King William had invaded the lands north of Talisand, capturing Carlisle, held by the Scots for more than a hundred years. Alex, Rory and Guy had gone with the king though they found the prospect of seizing Carlisle distasteful after the agreement with the Scots they had witnessed the year before.

By the time Alex and his men returned, little Rennie had been born. Alex had been frantic with worry for her and the babe, but she had been able to greet him with a warm smile and assure him both she and his babe were well.

Once she was up and around, she continued Cecily's lessons all through the summer. Joined by Ancel and Tibby, the three of them had become good enough for real arrows.

But it was Lora's good news that made her smile. Merewyn always looked forward to Christmas and the feasting and celebrations it brought. But this year would also see her closest friend's marriage to Sir Jamie blessed by Father Bernard.

"So you have agreed to a Christmas blessing on your marriage?" she asked Lora.

"Aye, it was Jamie's wish and since I made him wait so long, I could hardly say him nay. Now that my father has returned, my whole family will attend the feast."

"I am glad for it, Lora. Jamie is a good man and an honorable knight. He will also be a good father."

Lora stared down at Rennie, who had fallen asleep in her arms. "I want children and so does Jamie." Raising her gaze to Merewyn, she added, "Just think, our children will be raised together."

"Aye, and they will be watched over by my students of the bow. Cecily's skill will one day rival Lady Serena's and then there are Tibby and your brother, Ancel, racing to catch up."

"Those three may lead our little ones into trouble!" Lora remarked.

Merewyn chuckled. "You are right. We will have to watch them all."

Just then, the door from the bailey opened and Alex and Jamie stepped in, brushing snow off their shoulders. Hanging their cloaks on the pegs next to the door, they strode to where Merewyn and Lora sat.

The heavy tread of their feet woke the pup sleeping next to the hearth. He rose from the floor and went to Alex, who reached down to scratch the pup's ears. Alex smiled at Merewyn, then went to Lora and accepted the sleeping Rennie from her.

Holding the babe close, he looked into his face. "Made himself tired, did he?"

"Aye," said Merewyn.

Jamie leaned over to kiss Lora's cheek. "You looked quite at home with Merewyn's babe in your arms."

Lora blushed and flashed him a smile.

Alex took a seat beside Merewyn, kissing her temple. His lips were cool on her skin that had been warmed by the fire. "Good eve, love," he whispered to her.

She looked at him holding their child and her heart melted. Touching the soft skin on Rennie's cheek and then the rougher skin on Alex's manly face, she said, "Father and son, my loves." She rose and walked to the trestle table a short distance away. "Maggie has made a new batch of the spiced cider," she told the men. "I think 'tis her best thus far."

Handing each man a cup, she said. "Soon it will be Christmas and the hall will be filled with our friends and families. I can hardly wait."

"All my brothers are home for the feast," added Alex.

Jamie reached over to take Lora's hand. "And we will finally have our marriage blessed."

Merewyn sighed with happiness. All winter long, they would burn the candles and share stories around the hearth fire. Some of the women would embroider and stitch while Merewyn and Lady Serena would make fletchings. When the work was done, there would be games and, mayhap, dancing. Some evenings, she and Alex would take walks in the snow and admire the stars.

The life she had always wanted, but never thought possible, was hers and, for that, she was more grateful than she could say.

Alex stood and, with his free hand, reached out to her. "Come, love, let us put the babe to bed and leave Jamie and Lora to the fire."

She rose, bid their friends good eve and walked with Alex through the wide opening that led to the manor and up the stairs. What Alex had not said, but she knew he was thinking, was that it was time for them to go to their bed, as well. Long winter nights and a sleeping child meant hours of loving for them.

"Come, Magnus," said Alex, and the pup scrambled from the floor, hurrying to catch up.

AFTERWORD

Thank you for reading *King's Knight*. I hope you enjoyed Alexander's story. If you haven't read the other books in the series, you can find them on Amazon.
amazon.com/Medieval-Warriors-3-Book-Series/dp/B01G5QSA90

Want to keep up with my new releases?

- Sign up to get my newsletter (I give away a book each quarter from those signing up): www.reganwalkerauthor.com
- "Follow" me on Amazon: amazon.com/Regan-Walker/e/B008OUWC5Y
- "Friend" me on Facebook: facebook.com/regan.walker.104
- Join the Regan Walker's Readers group on Facebook: facebook.com/groups/ReganWalkersReaders

If you have a moment, please review *King's Knight* on Amazon and Goodreads. Reviews help both authors and readers and are so appreciated. And turn the page for an excerpt from *The Red Wolf's Prize*, the story of Sir Renaud de Pierrepont, the Red Wolf, and Lady Serena of Talisand.

EXCERPT FROM
THE RED WOLF'S PRIZE

The wolf will hunt for the jewel hidden among the stones, and if he finds it, his cubs will advise kings for generations.

– Maugris' vision, September 1066

CHAPTER 1

The North of England, spring 1068

Serena contemplated her reflection in the small silvered glass.

Soon I will be another woman. Soon I will have another life.

While she could not change her violet eyes or her curves of a woman full grown, her flaxen hair was another matter. Undoing her long plait, she let the loose waves fall below her waist to shimmer in the early morning sunlight streaming into her bedchamber through the open shutters.

With a sigh, she lifted her hand to touch the gilded frame of the silvered glass. She could still hear her father's voice when he told her he had bought the extravagant gift from a Spanish merchant who claimed the Moors had made it. No one at Talisand had ever seen such a magnificent wonder before he brought it home to the manor. Tears came to her eyes as she remembered the look on his face, the warm smile reflecting his love.

Her father had been her protector and teacher, a man of great wisdom and a thegn dearly loved by his people. Deprived of his guiding presence, and with her brother in Scotland, Serena was all too aware she alone of her family was left at Talisand. Fear crept over her like a winter chill as she remembered the messenger who had come with a writ from the Bastard King.

She was to become the bride of the new Norman lord of Talisand. *Nay, I will not!*

But how could she deny so fearsome a warrior as the knight they called the Red Wolf?

Serena's brow puckered in consternation. And what would become of the other women at Talisand? Would not the Norman conquerors claim them as spoils? Peasants fleeing the advancing horde the year before had spoken of the knights' villainy. Women were merely vessels to satisfy their lust.

Anger flared in her eyes staring back from the silvered glass. She would not have it! The young women of Talisand would not fall victim to the rampaging knights if she could help it.

But what choices were left? Some English women had taken the veil, but she was not suited to the cloistered life and that would not be a choice for the maidens at Talisand. But mayhap she could save the most vulnerable.

The door opened and Cassie, her handmaiden, entered with her mother, Maggie.

" 'Tis ready, m'lady," said Maggie, handing Serena a leather flask. "I have made ye the dye from walnuts."

Serena accepted the flask and poured the dark liquid into a bowl.

" 'Tis a shame to dye such beautiful hair," remarked Maggie.

"She must, Mother, if she is to look the part of a servant," Cassie insisted. " 'Tis nay just her speech and her clothes that make her stand out. 'Tis her hair that tells all who she is—like a pale flame on a dark night."

Maggie nodded, resigned. "Then oil yer hands and the skin around yer face, m'lady, before ye apply the dye. It will make yer hair brown like mine, but ye will have to add more as yer hair grows. And remember to keep yer hood up should it rain for water can make the dye run."

"I will, Maggie, and thank you," said Serena as she spread the oil on her face and hands.

Cassie oiled her own hands and began to work the dye into Serena's hair. "I know the messenger said ye were to be the new lord's wife, but it might be well ye are leaving. The tales of the Normans' brutality are frightening. Ye must be safe."

"To be sure," echoed Maggie, "the Norman who comes isna a man yer father would have chosen for ye. Mayhap it will be easier for us to accept his yoke, knowing ye and yer brother are beyond his grasp and safe in me own homeland."

"I could not bear to take a Norman as husband," Serena said with firm conviction. Cassie poured the last of the dye onto Serena's head and she let the dark liquid drip from the wet strands into the bowl. She was glad she would not have to color her brows. Like her lashes, they were already dark. "It is not enough the Bastard from Normandy has taken my father and my country. Now he would give my family's lands to one of his knights."

"If the traveling cottars' words be true," offered Cassie, "the one who now claims Talisand is one who fought with the Bastard at Hastings. He might even be the knight who slayed yer father, the thegn!"

"Yea, 'tis a hard time that has come upon the land," said Maggie, regret showing in her eyes, the same vivid green as her daughter's. Then shooting a glance at Cassie, she added, "When I think of the men the Norman lord brings with him, I fear for me own daughter as well."

"I want to go with Lady Serena," the flame haired Cassie blurted out while she squeezed the excess dye from Serena's hair. "She will be saving me and the others from certain rape."

Maggie smiled sadly. "Aye, but will ye be safe?" She handed the drying cloth to her daughter. " 'Tis a long road ye travel. I worry for ye both. The woods are full of thieves."

"Nay, Maggie," insisted Serena. "The woods are full of fleeing Saxons."

Cassie wrapped the drying cloth around Serena's head. "Would it not be better for us to flee than to stay and fall prey to the Bastard's men? Have we not heard the tales of their terrible deeds as they ravaged Wessex?"

Maggie nodded, her countenance fallen. "Aye, I have heard of the killing and the burnings. They even robbed churches. 'Tis a gift from God we have escaped such, and only because Talisand lies so far north. I pray the new Norman lord will not harm the villagers. They will now be his villeins, caring for fields that are his."

"I will worry for you," said Serena fighting the urge to stay even as she knew she must go.

"Ye must not worry about me and Angus," said the cook. "The Red Wolf will need me to feed his men and Angus to keep his horses shod."

Cassie nodded to her mother. "Aye, ye both will be needed."

"At least the young women I take with me will not be here to face the Red Wolf and his men," encouraged Serena. "We will search for my brother and accept the sanctuary offered by Scotland's king." Serena finished blotting the moisture from her dyed hair and unwrapped the drying cloth. "I wish I could take all of the women, but not all want to go. Like you, Maggie, some have husbands."

"Do ye know where yer brother, the young master is, m'lady?" asked Maggie.

"Steinar's last message said he was at King Malcolm's court in Dunfermline, north of Edinburgh, where many Englishman gather, hoping for an opportunity to return to fight for Edgar Ætheling, the true heir to the throne."

Maggie sighed. "At least ye and the young women will have protectors traveling with ye. And I will pray ye stay safe."

"We welcome your prayers," said Serena. Looking into the faces of the two women who were so dear to her, she added, "I am glad for all you have done for me. Your friendship has meant more than your service. And your company, Cassie, will be most welcome." She thought of those women who would travel with them, and the face of another rose in her mind. "Do you think Aethel would want to go with us? Her knowledge of herbs would be welcome."

"Aethel? Nay lass." Maggie gave Serena a wry look. "That one would lift her skirts for any Norman who would have her. She'll nay be running from them."

"I suppose you speak the truth," Serena admitted. "Since she went to my father's bed, she has not been the same."

"Or ye just didna see what she really was all along," chided Maggie.

The words saddened Serena. It was true that after being rejected by Theodric, the captain of Talisand's guard, Aethel had changed. The dark-haired beauty attracted many men, including Serena's father, the lonely thegn, but Aethel did not seem to be happy even with him.

"That leaves only Cassie and me and the three other women," said Serena. "Leppe and Alec will go with us, disguised as village cottars. Of the Talisand fighting men that still remain after the slaughter at Hastings, they are among the best and will be faithful to protect us." Wanting to assure Maggie they would have protection, she added, "Theodric and the other guards will stay to defend Talisand, if need be. I have asked steward Hunstan to visit the other manors to warn them of the Normans' coming."

"How soon do they arrive?" Maggie asked, glancing anxiously in the direction of the main gate.

"I know not the day," said Serena, "but I expect it will be soon, so we must be away this hour. I fear I have waited too long as it is."

Maggie nodded and looked at her daughter. "Send word as soon as ye're able."

Cassie's eyes filled with tears as she embraced her mother. "I will."

Blinking back her own tears, Serena sought to keep her voice steady. "Do not worry for us, Maggie. I have my bow and my seax. We will be well. And we will see you again, for I intend to return with Steinar to chase the Normans from Talisand."

Serena glanced once again at her reflection. Her hair now bore the color of the brown stain and was nearly dry. She felt changed inside as well as out.

"Ye look so different!" exclaimed Cassie as she formed the newly dyed tresses into a long plait.

"Aye, she does," said Maggie. "But the color does not hide her beauty." Mayhap a plain tunic will help. Maggie handed Serena a dark green tunic, and she slipped it over her shift.

As the folds of the rough wool settled around her, she felt her new life settled around her as well. The servant's garment was a stark contrast to the soft wool of the fine gowns she had worn as the Lady of Talisand. She looked down at her ankles that showed beneath the hem. The borrowed tunic did not fit well, either.

Seeing her shrug, Maggie said, "It will do 'til ye reach Scotland."

Serena sat on the chest at the end of her bed and pulled on the woolen hose and soft leather half boots the female servants wore. Cassie handed her a leather belt, which Serena wrapped around her waist. She secured to it her seax, the single edged blade her brother had given her last Christmastide. Grasping the polished wooden handle, she silently vowed to use it if threatened.

"Let me help ye with yer cloak." Cassie said, draping the dark wool mantle around Serena's shoulders and fastening it with a plain metal brooch. " 'Twill serve to keep ye warm against the night air." Smiling, Cassie took a step back and examined Serena's disguise. "Ye make a convincing servant, m'lady, dressed as ye are. Except ye're too fine of feature. So remember to keep yer head bowed and yer eyes down should we encounter any men. And since yer speech is a wee bit proper, say nothing, lest they wonder if ye are truly one of us."

"I will try and do as you say, Cassie. In time, I might be able to disguise my speech as well." She would do whatever she must to escape the plans the Normans had for her. "You will have to be my guide in this new life."

"It is time," Maggie said, turning toward the door. "I will have a word with Leppe and Alec afore ye go, though I know those two will protect ye with their lives."

An hour later, Serena left the manor to begin the journey north. Seven walked along in silence: Serena and Cassie, three other women and the two men. The morning mist still clung to the wild grasses under Serena's feet, dampening her leather boots. She was glad her borrowed tunic was as short as it was, else her hem would also be wet.

When they reached the edge of the woods, Serena paused and looked back. The sun cast its rays on Talisand, making the manor, hall and thatch and wattle cottages appear to glow. To Serena, it was like something out of a dream, like a village descended from heaven. The place of her home and her heart and the memories of all she held dear.

Tears brimmed in her eyes and escaped down her cheeks. Would she ever see her beloved Talisand again?

Garbed in a belted tunic and short brown cloak a shade darker than his long hair and beard, Leppe gently touched her arm. "My lady, we must hurry."

She nodded and let him lead her away. Away from her past and the dreams she had once for her future. Soon the fierce knight called the Red Wolf would descend like a devastating storm to claim his spoils.

Nothing she could do would prevent it. Concern for her people weighed heavy on Serena's shoulders. The Red Wolf's reputation was that of an undefeated warrior, as vicious in battle as the animal whose fur he wore.

She prayed he would not harm the people he would need to work the land.

AUTHOR'S BIO

Regan Walker is an award-winning, bestselling author of Regency, Georgian and Medieval romances. Her stories have won numerous awards.

Years of serving clients in private practice and several stints in high levels of government have given Regan a love of international travel and a feel for the demands of the "Crown". Hence her romance novels often involve a demanding sovereign who taps his subjects for special assignments. Each of her novels features real history and real historical figures. And, of course, adventure and love.

Keep in touch with Regan on Facebook, and do join Regan Walker's Readers.

facebook.com/regan.walker.104
facebook.com/groups/ReganWalkersReaders
You can sign up for her newsletter on her website.
www.reganwalkerauthor.com

BOOKS BY REGAN WALKER

The Medieval Warriors series:

The Red Wolf's Prize
Rogue Knight
Rebel Warrior
King's Knight

The Agents of the Crown series:

To Tame the Wind (prequel)
Racing with the Wind
Against the Wind
Wind Raven
A Secret Scottish Christmas

The Donet Trilogy:

To Tame the Wind
Echo in the Wind
A Fierce Wind (coming 2018)

Holiday Stories (related to the Agents of the Crown):

The Shamrock & The Rose
The Twelfth Night Wager
The Holly & The Thistle
A Secret Scottish Christmas

Inspirational:

The Refuge, an Inspirational Novel of Scotland

The photograph of Merewyn on the back cover of the paperback is used with the permission of artist Laura Olenska (all rights reserved 2013) – www.laura-olenska.com

243